W9-ANE-966

ALSO BY TODD GITLIN

The Twilight of Common Dreams:
America Is Wracked by Culture Wars

The Murder of Albert Einstein

The Sixties: Years of Hope, Days of Rage

Watching Television (editor)

Inside Prime Time

The Whole World Is Watching: Mass Media in the
Making and Unmaking of the New Left

Busy Being Born

Campfires of the Resistance:
Poetry from the Movement (editor)

Uptown: Poor Whites in Chicago (coauthor)

The
Why A

The

The W

sacrifice

sacrifice

A Novel

TODD GITLIN

METROPOLITAN BOOKS
HENRY HOLT AND COMPANY   NEW YORK

Metropolitan Books
Henry Holt and Company, Inc.
Publishers since 1866
115 West 18th Street
New York, New York 10011

Metropolitan Books™ is an imprint of
Henry Holt and Company, Inc.

Library of Congress Cataloging-in-Publication Data
Gitlin, Todd.
Sacrifice : a novel / Todd Gitlin.—1st ed.
p.   cm.
ISBN 0-8050-6032-4 (hardbound : alk. paper)
I. Title.
PS3557.I82S23   1999
813'.54—dc21   98-46155
                                                      CIP

Henry Holt books are available for special
promotions and premiums. For details contact:
Director, Special Markets.

First Edition 1999

Designed by Paula Russell Szafranski

Printed in the United States of America
All first editions are printed on acid-free paper. ∞

1   3   5   7   9   10   8   6   4   2

Again to Laurel

We are the monuments left to an alien,
unlived life that is scarcely ours.

—OCTAVIO PAZ

sacrifice

In the seventy-sixth year of his life, on a sweltering August afternoon, Chester Garland, the distinguished psychiatrist, author, and campaigner for human rights, was struck by a subway train and died.

The death of an old man is not astounding, but the circumstances of Garland's death shocked everyone who knew him. Heart failure, on the other hand—heart failure would have been plausible. Four months earlier, he had undergone open-heart surgery, spent five days at New York Hospital, in pain, feeble, exhausted, then six weeks bedridden, flattened by depression, at home on the Upper East Side of Manhattan, listening to Scarlatti.

"I've left the world, only my body doesn't know it yet," he said on one of those days to his son, Paul, who, on turning eighteen, had lopped off his given name, Michael, and taken his grandfather's surname, Gurevitch. Paul, now thirty-four, had sat at the foot of his father's bed, trying to understand what this man, older than himself by two generations, heard in the spattering harpsichord music.

"Compression," Garland said, as if reading his son's mind.

Paul wasn't sure he'd heard right. His father's voice was diminished. He seemed, as was his habit, to be addressing someone else, a presence just over Paul's shoulder.

"Compression. Scarlatti is the master of compression." Garland seemed annoyed that his son didn't understand. He cleared his throat. "Listen to all the notes he compresses into a few bars. It reminds you how much life there is to live in every second."

How much life? Scarlatti with all his scampering made Paul think of a hamster spinning its wheel. Anyway, what kind of value was compression when expounded by a man of multiple careers, serial marriages, a hodgepodge of reputations? A man who had smashed up his—that is, Paul's—one and only family? A man with a penchant, when Paul was a boy, for breaking off conversations to get back to his writing? True, Dr. Garland also relished order, spoke in measured tones, kept his files tidy and his journals in bound volumes arranged chronologically.

Paul, for his part, was a connoisseur of disorder. He was in the habit of grazing among three or four TV channels, sampling techno, jazz, and Gregorian chant at random on a five-disc CD player while chatting on-line with various passing acquaintances. Paul made an acceptable living as an on-line consultant and designer of software, which in his off hours he tested out on his unfinished comic strips—splicing together sound tracks, linking them into hypertexts. His father had told him that these loose constructions were rationalizations for his habit of not finishing projects: books, scripts, relationships.

"You're coming back to the world," Paul said, hoping the old man would appreciate a good-faith effort to cheer him up.

His father fell silent. Paul struggled not to feel judged by the silence. Chester said dryly, "Civilization is discontents, all right.

The Aztecs at least had the courtesy to eat your heart once they opened up your chest."

"You sound better," Paul replied, not insincerely.

"Do me a favor, son. Close the blinds. I don't want any more spring."

Paul hesitated. It was a crystalline day, the light pouring into his father's bedroom so generous, the air so clean, it seemed to have been pumped in from upstate valleys. Still, this was no time for argument, so he did as his father asked.

Chester Garland's thin lips sagged into a weak smile. Paul read—chose to read—his expression as an acknowledgment, and felt relieved.

"The notes fly all over the place, but it's the forward energy that makes the difference," Chester said slowly. "Perseverance."

Perseverance and compression! So that was the trick. Those were the gems of paternal wisdom for which Paul had been waiting thirty-four years. His inheritance.

"This Scarlatti was the son, you know," Chester said. "Domenico. His father was an important composer, wrote many kinds of music, but the son ended up surpassing him."

Paul thought later that his father must have meant to encourage him.

"He's speaking in whole sentences again," he said to his stepmother, on his way out. He didn't add, *like one of his books.*

I should talk, he thought on the subway ride home. I churn out fragments. I finish nothing.

Walking up the stairs to his apartment, he thought, Failure's my art form, and I still haven't reached my peak.

His father recovered, "as well as could be expected," in the surgeon's words. After six weeks, Chester Garland began to see patients again. His doctors, his wife, and his closest friends all thought that the sooner he went back to work, the better, though he was still forgetful and concerned about his ability to listen. His closest colleague, Howard Spain, thought he should be on antidepressants. Spain convinced Chester's wife, Grace, who convinced Chester, and he began taking the pills. After a week he felt better; after two weeks, much better. Still, he didn't go out much—a stroll to the park, to the newsstand, to the bookstore. He saw three patients the morning of his last Thursday on earth. He had been seeing each of them for some time, and all told the police they hadn't noticed anything wrong or "unusual." His appointment book showed that he had his normal full mornings inked in for weeks beyond the day he didn't come home from lunch.

His mangled body was recovered shortly before three o'clock in the afternoon on the uptown express track at Grand Central Station. The police found a sweeper, a woman who happened to notice an elderly white man standing alone by the track as a train pulled in. She thought it odd that he stood without moving as passengers got off and on the train. When she looked up, he was still there. She asked him if he was all right. "I'm all right," he replied. "Thank you for asking." "He looked," she said, "like a man with a burden." Her back was turned when the next train pulled in, so she only heard the screech of brakes and the *thunk* of the train meeting the body. No one else, not even a token clerk, could be located who had noticed Chester Garland. No one was evidently close enough to have pushed him. No one but the motorman seemed to have seen him jump, or fall, or whatever he did to die.

The policeman assigned to the case, a somber young man named Ramos, related these facts to Paul as freely as if he were conveying directions to a lost tourist. "What was his state of mind?" Ramos wanted to know.

"He'd been depressed but he was getting over it. The doctor said he had good odds. But my father was the kind of man who hated the thought of being the subject of odds. Any odds at all."

"Tell me, do you have any idea why he came down here in this heat? A man with a bad heart?"

"No idea. I didn't talk to him beforehand."

"Why he didn't take a taxi?"

"No idea. It doesn't . . . doesn't compute."

Ramos nodded slowly. He was doing his job, collecting impressions. Puffy eyes, distracted speech, a certain defensiveness—Paul was not the first bereaved relative Ramos had met who, while obviously not under suspicion, showed signs of guilt.

"Are you sure it was an accident?" Paul asked.

"He might have tripped. People faint in this kind of heat. They crumple up. Accidents happen. You see it all the time."

"My father didn't believe in accidents," Paul said suddenly. "He believed in explanations."

"Accident. That's an explanation."

"The funny thing is"—Paul drifted on—"he was always bumping into things."

"No kidding."

"He was good at a lot of things, but noticing wasn't one of them."

One minute, Paul is stumbling out of the police station, in a daze; the next, he's trudging through the late-afternoon heat to his father's apartment, the place where he spent his first eight years. He arrives with no recollection of how he got from point A to point B. If this were a video game, Paul thinks, they would leave out the grief scenes, which only impede the action. His stepmother is not home. In shock, she has been taken in by her

7

daughter across town. Paul gets a considerate doorman to let him into the apartment.

In an alcove off the living room, a modernist ivory chessboard is frozen in mid-game. White, Paul sees, without having to study the position, has strong lines of attack despite a congested center. But who, he wonders, was white, and who black?

He heads for his father's office, past the separate entranceway that leads from an outer corridor into a narrow waiting room. The magazines are current: *The New Yorker, Human Rights Review, Index on Censorship*. The people Paul knows would never bother reading *Index on Censorship*. Their tastes in communication run to voice mail and search engines, e-mailing confessions and jokes around the world in a split second. At that pace, no wonder painstaking psychoanalysis is on its last legs.

He pulls open the heavy, brightly varnished oak door to his father's office. More than once, his mother instructed him to stay out of this room. That's where your daddy works, she would say, as if that explained much. That's the cave where your father hides, was more like it. Your daddy works in that room, and you have your own room. Funny thing, that a man should go to work at home in a room inside a room, sealed off by a door behind a door. Freud didn't need such elaborate precautions. Soundproofing came along later, when the crazy belief spread that something ought to be done about human unhappiness and a whole profession was organized to listen in private.

Paul pushes open the second door, beautifully balanced and soundless on its hinges, and steps into that room of dust, Chester Garland's chamber of reason. It's more compact than Paul remembered. When his father used to summon him for the occasional audience, he was overwhelmed by its strangeness. Gravity, he notes, is the motif. Gravity and darkness. A room that sunlight cannot penetrate. Dark paneling. A bloodred Persian rug. The sole window opens onto an air shaft. Against one wall, that memorial to thousands of hours of confession: the analytic couch, looking long unused, covered with a striped afghan crocheted by Grace. Filing cabinets. His great glass-topped desk of finely grained oak with burgundy blotter and Mont Blanc pen. An IN box filled higher than the OUT box. In Plexiglas frames, a color photo of a beaming Grace and a black-and-white of little Paul standing stiffly in front of a jungle gym, Chester beside him, his hand on Paul's shoulder. The picture is cropped close to the border, where, Paul supposes, the image of his mother once was. Behind the photos, his father's minor trophies: an ebony African godhead, a brass Buddha, an angular Cretan goddess, and other objects of indefinite provenance. This is not the room of a man who didn't intend to return.

Next to the desk, two identical black revolving Scandinavian leather chairs inspect each other. Between them, the no-man's-land of a footstool. Visible only from one chair, obviously his father's, is a brass wall clock with a nautical look. Paul places himself in the other chair, stretches out his feet, and surveys the room from the sufferer's point of view. He notes the ceiling-high white bookcases, full of somber sets of Freud and the lesser classics, years' worth of psychoanalytic quarterlies, multi-volume histories of Judaism and Christianity, Bible studies. There, too, are his father's three books, bound in maroon leather, beside bound sets of Dostoyevsky, Mann, Proust, Lawrence, Sartre's *Roads to Freedom* trilogy, and the *Confessions* of Augustine and Rousseau. There are several ordinary copies of *Abraham, Isaac, Esau,* the best known of his father's works, in English, and eight or ten translations including, it would appear, Japanese. Within each section, the books are arranged alphabetically by author, each author's work chronologically. On one wall without books, a silver-framed reproduction of a Blake lithograph: a swirl of angels dreamed by a sleeping monarch, a continuous curve of deliverance filling its upper reaches. And then, next to it, the pièce de résistance: Herbert Spector's wooden triptych, commissioned for the frontispiece of *Abraham, Isaac, Esau*.

Stillness and safety, as much as a room can offer. Please have a seat. Compassion and knowledge have been accumulating for decades, awaiting the next fifty minutes of your suffering. Welcome to Chester Garland's quick, curious eyes, silver hair, and Lincolnesque fringe of beard, the creases that stamp his forehead with authority, the vertical crevices knifing toward his mouth, his low-pitched, damped-down voice. There is nothing so terrible that it cannot be said in this room. I have heard worse than you can imagine. His wistful and benevolent smile: How may I help you?

His son thinks, Dear Father who art in heaven, I'll bet you said that to all the paying customers. What do I do now, Chester, in a fatherless world? The grief—or whatever it is—feels like dry mud caked in his chest.

Paul stands up and inspects the framed certificates on the wall by his father's desk, a gallery of honors that patients would see only in passing but Chester Garland was free to contemplate whenever he wished. Paul can remember times when this wall was bare, times when it was filled with Cézanne prints, and times when it was clogged, as now, with a full panoply of testimonials laid out in perfect horizontals: honorary degrees; book awards; a photo of him receiving a medal from President Carter; photos with Julius Nyerere, with Andrei Sakharov, with Kim Mbela, Hassan Izmet, and other human rights activists. His father's service award from the Society for the Rehabilitation of Victims of Torture. His three book jackets, framed: *The Transmigration of Souls: A Psychoanalytic Account; Abraham, Isaac, Esau; The Silence of God and the Silences of Men*. All in all, a sort of home page of self-advertisement. No, shrine was more like it: what an exemplary human life was supposed to look like. Did he imagine his wall of pride having some healing effect on his patients?

Be fair, Paul. Chester Garland was good to sufferers—at least, those to whom he wasn't related or who came to him with a good reason to suffer.

Is that the best you can do? No. Restart.

He can remember one time when Chester embraced him in a full-bodied way. The arms of that younger man and the slightly musty smell of the elderly one mix in his mind. Paul is not sure he should trust such memories.

The Garland Museum, Paul thinks, or says (he's not sure which), and winces—the body is barely cold! He wonders suddenly what his father's patients are going to be told about how exactly their savior walked out of their lives. Will they be in a forgiving mood? That their doctor died is bad enough. Some of them have undoubtedly been in psychotherapy long enough to be convinced that there is meaning in every event. They are not going to believe in accidents; no, they know accidents are symptoms, and symptoms are revelations, and revelations are the means to mental health, or maturity, or integration, or whatever the goal is these days. They are going to think suicide. They are going to be saddled with guilt and rage for years. Shrinks all over Manhattan will batten on the domino effect. There will be hushed conversations among learned figures in leather chairs about the responsibilities of the profession. They will blame themselves or talk themselves out of blaming themselves, with equal flair.

His father must have been hurting so much, he wasn't thinking of his patients when he jumped.

If he jumped.

Forgive me, Father. I need to be forgiven. As I have forgiven you. Correction: As I shall forgive you someday.

If his father were sitting here, Paul knows, he'd hold him in his wise, sad gaze and with compassion and condescension in equal measure say, "You're too brittle, son."

Like the hard peanut candy that you break off with your teeth. Brittle, brutal.

The gentle man, his mother had called him, in Paul's hearing, not long after Chester bolted.

Paul remembered asking her once, years later, when she was living alone and claimed to enjoy it, what had first attracted her to Chester. "He didn't raise his voice," she said. "He was patient. He listened, and he was tender, and he had a way of fixing those gray eyes on me and patting my cheek, and all my resistance melted away. Oh, Paul, it's so sweet to be patronized when you're young."

He can no longer be sure those were her words.

Suddenly, Paul looks up at the wall, spooked. He has the impression that the triptych is watching him. He flicks on the light. Dust streams across the spotlight in the ceiling. He steps to the wall and studies the roaring colors and Expressionist outlines of "Abraham, Isaac, Esau." The name Garland appears nowhere on it, and yet Chester was in a real sense its author. It was he who commissioned Herb Spector, his childhood friend, to paint it, and the design must have been his own, since it seems to cover the same ground as his famous book—

—at least what Paul assumes about the book, since he hasn't read much beyond the flyleaf. When he was thirteen, his father had ushered him into this room and ceremoniously presented him with a copy, which Paul took back to the apartment where he and his mother lived and tossed on his desk unopened. As if it were a gift for his nonexistent bar mitzvah. Days later, he had picked it up, noted the dedication— "To my son: May he call a halt to the sacrifice"—and flung his inscribed copy full force against the wall. Thus the *Abraham, Isaac, Esau* on his own shelf has a wounded spine.

The left-hand panel of Spector's triptych shows Abraham, sweat in beads on his brow, a wild look in his eye, knife raised over Isaac, a plump boy of twelve or thirteen stretched out on a flat silver-bright stone, oblivious to the feathery angel swooping toward him or the stag caught in a bush, lower left. The angel has the tender face of an androgynous sprite, bearing a certain resemblance to Isaac, who lies on his belly, perhaps so his genitals won't show, and stares out of the frame, his face distended with fear. Near the edge of the painting stands an older youth, apparently startled, his bow drawn taut. He seems to have just noticed the sacrificial scene. A scrawl reads "Love and Infanticide."

Isaac stumbles out of the frame of the centerpiece—entitled "Fathers and Dispossession"—forearm raised, eyes averted from a ram sprawled on the altar, its throat slit, its horns in a pool of blood. Lit by a beam of light, Abraham stares at the ram. He looks as if he had no idea what came over him or what lesson he's supposed to have learned. And what lesson, Paul wonders, would that have been? Why in the world was his twentieth-century father interested in this ancient myth? The hunter, Paul notes, has vanished, and of the angel only a wing and a half smile can be seen through the steam, or fog, that rises—or falls—in the background.

In the final panel, "Betrayal and Vengeance," a grinning young man—possibly Jacob, if Paul remembers the story accurately—his hands in fur gloves, bows with mock servility to an aged man, presumably Isaac, whose milky pupils stare blankly at the viewer. Isaac's face is cracked, as if he's smoked too many cigarettes for too many years, but his cheeks have the plumpness of a child's. A sullen young man with a bow under his arm—but not the archer of the first panel—slinks off to the left, looking over his shoulder at a tent the silvery color of the altar on which Isaac lay. A sweet-faced stag looks on from a thicket, for God knows what reason. The angel, with whitening hair, his eyes lit with pity, hovers over the scene. With whom, in this painting, did his father identify? Not, surely, the demented Abraham. The elderly angel? Paul feels a surge of bitterness. *I know angels, Mr. Shrink, and you were no angel.* Nothing in his mind, Paul knows, stays serious for long. Even his father's death, even his father, quickly becomes a bad, bitter joke.

He looks at the triptych. Focus, he tells himself; think of it as a comic strip and focus. The landscape, he notes, is finely etched and diminutive, as in a Renaissance portrait, the olive trees and dunes outlined distinctly. There's a glow in the flesh tones, each human being and the angel illuminated as if by a source of light deep within the slashes of paint that make up the figures. God the Father is absent. There are no women anywhere.

Paul is aware of the tick of the nautical clock, and it unnerves him. Between the painting and him, a force field seems to vibrate. He feels the onset of some nameless, indescribable doom and then a sudden tremor, a tiny electrical spark, and he finds his mind untethered. It feels as if something in him has been zapped away. He takes a step toward his father's chair. Nothing happens. Two, three. He stands behind the chair now, massaging its smooth leather back, which is cool to the touch. He spins it wildly and then, with the touch of a finger, brings it to a standstill and swings himself into the seat. It does not feel like sitting but falling—plummeting into a hole that feels unsettlingly familiar.

sacrifice

So this is what it feels like to be an orphan. Not much different. You fall alone as you stand alone.

He sits, lost in time. How did he get here? He thinks, I should call someone. Who? Why? To hear me scourge myself?

The air is cool in his nostrils. He reaches into his pocket for his red western handkerchief and mops his eyes without quite knowing if he has shed any tears—why should he shed tears? Nothing has changed one iota since his father jumped in front of a train—and without exactly forming the thought that this is what he wishes to do, he goes to the bookshelf, pulls out a copy of *Abraham, Isaac, Esau,* one whose spine is in perfect shape, one never sacrificed to the god or gods of filial wrath, and sits back down heavily in the patient's chair, the petitioner's, opens the book in his lap to a random early page, and begins to read.

ABRAHAM WAS AN old man, burdened by days.

We know little of him but for a sketchy report of some of his actions. The Bible is sparing with details, but centuries of graven images have left their mark. We think of Abraham sun-baked, bearded, solemn, his face long, his hair matted, his eyes burning. It is difficult to imagine this Abraham as a cherub plump in his mother's arms, or as a boy who scampers about stealing dates, spitting out the long pits, or shaking gnarled trees to collect ripe olives from the stony ground. No, Abraham seems to have been born grave and deliberate, an ancient from his first moments on earth. He is consumed by his purpose. It is not the desert heat alone that drives his eyes wild. He is a fanatic.

This fanatic burns for one thing and one thing alone: to found a people. Abraham sorely desires what God promised him: sons, sons, sons who will bring forth ever more sons. Yet this same progenitor is always casting his sons into the wilderness! Surely this anomaly is the key to his character. The question is, what does that key open? How does a father reveal his love?

What a difference between a week ago and now. Then Paul would have resented his father for asking such pompous, condescending questions, while now he feels their poignancy.

For reasons that are obscure to him he suddenly feels like leaping up and fleeing the room.

By sheer force of filial will, he keeps reading. What was it his father used to say when he couldn't concentrate on his studies? "Persevere when it's the last thing in the world you want to do. You may discover something about yourself."

So he will persevere. But he does yield to the urge to skim ahead. Abraham builds altars, goes to Egypt, gives his wife to the Pharaoh, whom God proceeds to punish with plagues, Sarah is barren, and so on and so forth.

IN THE DESERT, Abraham made a life of abundance and sacrifice. He fought wars; he won victories; he settled land. Still the land was barren and Sarah remained barren. Why did Abraham go on believing? Because the Lord did not quite abandon him. The Lord brought him victories, and the gift of more promises, and told him to fear not. Bring Me a heifer, a she-goat, a ram, a turtledove, and a young pigeon, said the Lord. Abraham did more than the Lord required of him. He had heard of the days of Noah and the coupling of beasts. He gathered the beasts for the Lord, and brought them to his altar, and sliced them in half. And Abraham said, O Lord God, Your love is beyond question, and though I shall die childless, Your love is my shield. And the Lord said, Know well that your offspring shall be strangers in a land that is not theirs, and they shall be enslaved and oppressed for four hundred years. Without limits is my love, Abraham

sacrifice

said, because the time of sacrifice shall not go on endlessly. In the fourth generation, said the Lord, your offspring shall be free, and prosper, and shall return to this land, once the people who now dwell here, the Amorites, are done with their iniquity.

In dread did Abraham hear the word of the Lord. After all these years, he was only beginning to understand what was at stake in a father's love for his son.

Sarah asked, Why must we wait? And Abraham said, The Lord is my Master but not the Master of all events at all times. . . .

Paul's eyes glaze over when the Amorites make their appearance. What was Dr. Garland driving at in this strange retelling, or allegory, or—what is this book anyway? Fiction with a prefabricated plot? So much like, it occurs to him, psychoanalysis. In fact, Chester had once told his son that he'd wanted to be a novelist, when young, and had written short stories throughout his college years, only to give up fiction for truth-telling in medical school.

But isn't it obvious? A barren wife who gives birth at an advanced age? The book is his father's confession. The logical next step would be to show Abraham the righteous father of Jews, Christians, and Muslims botching his flesh-and-blood fatherhood. . . . Paul hasn't the heart to go on. He carefully reinserts the book in its niche, leaving no evidence that he's ever invaded the inner sanctum. He closes both doors on his way out, sealing his father's vault airtight behind him.

Early the next morning, the phone rings. Paul lies in his tangled sheets and listens until it resoundingly stops. A few seconds later it begins again, and this time he answers.

17

"Am I speaking to Paul Gurevitch?" says a composed voice. Paul mutters something. "This is Cavender." Bill Cavender—William Cavender, Jr.—his father's lawyer. Mainly Paul remembers them playing chess in the enclave off the living room, long hours when his father was not to be disturbed. "I don't have to tell you how sorry I am."

Suddenly Paul is awake. Electrically awake. "No, but thanks anyway. I'm sorry on your behalf, too," he hears himself saying.

"Of course this is not an ideal time to intrude, I know, but your father asked me to speak with you."

So the time has come to clue the son in on his father's will—before the body is even vaporized! Does Cavender think he can't wait? Did his father?

Cavender clears his throat and says, in that carefully modulated voice that must have measurably increased his billable hours, "I have something for you. Something your father asked me to pass on to you, should anything happen to him."

"Excuse me?"

"If you can arrange to come to my office at your convenience, I will explain."

"You have something for me," Paul repeats stupidly.

He has nothing else in the world that urgently needs doing, and so makes an appointment to receive this something as soon as seems decent, the day after the funeral.

"We were not just happier for his company," Rabbi Gerstein is intoning, "but somehow more honorable. Now that he is no longer here with us on the material plane, we can understand—perhaps only now in the depths of our being—that he was truly a just spirit, not only a man for all seasons but a man who made every season into his own."

sacrifice

In his mid-sixties, Gerstein is not one of those smooth suburban rabbis with assimilated faces. He has tended to his spiritual hunger. Yet with his huge gut, his booming voice, and his eager, bulbous eyes, he is also distinctly a man of appetites. The black yarmulke on his hairless skull looks like a raft cast onto a great bald sea. The skin beneath his eyes is baggy, but the eyes are fierce and don't care. Gerstein is the sole reason why this service for the (so far as anyone knows) atheist, agnostic, or indifferent deceased is taking place in a temple of worship. For years, Dr. Garland found Gerstein a valuable colleague in the struggle to keep torturers from inflicting acute damage upon the human body and spirit.

"Do not remember him as the man with the ailing heart, whose best years were behind him!" Gerstein implores. "Remember Chester Garland as a man with the strongest and most committed of hearts, committed first of all to his beloved family"—he dispenses a soulful glance at the front bench, where Paul, to his displeasure, makes eye contact with him—"but also, and far more remarkably, to his extended family: the multitude of readers he inspired and, above all, the many, many unfortunates wasting away in prisons, in wretched concentration camps on every continent, men and women whom he never met but who were as real to him as you or me. And then, of course, there were the victims, whom he campaigned tirelessly to rehabilitate, to bring back from living death. They will never forget him; they are his—well, not his children but his living memory. We who had the good fortune to live in his company, we may have thought we knew this great and good man, but I wonder if we truly did. I wonder if even today we know just who Chester Garland was and what he gave us."

Paul has the sensation now that Gerstein's eyes are blazing directly into his own. Who does Gerstein think he is, scrutinizing Paul for his reaction? Paul tries not to blink, but he knows Gerstein's questions are fair: Who *was* his father, and what *did* he give Paul besides grief and disappointment?

"We all sensed, when we met Chester Garland or read those profound books of his, that however great was our own travail, he knew, if not how to master it, how to find the meaning of it and how, if necessary, to live with it."

Out of the corner of his eye, Paul watches his stepmother absorbing the rabbi's oration. Her red eyes intent, her handsome head tilted up, she gazes through a film of tears and wonderment as if she were hearing the rustle of angel's wings bearing her husband to heaven. There were angels in the artworks on Chester Garland's walls, after all, and at birth Paul himself was named (after a dead great-uncle) Micha-El, archangel of God, guardian, if he remembers rightly, of the soul of Abraham. But Paul preferred—prefers still—to leave any preoccupation with angels to his already sainted father.

"He was a man of his word and a man of healing words," Gerstein goes on.

Shall we talk for a moment about some words that don't heal? And then bring on the anesthesia?

For example: "Mom, where's Dad?"

"I told you, away on a trip, Michael." Marion Garland, knitting a sweater, speaks crisply, her anxiety wrapped tight, like her needles in yarn. She wears no makeup. He likes the mommies who wear lipstick, but his mother is different. "He's in Paris. France."

That seems a funny place to go. "When is he coming back?"

She lays her needles down carefully on the coffee table and says quietly, "Soon. Soon, Michael."

She must have been chagrined, Paul thinks, that her son

should have cared so much about the whereabouts of a father who put so little of himself forward when he was home.

She tucks her hair, her long, dark, limp hair with its silver streaks that look like scars, over her left ear and goes back to knitting.

"Why did he go to a convent?"

"A convent?" She laughs her throaty laugh. "Oh, Michael, no, he went to a *convention*. He'll be coming back as soon as it's over." He can hear the peculiar hesitation behind her crisp voice. A lot of things have been peculiar lately.

"When is it over?"

"It is over. It's over now. Actually, it's over, but—"

"But what?"

"Enough, Michael."

"Is he coming tomorrow?"

"It might be tomorrow. I don't know." Then, more sharply: "Please don't keep asking."

"Daddy's not coming back."

"Of course he is, darling."

Paul doesn't want his mother to cry and yet he does. She's been crying a lot recently. She has a strange way of crying silently. When she cries, he feels awful for her. He wraps his arms around her, and then she lets him do anything he wants—go to a movie, buy more candy bars.

She carefully places the bundle of wool and needles on the coffee table. She cups the back of his head in her hand and holds him as if he were a sacred thing against her breast, and everything he is or has ever been dissolves and flows into her, into the room, and the room melts away. Later, after his eyes run dry, he lies in her lap, his mother's hand stroking his hair, her arms and her warmth enveloping him, her heartbeat a rumble in his own chest, and he listens for the rattling moan that wells up from her when she pauses to breathe.

21

. . .

Three hundred mourners summon up memories. The analysts and the analyzed, the ex-patients in shock, the bereft, the puzzled, the curious and admiring—three hundred busy, not vastly religious souls ducking out of their respective working days, taking refuge in a synagogue to feel their loss and, in the process, assess the company they're in. Three hundred bodies defeat air-conditioning as they heat up the chapel a fraction of a degree at a time. The varnished cedar casket reminds Paul of the door to his father's study. Even Jesus Christ got only one resurrection. The second time Chester Garland was destroyed—destroyed himself—was for good. He did a more thorough job than the surgeons. That's why there is no open casket and no chance to ask his preternaturally smooth face for forgiveness—or some last favor—or to leave a final kiss on his icy forehead.

"Many of us were gathered to Chester Garland by his gift for words, which reflected the quality of his soul." Rabbi Gerstein lumbers on. "He did not heal by passing on formulas sanctified by his elders. He *earned* his words. His only orthodoxy"—Gerstein sticks up his forefinger and waves it around like a pointer—"his only orthodoxy was the unorthodox. When he wrote his remarkable *Abraham, Isaac, Esau,* he knew there would be some who would not understand, who might be offended, who would call it heresy, even if they did not use the word. And then, when he added the subtitle"—Gerstein, a pro, pauses for effect—"*Love and Infanticide,* well, such audacity was not calculated to win him many friends in the seminaries." Gerstein shows a grin full of big teeth and waits for the titters to pass. "They thought the Old Testament was *theirs,* but Chester knew better. So he was not so interested in the fancy commentaries and interpretations that had piled up over the centuries to improve the Bible—that is what he thought

of the midrash. Obviously he was no calculator of consequences. He had his calling and that was that. I never heard him
complain about being misunderstood. That came with the territory. He took his critics lightly because he knew that actions
produce reactions."

And there, not eight feet away, is the polished box containing the heap of mangled flesh and bone that is all that remains
of Chester Garland's last action. Paul remembers drawing a
comic strip in high school under the influence of Poe. The story
took place in Spain, in a time of religious wars. A castle is under
siege; the few men who survive are running out of food.
Improbably, they have obtained a cease-fire to transport their
dead to a cemetery. One man bearing a message volunteers to be
smuggled out in a coffin. His coreligionists will know where to
dig him up. All goes well until the wagon that bears his coffin
runs into a roadblock. His side has won an unexpected battle,
whereupon his coffin is diverted—to the wrong cemetery! The
man is only aware of the procession stopping, then starting
again. The last thing he hears is the sound of earth thumping
against the lid of his coffin.

The young Paul loved leafing through the one-volume complete Poe in the living room bookcase. On the flyleaf, Chester
Garland had written, in a meticulous hand, *My darling, my darling, my life and my bride.* Poe's words to his dead wife.

Chester Garland's casket gleams by the light of a dim chan-
delier. These words drop into Paul's mind: *You're burying the
wrong man.*

"He was truly one of the devout, one of the just, one of the
writers of the book of our people!" Gerstein is soaring now. "In
the end, his great, good heart failed him, yet it never failed us."

Paul thinks, As if it were a faulty ventricle that killed him,
not the East Side express.

"Yitgadal v'yitkadash sh'may raba b'alma d'vera chirutay,"

Gerstein intones. "Let the glory of God be extolled, let His great name be hallowed, in the world whose creation He willed." The tone is flat and anticlimactic, like—it occurs to Paul—the credits rolling at the end of a movie.

Is there glory? Is anything hallowed? Paul wonders what his father believed in his final days. He wishes he had asked. Already he misses that smile, the one where his father looks as though he's squinting into the sun. Paul would like to remember him as a man who could rescue himself. Who would not have been chewed up by so much sour motionless agony that he would stand at the lip of a subway platform, his back turned to his family and the rest of the living, listening for a muffled vibration to swell into a roar that would be the last sound he would hear in this life.

"May His kingdom soon prevail"—Rabbi Gerstein's voice trembles—"in our own day, our own lives, and the life of all Israel, and let us say: Amen. . . . *Oseh shalom bimromav, hu ya'aseh shalom aleinu v'al kol Yisrael, v'imru: amen.* . . . May the Source of peace bring peace to all who mourn and comfort to all who are bereaved. Amen."

Throughout the hall, sobs and coughs break out, along with rustles, fidgets, positional relocations, and throat clearings that have been postponed until the eulogy's end. After a deep breath, Gerstein introduces the next speaker, Hassan Izmet, a small gaunt man with olive skin and high cheekbones, wearing an ornate embroidered yarmulke. He walks down the aisle, limping slightly, past women in straw hats or bare-headed fanning themselves with programs, past men in suits and men in polo shirts. Izmet's voice seems especially high and delicate after the rabbi's. "Dr. Garland learned of my situation and campaigned to have international organizations take up my case," he begins. His vowels bear traces of English schooling. "He wrote to me expressing solidarity. I wrote to him that the winter was cold.

He wrote back reassuring me about the coming spring. He understood my meaning perfectly. I wrote to him that the situation of philosophy was uncertain. He wrote that the proper appreciation of uncertainty was the burden of humanity. And so on. I was in the seventh year of my imprisonment for pleading the cause of the Kurdish people. I had published books, you see, saying that the problem of the Kurds was not psychological but political. This was my third year of solitary confinement. They beat the soles of my feet with sticks. On a summer day, the guard threw open my cell door and told me I had a visitor. I was astounded. I had not been permitted a visitor in six years, not even my family. I was taken to a small room. There was a man I did not know seated on a wooden chair on the other side of a table. It was, of course, Dr. Garland. We were not permitted to shake hands. He seemed very much at ease. He was on vacation nearby, he said, when he thought to look in on me. I came to learn later that he had been warned not to come. 'What are they going to do to me?' he said. We talked about poetry. We discussed the life of Abraham and the principle of *amor fati,* the love of fate. He said he admired my work on Hagar and Ishmael. The guard said to me later, 'This man is an American imam?' I said, 'Not exactly.' 'Your imam?' I said, 'Not exactly.' This guard held me down on the chair while another guard broke my ribs."

When Izmet pauses you can hear the stillness in the chapel, like the background hush that fills the spaces between words on tape. Izmet says that later, after Dr. Garland had invited him to America to work with the Society for the Rehabilitation of Victims of Torture, he found out that the doctor had proceeded to a dinner at the American embassy in Ankara and drunk a toast to Izmet's health. A representative of the Ministry of Justice was present and walked out. A diplomatic scandal! Soon afterward, Izmet was released. He speaks of himself as one of many who owe their lives and their sanity to the work of "this great and generous doctor."

Grace's sweet face has lost its shape, like a crumpled beach ball. Paul wonders what he looks like when he's weeping. But he is not weeping. What he feels is primal anxiety. Adrenaline has taken over his being, pools of it. He rises to his feet, lurches forward, and ascends the steps to the rostrum, the scaffold. He thinks, Here goes nothing, pulls three typed folded pages out of his inside jacket pocket, lays them on the lectern, and runs his hand over them to press out the creases. He looks out into the hall waiting for . . . some kind of climax? For him to prove himself? Or flop? He sees a room full of summer suits: analysts, theologians, the human rights establishment. His suit—the only suit he owns, the one he buried his mother in nine years before—is navy. His tie is black, courtesy of the funeral chapel. The hinge of his mouth is tight, like the spring of a trap. What do the guests see, his anxiety? The hawkish beak of his nose? The maladroitness that would have shamed his father? Paul feels the tightness seep, as if it were liquid, into the back of his skull. At least this is the last parental eulogy that will be required of him.

There is a tingle in the hollow behind his eyes, and at this precise moment the words directly in front of him start to blur and shimmer as if he were staring at them through water. The ones on the periphery are still clear enough, but no matter how painstakingly he composed and recomposed them, the rest are jiggling just when he needs them. He waits stupidly, helplessly, in silence for the words to come back into focus, but they seem to ignite, flare up, and double. He recognizes with a familiar horror the onset of a migraine—"a classic symptom," his doctor had once told him with a smile, as if he should feel proud to be in touch with the classics.

He adjusts his clear-framed glasses, as if some action might help, looks up from his useless pages, and calls his father "a noble man—a kind of Jewish nobleman" and "an aristocrat of the people." He says Chester Garland taught him that anything worth doing was worth doing meticulously, that "the angel is in the details." Michael Paul Garland, he thinks as he gropes for something else to say, absorbed that lesson well, applying it with care in the early cartoons of what might pass for his career. When you flipped the pages of these porno flash books, his extraterrestrials fucked with remarkable precision and verisimilitude. He had dropped out of college to do more of the same under the name M. Paul. Not the line of work a father advertises. Perhaps Chester Garland felt a certain relief when his son dispensed with the name his own father had adopted for membership in America forty years before.

Soon, Paul Gurevitch, aka M. Paul, had lost interest in down-and-dirty sci-fi stroke books and graduated to philosophical erotica—busty maids sprouting wordy talk balloons about the doctrines of eternal recurrence, the limits of lived experience, or the need to remain silent on matters about which one could not be intelligible. By twenty-one, inspired by R. Crumb and the Situationists, he had drawn 110 panels of a strip called "A Season in Tedium," 172 of "My Life Is My Drug." He showed his parents selected panels and his mother used the word "proud" while his father allowed "promising." Neither was permitted to see what Paul called his black box, the 44 panels of "Fuck More, Bitch Less." By twenty-two, his stuff, always labeled "in progress," was appearing in group publications under names like *Enlightenment Comix* and *Ecstasies of Communication*. He picked up admiring notices in *Playboy* and—to his embarrassment—*Hustler*. He was denounced in *Ms.*—"permanent arch

adolescent . . . gives new meaning to the word 'objectification.' "
All this without making much money to speak of, which was
fine with him.

Fast-forward two years. He composes elaborate, Rube
Goldberg–like strips about failing to finish his stories. He begins
a "graphic novel" called *Bizarre Success Artistique,* about
Hollywood in the lives of Irving Berlin, the Russian Jew
who wrote "God Bless America"; Louis B. Mayer, the Russian
Jew who adopted the Fourth of July as his birthday; and
Thomas Mann, the German who wrote about the demonic-
slash-romantic soul of art from his exile in Pacific Palisades. His
mother is wasting away from ovarian cancer. He visits her every
day for a year. Income trickles in from European and Japanese
editions of his comics. He finds he has not produced enough
work to be collected. Under the name Gurevitch, he picks up a
regular strip in a computer magazine. He carries on multimedia
experiments, with computer-assisted design as a sideline. He
decides that living in a rent-controlled apartment is as much
success as he can handle. His father has long since ceased to ask
when he is going back to school.

Paul's migraine is shifting to the headache stage. Tiny nodes
of pain in his temples sharpen like red-hot pencil points. The
faces before him blur. Everything shimmers in its doubled state.
He finds a glass of water on a shelf of the lectern and takes a
swallow.

"We failed him," he says. "That may seem harsh, but he
liked blunt statements. This one is as blunt as they come:
Together we failed him and separately we failed him. I don't
think we have to torture ourselves about our failure, but I think
we have to stare at it straight. Let's admit it: He was an easy
man to fail. Chester Garland demanded a lot of everyone
because he demanded a great deal of himself. Governments
failed him, so he did something about them, as we heard from

our Turkish friend. I don't have to tell you what he did for immigrants, asylum seekers. We could stay here all day and hear from desperate people out of all kinds of hellholes—I am sure many of you are here."

Paul glances at his text, pointlessly. Somebody coughs.

"Chester Garland was not a perfect man." Paul rumbles toward his unknown conclusion. *As he was perfect enough to remind me more than once.* "Now we have to suffer without him. And to do what we can to relieve the suffering of others, which, as my father knew, will help us relieve our own. But now we will have our summering"—he stops still, horrified—"I mean our suffering, to ourselves."

He has failed—failed his father—again. He slumps back to his seat, hot nails of pain piercing his skull. *Summering, suffering.* It seems a reasonable summary of a life, when he stops to think about it. Possibly even his own.

He is barely present for the rabbi's closing words and the final movement of Beethoven's last string quartet, the tense and not obviously consoling passage that had been his father's sole ceremonial request.

The less said about the cremation, the better. Blood boils, brains evaporate. At the bone-white marble pile of a crematorium in a Jersey suburb that seems to be consecrated to the disposal of bodies, the air-conditioning is excessive to ward off the August heat. And yet there are thousands of degrees Fahrenheit on the other side of the brick wall. As in—well, Auschwitz. The mass murder of Jews should not be converted to a casual analogy, but there it sits, the uninvited guest. Zero is the solution. Chester Garland is history.

The ashes will be scattered off the beach in front of the summer house on Cape Cod.

. . .

Cavender's office is on a cross street around the corner from Park Avenue, on the second floor of a narrow brownstone, the remains of a more genteel New York now wedged between new sleek office buildings. The entrance to Cavender's building is a few steps below street level. The elevator is intimate, with a gate that has to be closed by hand. This was the Strong mansion, says Cavender before Paul asks, taking his elbow, ushering him into his inner office, as if Paul knew who Strong was. Cavender wears a pin-striped suit, double-breasted, with a red tie pulled taut at his weathered neck. Paul is wearing a white shirt, collar proudly frayed, no tie. Black jeans, plain white sneakers.

Cavender extends a long-fingered hand. More distracted than usual, Paul gazes at a point slightly above the other man's eyes and tries to read his mind. Probably in his early seventies, the lawyer is only of medium height but his way of holding himself erect gives an impression of stature. He has shrewd blue eyes. His hair, once a metallic blond, is thinning and gray, but enough remains for a pompadour in front. His mustache is trimmed precisely; his cheeks are hollow with age. He radiates reliability. Once he must have been dashing, and he has lived long enough to see that style gray with him. Still, his manner is fragrant with skill and understanding. He is exactly the man Chester Garland would trust to break bad news graciously—a bequest, say, in the form of a trust hedged about with caveats and an executor.

"Thank you for coming. My condolences again. Please sit down, Paul."

"Thank you."

"I suppose you remember the period many years ago when your father took his"—the pause lingers for the correct number of seconds—"leave from the family." Cavender sits behind a wide mahogany desk that has been cleared of all but a single small stack of paper and, directly in front of him, three battered books bound with a thick rubber band. He forms his fingers into a steeple of concern.

"His extended leave," Paul offers, in the spirit of what Cavender might call a clarification.

"His extended leave," Cavender concedes, with a whiff of irony.

"It's not the sort of thing a child forgets."

Cavender is used to being held accountable for his clients' shortcomings. "Surely not. What I'm about to tell you concerns that—that turning point in your father's life."

"Not only his."

"Please understand, it is not my place to make judgments."

"Of course not."

"I am here strictly as an instrument of your father's wishes."

Paul shivers, his skull tingles, and he fears that another migraine is on its way. Chester Garland had that effect on people, he thinks. They wanted to please him. Of course, the hard part was to know what his wishes were. When he walked out on his family, for example, or when he wrote *Abraham, Isaac, Esau*, or when he went down to Grand Central Station.

"I'll get right to the point. Your father left these notebooks in my possession."

As Cavender gestures toward them, Paul has the sensation that his mind is floating upward out of his skin. He compels himself to pay attention. It registers on him that the top notebook is blue with gold decorations.

"He kept a journal. What he told me is that it concerns—well, as I said, that difficult period in his life. He thought these materials were yours by right. He wanted you to have them."

"Jesus Christ," is all Paul can say. The tingle in his skull no longer feels like the prologue to a migraine. It feels like something else, something unfamiliar: spectral, even.

"They're your property now." Another carefully calibrated pause and then: "In case you are wondering, it was not my place to read this material, and so I have not." Cavender's blue eyes gaze at Paul with a slight twinkle. He is a connoisseur of other people's surprise.

"Your father is full of surprises," said Marion Garland with considerable restraint, during one of her better days on the Cape in that time of abandonment. Surprises include: birthday parties, sneak previews, a trip to an underground cave, your father going off on a trip and not coming back. "I wouldn't have thought he could do this to us, Michael. Such a steady man. Would you have thought it?" Paul is impressed that his mother does not raise her voice.

In the attic, Michael Paul spots a frame face down on a trunk. When he turns it over, he finds the portrait of his father that used to sit on his mother's dresser, now without its glass mounting. Scrawled on the face in a black magic marker: POR- TRAIT OF A MAN ABOUT TO LEAVE.

"Where is he really, Ma?"

Michael Paul's first big piano recital is coming up in October. He's considered young for the challenge and honor. He begins every day with a queasy stomach. All his friends and classmates have stepfathers, at least. A lot of them have fathers. His mother has bought him an unwanted new suit and a Looney Tunes tie to make up for the discomfort.

"Your father is finding himself, Michael."

Michael laughs at the absurdity of it—his father, whom he hadn't known to be lost, having to find himself.

For days, his mother drags around, a phantom barely filling space. Paul has the run of the house. But one day, he hears a crash from the kitchen. He runs downstairs and finds her standing amid a scatter of glass shards. She reaches up to the shelf where the ceremonial goblets are kept, picks up a thin blue fluted glass, and tosses it onto the floor with a certain delicacy, a flick of the wrist. It breaks with a tinkle, as if it hadn't been solid to start with. There is nothing frantic about her, only a pure, controlled desire to see things break. The moment of satisfaction passes, and she reaches for another ritual sacrifice.

"Mommy, stop, stop it." The boy is crying, throwing his arms around her waist. She makes no effort to push him away. Whatever has broken in her husband on the other side of the world is now breaking in her. Michael Paul lets go of his mother, goes to the closet for the broom and dustpan, and starts sweeping up fragments of glass, but his mother cannot abide the sight of her fumbling little boy prodding a heap of broken glass with his pianist's fingers. She takes the broom from his hands.

Chester Garland, the abandonment years.

Michael Paul did well at the recital. There were comments about his maturity.

Paul gets into a taxi, holding the notebooks in one hand, thinking they ought to be wrapped in newspaper like the Maltese Falcon. The blue notebook, slightly frayed, is covered in stiff pebbled cloth; its four corners are imitation gold leaf curlicues connected by straight gold lines, giving Paul the impression of a faded Victorian version of something vaguely Persian. The second notebook is smaller and thinner, with a yellow cloth spine. The third, also thin, has a plain tan cardboard back cover; its corners are worn.

He desperately wants to tear open this unexpected cache, yet fears what he might find—as if something loathsome might be putrefying inside, as in *Tales from the Crypt,* that sort of thing. He starts to roll the rubber band off the notebooks, and it snaps in half. He opens the blue one. The first entry is dated July 30, 1973. Paul was eight; his father was, what, forty-nine? The thick pages are still milky white, rag paper; this is a man who, after all, bound his prized books in leather. His father's handwriting is elegant and precise, surprisingly diminutive for a bold man. The pages are unlined, but his sentences inch along methodically in nearly perfect horizontals. The ink is black; the nib of the fountain pen must have been narrow. A few words are crossed out, boxed out actually, by little crosshatched black rectangles—coffins, Paul thinks.

"You've got to bring out the fine grain," his father once said, speaking of what he called the art of therapy. Paul had started to draw in earnest and Chester was looking for a language to make a connection.

It suddenly occurs to Paul that Cavender said nothing about his father's will. Surely his father left him—what is the phrase?—"well provided for." No, the will must hold no surprises, for otherwise Cavender would have brought the subject up himself.

It occurs to Paul that he didn't ask, either.

His father's body is bone chips and ashes. He holds the actual remains in his own clumsy hands.

Home in his one-bedroom walk-up, Paul grabs a sketch pad and a tray of oil crayons off his easy chair, takes off his sneakers, and stares at the grain of the blue cover. Flooded with dread and excitement, he sits down on his bed and opens the first book. Next to the outer edge of the inside front cover, undated, in a free hand that is nevertheless his father's, is a single sentence: *Wherever a man finds himself, there is a way by which he came and a way by which he can leave.*

The notebook pages begin.

THE FLIGHT PATH announced by the captain will take us up the coast to Newfoundland, then out over the Atlantic. The actual ocean crossing will last only two hours and some. Expect a smooth flight, so sit back and relax. For millennia, men wanted nothing more than to take leave of the earth. Today, the traveler departing the ground feels, at first, a sort of rupture, expulsion, a rush of pleasure, and then a diffuse nothing. We are launched but we are not exactly anywhere. We sit but we move—are moved. Nothing much will happen to us. If anything does happen, it is nothing over which we have any control. Thirty-some thousand feet above the earth we find ourselves in an administered receptacle run by a smooth voice, like a psychiatric unit. The trip is a therapeutic lull.

I remember with fondness the apprehension I felt before earlier psychoanalytic congresses—apprehension that gave way to pride, because I was bringing my materials to the grand old men, because I was going to win a nod from them, because I was considered promising (at the least). Not so long ago, I was a comer; I made impressions. I was early to resurrect the subject of the uncanny, in neurotic conflicts and particular times of life—eight years ago—"The Uncanny as an Undertow in the Male Hysteric." The subject was generally not approved of— the diagnostic category rather unorthodox and the concept of undertow too "poetic," some said—but I was pleased that the paper was noticed at all. Even my critics admitted that I cast new light on the flying saucer cult. Not everyone was thrilled by my emphasis on the male hysteric, but that didn't detract from what was seen in the profession as a young man's triumph. In the light of our present cultural upheaval, I was credited with foresight.

I followed this up in Vienna, two years ago—my talk on astrology, "The Routinization of the Uncanny." The starting point was simple: Here were rebels, or at least a great number of young people who thought of themselves as rebels, using pseudoscientific astrological charts to put themselves "in touch" with what they thought was ancient learning. First, I began to run into this strange phenomenon with younger patients. Then I ran into it with Marion's friends. "I don't really believe in this stuff, but you know, I had my chart done, and the most amazing thing. . . ." By throwing around a lot of numbers and Latin words, these women—most of them in my experience <u>are</u> women—pretend to be scientific, even while they think they're antiestablishment and "into" primal forces of nature. There are more of these delusional notions in circulation every day. Jung is all the rage. The fatalists and irrationalists are masquerading as scientists. What is this really about?

Transmigration, for example, is a denial of death and a rationalization for splitting off unacceptable parts of the self. My little book on the subject was not bad.

The case of astrology is particularly interesting. The ego uses technical-looking charts to try to assert rational mastery of instinctual forces. Most of the signs of the zodiac are animals— which stand for unmastered forces of one's own nature. By taking on his "sign," the believer identifies with an unconscious force and still believes there is a rational system by which this affiliation is determined. Yet astrology comes up against a paradox that it does not want to face: The ego it seeks to strengthen turns out to be helpless because everything is really foreordained. The believer thinks he knows what it is important to know, and that knowing is all he needs. So he is a fatalist with a pseudoscientific alibi. <u>He doesn't understand that our problem in modern life is only sometimes ignorance; it is more that we don't know what to do with what we know.</u> "The stars impel, they do not compel" is a slogan meant to sugar-coat this surrender. With astrology, the romantic gets to imagine himself a rationalist. All this seemed rather obvious, but for some reason it was treated as a not insignificant contribution to the psychoanalytic literature.

This time, my paper generalizes about the new so-called body therapies: Wilhelm Reich, "bioenergetics," meditation rituals, kundalini, tantric yoga, etc. The point is that the return to the body is tantamount to a regression—a flight to narcissism, in which the individual hopes to return to an ideal of self-sufficiency and is torn away from relations to other human beings. In body therapy, the patient escapes the need to confront the transference and is encouraged to remain immature. . . . Some of the elders are grumpy with me because they think this is obvious—and in a sense they're right. "What's got into Chet?" they're asking. Spiegel thinks it regressive to revisit questions that were settled decades ago. Let it be, as the young people say. My paper is written.

There was a time when the prospect of a week in Paris on my own would have filled me with uncomplicated happiness, but this is not my mood.

The young woman in the seat to my left turns and asks me, "Is this as fast as planes usually go?" She is chubby and wears a safari hat and an unflattering T-shirt. I observed early in my own training analysis that the noncommittal tone is usually reassuring. "So far as I know, this is the usual speed," I say. "Well, that's very good," is her answer, and she draws a conspicuous though shallow breath and looks at me expectantly. I seem to be in the know. Now she obviously wants me to ask her where she is traveling on her first air flight.

To avoid this conversation, I open a journal and find, almost at random, an article on the evolutionary history of sex. Why, the author asks, must sex be ecstatic? Why was natural selection not satisfied simply to make sex rather pleasurable, so that those who liked it reproduced more than those who didn't like it at all, leading to a sort of acceptable plateau? The author speculates that, if sex were merely pleasurable, men would not have gone to the trouble to reproduce the species. After all, many patients experience sex or think about it with mixed feelings of disgust as well as pleasure—it is thought to be "messy," "dirty," "slimy," associated with excretion. The pressure to perform commonly overburdens a man, leading to impotence, not to speak of a primitive fear of dissolving into the mother and losing one's masculinity through a sort of castration. The author asks whether distaste toward the sexual act, mixed with indisputable pleasure, might produce a profound ambivalence. A good question.

Dinner. Feeble nourishment. I've gotten off the ground with only minor damage.

Awoke with a faint abrasion of my lungs, a stale dryness filling my mouth and nasal passages—the result of smoke, of course, out of the mouths of fellow passengers. A very strange business, this intimate relation among strangers. Connections without connection, like family life. This little society is a full barracks ripping through space six miles up. Two, three personal lamps are switched on, tiny nonoverlapping circles of light scattered throughout the plane. Everything else dark. We are over the ocean, reversing the direction of history.

I ring the call button, ask for orange juice. The stewardess is attractive, to tell the truth: long straight blond hair, unnaturally green eyes, and a mouth . . . a mouth as wide as desire—or, to put it bluntly, my desire. Would you like anything else? she asks with a rehearsed smile, also—or am I imagining it?—a flicker of something else. She appraises me coolly. My wedding ring, a little prop in our microscopic drama. We are fellow conspirators.

Nothing right now, thank you, I say. Her eyelashes lift, nonchalant.

sacrifice

How long is it that I have denied myself the pleasure of flirtation? This is an occupational hazard. Whenever a patient tempts me—and how many of them try, such being the cunning of transference—I know how to listen to myself as I listen to her, with the third ear. This is what comes of having been trained properly by a first-rate analyst. I felt no inhibitions discussing these feelings with Ida Resnikoff and have no need to trouble myself by acting them out. No, that sort of trouble I do not need. The result would be an altogether too predictable mess. What do you hear in yourself, Dr. Garland? Well, Dr. Resnikoff, since you ask, I hear a desperate playfulness. I hear the sound of a man trying out an unaccustomed role, but gracefully and without commitment. This man is watching a cage door slowly, slowly open. But from which side?

Read a few pages in The Possessed. Dostoyevsky's fevered temperament: It's this that makes him a founding father of the twentieth century. His advantage is that he knows the temptation of violence. His disadvantage is that he didn't know war. Tolstoy knew war and so could cultivate a certain serenity, at least in his writing—not in his sour, ridiculous marriage. But enough about that.

Awakened by plane shaking. The shuddering of a plane unlike any other sensation. The ting of FASTEN SEAT BELT signs coming on. The girl in the safari hat clutching my left forearm. It's all right, I assured her, it's normal, we just have to wait it out. The voice of the captain came on, speaking coolly of "bumps in the road." Smart way to put the matter; you can't drop through a road into free fall. "Do you mind if I hold on to your arm until this passes?" the girl asked. "Not at all," I told her. "Are you a writer?" she asked. "Not exactly," I said, and left it at that. "I see you're writing." "Yes, I'm used to taking notes. I'm a physician."

"A doctor! That must be scary." "I don't see any blood. I'm a psychoanalyst." "Oh!" That stopped her. "It's a very nice sensation," I said eventually, "when the turbulence passes and you go on in comfort."

The turbulence passed. Smoothness, a luxury.

The girl fell asleep still holding on to my arm. Wonderful obliviousness of the young. Some of them.

How long has it been since I devoted any energy to writing descriptions? I will try to pay closer attention. The physical world is a useful distraction.

According to the captain, we crossed Ireland near Cork, though without any visible evidence of what was beneath the sheet of cloud that has held fast from Maine on. We might as well have been flying over Nebraska. The girl in the hat read the airline magazine intently. I reset my watch, six hours ahead. The organized limbo called transatlantic travel.

The little window shutters snap open. We await breakfast, like children. Amusing, the helplessness of the passenger who has paid a large sum for the privilege of being looked after.

Surprise outside. The clouds are gone. The ocean's metallic gloss. Few of my fellow travelers look out the window. These surroundings too shall pass. Even the shadow of guilt shall pass. Though I fly over the valley of the shadow of guilt, I shall fear no evil, for Thou art with me—?

As much as Thou wert with Marty DeLong. Exactly that much, archaic God of the Patriarchs, God in Whom it would take a God to believe, in Whom my founder and font Freud does not believe.

I am turning into my own most interesting patient.

sacrifice

I have my limits. I cautioned Marty DeLong repeatedly, as needed. And patiently, so I thought. He did not appreciate the caution. He pitied me. Normal transference. He projected upon his "father" his own ego-ideal. The child cannot accept the frailty of the parent. But leaving aside my particular weaknesses, I recognize more and more the limits of psychoanalysis. I am reasonably talented at learning about my patients, but I do not know what to do with what I know. I am no longer sure that the patient benefits from his passage to knowing. Memory does not function the way Freud said. Repression is no lock and memory turns no key. There is no release. He who does not remember the past is condemned to repeat it, but at least does so with the pleasure of feeling original; whereas he who remembers the past is condemned in any case.

This is why we go to professional meetings: to flee this truth and pat ourselves on the back for doing so. Whether or not we are capable of helping a living soul, we are at least the keepers of the flame. Do priests hold conventions too? Prepare papers on nuances of the confessional process, brag about how many souls they have saved, gather in hotel lounges to confess their doubts to each other? Grope for each other in hotel rooms in the middle of the night?

A delicate business: how much doubt to communicate to a patient as fragile as Marty DeLong. You do not tell a drowning man that this frayed rope you are throwing him is not likely to hold although it is the best you happen to have on deck.

Paul rereads: "The child cannot accept the frailty of the parent. . . . my particular weaknesses." Not a word about his particular son and only the most glancing reference to his particular wife. Instead, this Marty DeLong. But Paul hardly needs a diary to tell him that his father's only begotten son, who wasn't a paying customer, was already a missing person by the end of July in the year of Our Lord, as his father might have put it, 1973.

He looks up at the day and thinks, Don't torture yourself. Put away these documents from beyond the grave that can only cause you more pain. He fishes a brand-new rubber band from a dish, double-loops the notebooks, and places them carefully, like evidence to be retained for a trial, on his bookshelf.

His apartment has brightened. The light rebounds off the back wall, painted glossy white and left unadorned but for a Vermeer print, the girl with the blue and gold turban, lustrous eyes, moist lips, shining pearl earring, caught turning toward you with an expression of—what? By the time Vermeer finished, that original moment had been burnt to a crisp. Still, Vermeer at least was left with something to show for his lost moments. Paul's watch reads 10:50. He considers getting some work done.

He pushes himself off the bed, brews himself a double espresso, logs onto e-mail, collects commiserations. There's a note from Geoffrey, publisher of *Cyberbia,* the on-line magazine he consults for. "I know you've got a lot on your mind but I've discovered (again) that you're indispensable." On the screen is a folder of photos, drawings, comics, and ads for the next issue. Paul is to massage them, mediocre as they may be, until they *move.* He nudges the fragments around on-screen. He digitally dresses women in skintight leather jumpsuits and equips them with spears, then disarms and undresses them. His eye catches a mocking article about family reunions on the Web. All over America, it seems, people are holding reunions without having to make plans months in advance or disrupting their lives. *Cyberbia* poses the question, Why leave the house at all? Imagine your second cousins as they would never be in real life.

He goes to the CD player, puts on a recent favorite by the Vanilla Buddhists.

You're high though you don't know it.
Too bad.
You're fucked though you don't think so.
Too fucking bad.
You had your chance but you blew it.
Didn't you know you were screwed?

He lies down on the bed and watches the chambered nautilus screen saver of his own design as it unwinds into a lithe androgynous body, a tiger, a Venus flytrap, and then dissolves. He imagines—as he has many times before—unwinding the Vermeer girl's turban. In slow-mo she picks it up off the chair where he's draped it and twirls it around her torso while crooning, in a contralto, "Are you blue?" "No," he says back, "why?" "Come here," she whispers, and lassos him with the blue and gold strip. . . .

To his surprise, Paul shuts down the fantasy right there, where he's never halted before, stops the CD, and in the silence that follows finds himself back at the bookshelf, where he pulls out his own copy of *Abraham, Isaac, Esau,* the one with the crippled spine, and, though he has no idea what possesses him to do so, goes to the spot where he left off reading in his father's office.

ABRAHAM WAS NOT at peace. Under the heat of the sun, a cloud of darkness came over him and he cried out to God, Who am I that You have chosen me? Did I ask for this honor? I have erected altars in Your name. I have sacrificed. I have foregone other gods. Have I been permitted to spawn the multitude, the nation of nations, as You promised? I have counted Your reward. It is nothing.

There must have been more than one such moment when Abraham, in his old age, despaired, and his despair turned to anger. One, two, three times and more, God had showered him with promises, and Abraham had gone forth, gathered his sheep, his donkeys, his cattle, and led them into the desert, moving them from a green place watered by springs to a place without water, into famine, into strife, into tribulation, remaining true to the one God, only to find that this God once again had failed to redeem His promises. Then Abraham would erupt: Why me?

At one of those times, God spoke to Abraham out of a whirlwind, saying, Because I am He Who chooses. You are *my* sacrifice.

Abraham said, Then leave me to wander in the desert with the defunct gods. I am an old man and weary, sick with argument. I have been brought low. Let me be, to the end of my days.

Because you placed your trust in Me, said the Lord, I am He Who made of your life something sacred. I am He Who Is. You are Mine. Do you understand?

In the full heat of the day, Abraham shuddered and was afraid. The sky descended and drew the land up after it. The land and the sky were one. There was nothing solid to rest on. There would come a time when Abraham would no longer exist. He wished to take up his hand against God, but his hand was stayed. . . .

Paul wonders what on earth his father was driving at. The helplessness of Abraham, the fatality of the tone—if this is some elaborate alibi, then for what? For a father too old to know what to do with a young son?

SARAH PERSEVERED, AND after many more promises from God, she gave birth to Isaac. Abraham was one hundred years of age.

Sarah did not want her son to have to share his patrimony. She told Abraham to rid himself of her servant, Hagar, and Ishmael, Hagar's son. Abraham was sorely troubled, for Ishmael was flesh of his flesh, conceived because Sarah had told him to cleave unto Hagar. But God commanded him to do as his wife had said, and Abraham did not argue. He trusted the Lord. As soon as Isaac was weaned and likely to live, Abraham banished Hagar and Ishmael to the desert. Hagar had done nothing but obey Abraham.

In all stories of the desert, water is of the essence. Abraham placed a skinful of water over Hagar's shoulder, along with her child. Abraham had not yet been asked to slaughter his son, not in so many words. Surely, he must have thought, the Lord would provide for the flesh of his flesh! Indeed, when the skin of water was empty, Hagar set her son down under a bush and sat at a distance and wept, for she expected her son to die, but God came, and made for Ishmael a well, and promised him a nation of his own.

All these sons, their ancient father, his banished lover—Paul finds even a few paragraphs make him anxious, but he suspects there's a code here he hasn't cracked, a code less than three decades old. This book might well have been called *Tales from the Cryptographer*. If Paul can crack that code—and there's always a chance, isn't there?—he might find out who that cryptographer really was. He skips ahead to an interlude called "Time, Psychoanalysis, and the Study of the Bible."

TO REWRITE THE Bible is to start the world again. It is to imitate God. It is to be reborn, without memory, without limits, fat with fantasies of omnipotence. And then, like God, you are left to rule the creation that you created. But because you were all-powerful once, you can never be all-powerful again. Not you, the father; or you, the mother; or you, the author; or you, the analyst. Once light is light and dark is dark, heaven is heaven

45

---

and earth is earth, you may not turn light to dark or heaven to earth. They are as they are. You created time, and time separates them forever. You created space, and space separates them forever. Because you were once the Creator, you can never be the Creator again. Your Abraham will always be the man who made his way with his trusting child up the side of Mount Moriah. You cannot send him back to his tent, with his son by the hand, to say to Sarah, Sarah, behold, I have returned with your son without taking a journey. You carry the weight of what you have done, forever.

Half bored, half anxious, Paul skips ahead again.

AND NOW, WHEN God had given Abraham that which He promised, He spoke for the first time of love, for in Genesis there is no love of Adam for Eve or Eve for Adam, of Abraham for Sarah or Ishmael. No, when it appears, love is coupled with sacrifice. God said to Abraham, Take your son Isaac, your favored one, whom you love, and go to the land of Moriah, and put him to death for Me.

What these wild-eyed people who dwelt in the wilderness would not sacrifice, so fervently did they yearn to live in a future when first things would be vivid again! Here are the ways in which the family of Abraham were ready to surrender themselves: At seventy-five years of age, Abraham gave up his home in Haran because God called him. He lived with Sarah when she was barren. When Lot's wife died at Sodom, the daughters of Lot, who were the grandnieces of Abraham, lay with their father to maintain his family line. Now Abraham, not knowing that Ishmael was still alive, prepared to give up his son to preserve favor in the eyes of God.

sacrifice

Abraham might have argued with God. He had argued with Him before.When God said that He would destroy Sodom and slaughter its people because they practiced abominations and would not produce children, He thought to inform Abraham beforehand, and Abraham stepped forward and told God to hesitate. He said to God, If there are fifty innocents in this perverse city, shall you destroy them too? And God said He would save the city for the sake of the fifty. And Abraham said, Will you not save the city for the sake of forty-five? And God agreed to forty-five. By these means Abraham had argued God down to ten, and God had agreed. Thus Abraham knew he had the power to convince God.

All night, Abraham fought against what he felt. He recalled how the Lord had renewed His covenant. He saw in his mind the image of his son whom he loved more than himself. He thought about the light in the fair hair of his tender boy. Then he asked himself, Who am I to doubt the Lord when He demands of me what I love most? And his answer was, I am he whom the Almighty, blessed be He, has singled out as the righteous one. I have not refused God in anything He asked me to do with my own hand. Now, the Lord asks me to bind myself to Him by doing what injures me most. The Lord is the Lord.

Abraham did not sleep, nor did he try to change the mind of the Lord. In the morning, he arose and split some wood. He took two servants and an ass, and a butcher knife, and the wood and a firestone and a rope. Sarah said to him, Where are you going? And Abraham said, To give thanks to the Lord Who has made us laugh. And why do you take wood? she asked. Where I go is exceedingly barren, said Abraham, but that is where the Lord has told me to go. Sarah put her arms around her child and said to him, Isaac, you shall be a man.

Abraham and Isaac rode two days to the mountain of

Moriah. There Abraham loaded his son with wood, and took the firestone and the knife, and told the servants that father and son would return together, and left the servants behind with the ass. As they climbed, Abraham listened. Surely God would speak again! But the Lord said nothing.

Abraham did not wish to speak to the Lord in his son's hearing. He did not speak falsely to God, as Cain had done. He was silent. This was the birth of thinking in secrets from God.

Abraham thought perhaps God had not commanded him but only prophesied: "You *shall* offer him up. . . ." Yes, that was it, a prediction! Abraham could prove the Lord mistaken without disobeying Him! This was the birth of interpreting the word.

Then Abraham thought, If I cut the throat of my son Isaac, whom I love, then who shall live to receive the land that the Lord has promised? No one! Then how can the Lord have commanded me to keep His own promise from being fulfilled! God does not mock. He is not perverse. This was the birth of reasoning.

Then Abraham thought, The Lord must know that my son Ishmael lives! Yes, it is *Ishmael* who shall be the founder of nations. This was the birth of wishfulness and distraction.

Then he thought, No, the Lord did promise that Sarah would give rise to nations; rulers of people shall issue from her. Sarah heard the messenger of the Lord make that promise. Is the Lord so cruel? And if the Lord is so cruel, what does that make of me? It makes of me the cruel Lord's servant. This was the birth of rationalization.

He thought, Shall I father a just people by refusing God? This was the birth of righteousness.

Abraham did not know what he intended. This was the birth of ambivalence.

Thinking in secrets, interpreting, reasoning, wishfulness,

rationalization, righteousness, ambivalence: All these things came into the world while Abraham said nothing.

Out of the corner of his eye, Isaac looked to his father and saw only the weathered, devoted face he knew. The sun beat on him as if on a drum. Finally Isaac broke the silence and said, Where is the sheep, Father, for the burnt offering? Abraham said in a hollow voice, God will see to the sheep. Abraham did not want to lie to his son any more than he wanted to lie to God. He thought, Surely there is much I do not know.

Isaac looked straight ahead and thought, My father is wise in the ways of the world. Surely he is wise in the ways of God. I shall trust in him. I would be no one if I did not trust. But I miss my mother.

They reached the heights. Abraham built an altar as Isaac watched. Abraham laid out the wood and did not ask for help. He stood between Isaac and the sun. Isaac stared at his father, and the sun was strong. He rejoiced to be free of his burden of firewood, but he was weak. Abraham felt the strength of two men. He took his son in his arms and laid him on the altar and took the rope and bound him. Isaac did not once take his eyes off his father. He said nothing. Abraham said nothing and looked away. It was dry and still, on the mountain.

Abraham reached out and grasped his knife in his hand. Isaac thought, Father, father, why have you forsaken me? But he did not call out. Abraham thought, Now, my son, you know what it is to be a man. Isaac called out that the rope was tight. Abraham put down his knife and leaned over his son and loosened the rope. Isaac did not cease to gaze at his father as Abraham picked up his knife again and lifted it high. He looked out over the far mountains, over the sands and the deep valley before him. He heard only the sound of his own breath. The sun drummed on him. Isaac closed his eyes and thought, I could untie myself and arise if I so wished. But I do not so wish. My will is to surrender.

Abraham looked upon the face of his son and thought, I have reached the end of my understanding. But understanding is not the point. He clenched the knife. His upraised arm was heavy as stones.

But he heard a voice calling, Abraham! Abraham! He said, Yes, I am Abraham, cursed among men. And the voice said, I am the angel of God Whom you love and fear so greatly that you would not withhold from Me your beloved. Abraham thought, Yes, I fear that much. As much as I despise myself. I am that strong. And the voice said, Do not raise your hand against the boy!

Abraham looked up and heard a rustling. He saw a ram caught in a bush by its horns. The angel did not have to tell him what to do. He cut the rope binding his son. He took the rope and bound the ram. He placed the ram on the altar and slit its throat. Isaac watched this sacrifice with big eyes and thought, *I am a man.* Abraham named the place *God sees,* and hence this is the place of which it is said, From the heights of God's mountain, much slaughter is seen, many mistakes are made, some last-minute reversals take place.

The angel called to Abraham now and said, "Because you have done these things, I will bless you and multiply your offspring, and they shall outnumber the stars and the sands, and they shall conquer their enemies. Because you obeyed, all the nations of the earth shall claim you and bless themselves by your offspring."

Paul's mind is racing, his thoughts snarled together. He closes the book. He is moved, pained, terrified.

Was he, then, the model for Isaac? Not that his father ever laid hands on him. No, Chester was understated, you could say that much for him. Still, he was clearly obsessed with the theme of the wrongful father and left grains of guilt sprinkled all over his book. *As many as grains of sand in the wilderness.* The book, Paul realizes, reads like an apology for failing his actual son, even if he turned his guilt into an allegory of civilization, or psychoanalysis, or something, and laid the blame on God. No, he only toyed with God as an excuse. He didn't really let Abraham off the hook.

Paul's questions pile up. What if Isaac doesn't stand for Paul after all? What if Chester was atoning for his own rebellion against Freud? What if he automatically sided against the son on behalf of the father who, in turn, intoxicated by righteousness, was bowing before *his* almighty Father? No, this makes no sense—the actual Chester was always adopting figurative sons and trying to rescue them from their torturing fathers.

There's a message here. There's got to be. Start again, Paul. Think about Isaac. Isn't Chester sympathetic to Isaac? Sure, but from way outside. Chester gives him a thought or two, but what does his Isaac do? Collaborate! Abraham lifts the knife, Abraham lays down the knife—and all this time Isaac can't even bring himself to speak up for his right to live. Take me, Father! Sacrifice me! At your pleasure, which shall be my pleasure! As for Sarah, she might as well be a stone. We hear almost nothing from or about her. So what was Chester doing? Yet again calling attention to—who else?—Chester? Chester and the glory of his struggle with God?

And yet his father reached out to him from bone and ash. And when Abraham refused to sacrifice the flesh of his flesh, Paul almost felt as if he touched him for a second.

Flesh of his flesh—what a weird expression. Does it mean that killing your own son is a form of suicide? Was Chester already in training for suicide back then? Did he, like Abraham, secretly despise himself? Wasn't he agonized? And therefore shouldn't he be forgiven? Because he knew not what he did?

Paul is swamped. Too much code, too few clues. He gazes down at the book in his lap.

No, he thinks, the key, if there is one, has to be found in the book his father left him and him alone. He closes *Abraham, Isaac, Esau* and tosses it to the floor, where it splays open. He undoes the rubber band from the notebooks on his shelf, flings open the one with the blue cover, and finds his place.

"WE'RE OVER FRANCE," the second officer just announced in a snappy voice. He was trying to sound matter-of-fact but there was still a little note of wonder he couldn't suppress. The junction where the sea meets the shore. The faint blue hint of land. Age forty-nine, over the territory of France—in a 747, not the troop transport that would have carried me over here if the war had lasted a few more weeks. For the girl in the safari hat, there is only one war, and that is a bad one. Age is her alibi.

[Here Chester had sketched a safari hat.]

Everyone has alibis. For example, even I can rationalize my failure with Marty DeLong.

"When you go to the dentist to fill a cavity," I remember him saying with a triumphant air, after several months of treatment, "you don't expect alibis, long apologies for the limits of dentistry. You can put that on my tombstone: No alibis, no limits." "You're very dramatic," I replied. "Brilliant deduction," was his response. "And why are you smiling? You look very pleased with yourself." "Neither displeased nor pleased," I said, trying not to look too displeased or pleased. "I'm concerned with what brought you here."

He had been a well-behaved teenager—good grades, normal haircuts, well-behaved friends—but the whole time he was plotting his escape, as he put it. "Pig parents had too much money," he said. I let that pass. He found his way into the radical movement. Plastered the playground with antidraft leaflets. Suspended from school. Marijuana, hashish. Joined a "collective," got "busted." LSD. Limits exist to be overcome, he liked to say. He quoted Blake at me more than once: "You never know what is enough until you know what is more than enough." Yes, I said to him repeatedly, but you will not find me to be the absolute, all-knowing father you crave. "We shall overcome," he said, with his wolfish smile. So much ironical armor, so little trust, so punitive a superego.

He came into treatment for severe depression. Small, frail, juvenile. Napoleonic potential. Son of an inconsistent and seductive mother who didn't know where she stopped and he started, so his ego-boundaries were always melting down. Distant father who liked to tidy the mess around him, including his son. DeLong had the baby narcissist's belief in his own powers: the other side of a rage against helplessness. An interesting contradiction. On the one hand, rage against hypocrisy: He wouldn't put up with a world that didn't match his ideals. The only honest thing to do was to shove its face into the ugly truth. He turned the father's love of order into a love of justice, the mother's seductiveness into a call for compassion. On the other hand, utopian lust for more of those mad oceanic feelings he experienced with drugs. He had a love of perfection fueled by infantile rage (anal fixation) which he tried to cultivate into political outrage. At demonstrations he liked to stand in the front lines and taunt the police. One time, when his girlfriend criticized him for provocative

53

tactics, he called her a coward. He was frequently impotent. She didn't stay.

"Why are you raising your eyebrows?" he asked me.

Answering directly wasn't my usual method but I was afraid that he was heading into a tailspin. "I'm struck by the fact that you chastised your girlfriend."

"Yeah? And?"

"I was thinking that that wasn't very gallant."

He snorted. "Gallant!"

"Yes?"

"That's what you understand."

"I see you're exasperated."

"Congratulations."

"I'm trying to understand what you're telling me."

"Understanding is the consolation we're left with when we're afraid to act," he said.

"That doesn't sound like Blake," I said.

"It's DeLong. Blake didn't have to deal with Vietnam, this scale of death. How can you stand what this country is doing? What makes you the sane one?"

I sidestepped. "There are a lot of people who feel as you do."

"Thank you very much."

"No one can stop the war by himself. We all have our limits."

"There you are with your limits again."

It was a delicate business all those months to suggest very gently that DeLong be realistic, to work to peel away his omnipotence fantasy and yet keep from undermining what faint realistic belief he had in himself. His narcissistic supplies were low, and he was afraid to give up his need for them. I suggested once that he look out the window, picture all the people walking around on a single block in New York, and imagine how hard it would be to mobilize them for the right sort of "action," as he liked to call it—to recruit them into "the movement"—even if

sacrifice

some of them might agree that American society needed radical change. Then was it realistic to think of turning them into a fighting force?

"You know what they said in France?" He smirked. "During their little revolution that failed?"

"What was that?"

He scowled. The ignorance he had to put up with from his psychiatrist! "Be realistic, demand the impossible."

We went around and around.

Must have dozed off. My legs cold, my feet cold. Wrapped my feet in a blanket.

An elderly man across the aisle keeps stirring and moaning in his sleep, his ropy neck shaking.

Breakfast. Stale roll, Styrofoam coffee. My fellow passengers seem not to mind. Sleepy and serene. Comfortable enough within their limits. Limits are cozy sleeping bags. For example, the overweight couple on the other side of the aisle, with a midwestern vacation look about them. Paris in their hearts— the Eiffel Tower, the Mona Lisa, cancan girls. Who can blame them? Plenty of room between them and their limits, room to grow into.

[At this point, Chester Garland had sketched a spidery Eiffel Tower.]

Something tickles at Paul's mind, and he leafs back to his father's description of Marty DeLong's—what was it?— "distant father who liked to tidy the mess around him, includ-ing his son."

An oblique reference to Paul? Or might that son have been Chester himself? He had never said much about his father,

Louis Gurevitch, who started out selling pots and pans from door to door on the Lower East Side and before he died was selling them from his own stores on the Upper West Side and in Brooklyn. From the few things Paul's mother had told him after the divorce, Louis Gurevitch had been an austere man with a passion for penny-pinching. Marion was too vivacious for him.

Distant, controlling fathers begetting estranged, out-of-control sons disconnected from women.

Paul goes on reading.

SOMETHING PECULIAR IS happening. I lift my hand but it might as well be a towel, a rope, something that isn't mine.

Dissociation is an interesting phenomenon. I command my writing hand to advance across the page, but it feels like a thing apart. I am a <u>what</u> more than a <u>who</u>. I feel like a dummy and don't know who the ventriloquist is.

I associate this observation with Marty DeLong's recurrent anxiety dream. He went to a circus sideshow. There was a ventriloquist with a well-trimmed white beard. After describing eight or nine variations of this dream, DeLong realized that the ventriloquist resembled a younger, more muscular version of me. He couldn't remember much about the dummy, except that he felt a peculiar attraction to it, as to a twin. At the same time, he feared it. It disturbed him. He didn't understand either the attraction or the fear but felt drawn to investigate. After the performance, he went into the tent. A guard asked him where he was going. DeLong forced his way into the dressing room—only to discover that what he had thought was the dummy was a midget ventriloquist, while the full-size figure was the real dummy. The sight of the midget would fill DeLong with horror and he would wake up in a full-blown panic. He didn't know what he was afraid of. I asked him to fantasize, but his fantasies sounded cooked to me: castration, crucifixion, torture on the

rack. He said the dream reminded him of a television program
by Hitchcock that he had seen as a boy. I told him I had seen
that program and had been a touch unnerved by it myself. I was
trying to reassure him. In fact, I was understating the matter.
That show had disturbed me deeply.

A textbook case of the uncanny, in other words. Freud gives
the very example of an automaton who is mistaken for a person.
(In the Hitchcock version, we have the reverse situation as well.)
The double is the beginning of all creepiness. DeLong's dream
was a paragraph straight from the master.

So without hesitation, in the second session about this
dream, I offered DeLong an interpretation. The midget represented DeLong's own fantasy of omnipotence. He felt like a creature—a marionette—of the radical movement because it had
gone off the deep end, yet his actual (i.e., sexual) impotence as
well as his more generalized feeling of impotence was partly a
function of his fantasies of absolute power, along with his
own unacknowledged wish for violence. Moreover, he wanted
unconsciously to displace me, to be his own father, and so feed
his fantasies of absolute independence, yet this reversal would
be extremely threatening, his feelings not being ego-syntonic—

Ego-syntonic. Here Chester broke off with a word that only
a bureaucrat could love. Did he reach for this deadening language every time he got near a straightforward feeling? No, give
the man credit. Paul has to concede that by the time his father
became the author of *Abraham, Isaac, Esau,* he was writing in
plain English for the general public. *Interesting coincidence,
Chester. You leave for Paris with jargon and a family. You come
back from Europe without either.*

"Ego-syntonic" doesn't appear in Paul's on-line dictionary.
He makes a note to look it up later in a psychiatric text and
then turns to the next page in the notebook.

SOLITUDE AT LAST, the whorls of my deeper mind. To spend some time with myself, I had to bring myself all this way, to the Luxembourg Garden, and sit among doves.

My room at the Hotel Lutétia wasn't ready. Just when the weary traveler needs rest, he can't have it. The clerk said she was sorry, but her blasé (a French word, come to think of it) tone said she was not sorry at all, since, after all, I arrived before check-in time, so I was the rule breaker and she was the rule keeper. I was not going to sit in the lobby, waiting to run into colleagues. So I walked to the Luxembourg Garden, where I am sitting in a freestanding metal chair painted green. I have moved it to a position in which the sun is full on my face—moved in order to face a baroque sculpture of an enchanted young couple embracing. The woman is beautiful, high-breasted, her hair flowing down to her shoulders, and she smiles radiantly. She is holding a baby who faces outward, eager, arms stretching toward a lamb—or a kid?—that lies at the man's feet. The man has a beatific smile and seems more or less to be supervising the family tableau. The baby is primed to pull the world toward him. Love starts the world again. The whole family group is set on a hillock of flowers, blue and red. A long time since I have noticed such things.

Such a civilized custom, the movable park chair! A park bench has its virtues—the unexpected flirtation, the uninterrupted nap—but a park chair has so many uses: face-to-face conversation, solitude, an encounter with a sculpture, just as you like. I sit in range of this stone felicity to write about Marty DeLong and his unsatisfactory outcome.

DeLong had a line into me. No other patient has ever gotten to me this way.

Clear from the start that he was a difficult case. (Howard always thought so.) Still don't think it was foolish to imagine I had some prospects. He trusted me (up to a point). He knew I admired his political commitment, even if I didn't share it. Unlike his previous therapists, I confirmed that his activities were at least in part authentic, not simply acting out. In this way, I hoped to bolster his defenses. And yet this meant he kept trying to treat me as his confederate, to draw me into discussions of therapy, of imperialism, of the limits of reason. He sought out my papers on astrology. Drugs had weakened his already weak defenses to such a degree that he developed a powerful feeling of doom, that it was his fate (he spoke of it as his "calling") to sacrifice himself for the greater good of mankind—his "Isaac complex," as he put it—which on top of his initial deficit in fundamental ego-strength—

Make notes for an article: the Isaac complex.

Interesting, Paul thinks, even moving—my father's feeling for weak young men. I should look for that article.

EVEN NOW, I am reluctant to face the reality that the outlook for DeLong was never better than fair.

There is a young man DeLong's age, but with thin lips, sitting on one of the nearby chairs, reading the newspaper, jacket draped over his shoulder, metal-rimmed glasses. Now he smiles to himself in that secret French way. Whatever pleases him goes on pleasing him. Fascinating. It's not, I imagine, that he's read something he likes. Rather, he's read something he knows he detests. It confirms his view of the world. DeLong had the same contempt but without the mirth.

Day after day, sullen DeLong sat across from me, clenching and unclenching his fist as if he were pumping up his vein to receive an injection. When he wasn't venting his bitterness, he had taken to carrying himself like an old man—stooped shoulders, drooping eyelids—and he spoke in a monotone. His fate was despair, he would say. Did I have something against him for that? he would ask. He contradicted himself. Sometimes he would maintain that he had been born in despair; at other times, that despair was his protest against the butchery in Vietnam. No matter how many demonstrations he marched in, the war went on. It was his personal failure. He claimed he had had too many successes too early in life (multiplying three-digit numbers in his head, chess championships, spelling-bee victories), that he wasn't cut out for the reverses of normal adulthood. A young man possessed by elderly despair—like the survivors of Ravensbrück and Auschwitz, who are the hardest cases I have ever treated. DeLong demanded to know whether I'd ever seen anyone like him. I mentioned them.

The air is sweet in the Luxembourg Garden. On a chair nearby, a girl is sitting on a boy's lap. They're in their early twenties, ordinary-looking. She's smoking. On another chair, a man has come to sit. Beret, dark beard, suit, what looks like a soiled vest. He places his briefcase on the ground, opens it, reaches in, pulls out a bottle of wine, almost empty. He stands the bottle upright next to his briefcase and waits. The girl throws away her cigarette and rests her cheek against the boy's cheek. The two of them are enjoying themselves. Life seems easy if you haven't had too much of it.

Paul thinks, The old man had his moments. Even after his heart surgery, I never heard him utter a syllable of self-pity.

BY APRIL, DELONG was in an acute state of depression. His principal sign of vitality was occasional agitation. Fitfully, he was willing to talk about his mother, who had treated him like a little god and left him with the feeling that he was destined to do no wrong—so that later, when he didn't accomplish his goals brilliantly, no outcome could ever be right. He was condemned to fall short. He didn't see this insight as progress. He saw only that he was doomed. He had nowhere to put his rage. He blew up at shopkeepers. Another girlfriend broke off with him. He was afraid to leave his apartment. He sought assurances that I wasn't keeping records on him. (I have my own suspicions of records and long ago stopped writing down more than the most perfunctory notes.) He thought his phone was tapped.

And maybe it was. During one of those demonstrations, DeLong went out in the streets, and after a few days of running around "trashing" stores (his term), he was arrested. His parents bailed him out, got him a lawyer, and told him they were sure he was coming to a bad end. It was then he started noticing funny clicks and odd patches of static on his phone line.

At any rate, by April most of his bitterness bit inward. Primitive rage. I asked him whether he didn't take some satisfaction from knowing that the war was winding down. That to him was a ridiculous question—millions of people had been killed and injured, and Nixon had gotten away with murder. He had fantasies of mutilating himself. He imagined that his brains were draining out of his head. He presented mysterious physical sensations. He was obsessed by a feeling that he was "dissolving." I put him on Thorazine. The agitation lessened. So did his vitality. He stopped bringing his dreams to me. I decided to tell him that he was ill but that the outlook was not at all bad. Around the end of May, the silences began. He sat in the chair and stared blankly for five or ten minutes at a stretch. He pressed his head back against the cushion. He wanted to bury himself. Therapy was pointless. I was pointless. I was out of it. I was too quiet. I didn't fathom his pain. I asked him, gently, to bring dreams. (Was I too demanding, intensifying his sense of failure because he couldn't even produce a dream for me?) "I'm a corked-up volcano," he said. "I've failed you too." I waited. Then I said, "Not at all." A dead look in his eyes.

I reassured him that it was common to feel this sort of frustration in therapy. He was not impressed. He didn't like to be common. "I'm on strike," he said. "What are your demands?" I said. "Everything. Nothing at all."

All I could do was try to hold his suffering and in that way say to him that if I could bear it, he could.

I consulted Howard, whose judgment I have always trusted above all others. He was puzzled. He, too, had patients with a high degree of disturbance who attributed it to the Vietnam war, though their numbers were by now waning. The war brought to the surface a great deal of repressed rage against pre-Oedipal abandonment, even on the part of angry radicals who had previously denied any attachment to the United States (just as they had denied their infantile need for their mothers). It was hard for them to admit that they felt abandoned by their country. "I don't know about you, Chet, but I feel more than a little disturbed myself," Howard said then. "We have to handle our feelings," I replied foolishly. "Handle?" Howard had said. "I told one patient it wasn't the worst thing in the world to throw a rock at a police car." I said, "These are not new problems. Freud had to share the same continent with Hitler. He handled his feelings. He plunged on, trying to make sick people well." "You don't believe your own words," he said. And rightly so.

Howard has published thoughtful work specifically on the treatment of helpless rage. We had long conversations about how to treat the dissonance of the world when it enters into the psyche. "Freud got up off the couch," Howard says. "He looked at World War One and the Nazis and decided to get to the bottom of it all, the sickness of civilization." "All very well," I said, "but I don't know what a better theory is going to do for Marty DeLong."

sacrifice

I spoke with Arthur Weinberg. In Arthur's considered opinion, America has been passing through a historic convulsion that is testing everything we ever believed about the power of psychoanalysis. I thanked him. Here was Marty DeLong with the bad luck to find himself on the wrong side of a historic convulsion. I debated hospitalizing him, but there was no particular crisis.

"I've disappointed you," he said one day, after a long silence. "That's my mission in life. Don't bother shaking your head. I do need a mission, don't I?" Another silence, and then, grim and melodramatic: "Don't worry, I won't spin my wheels forever." "You're not going to injure yourself, are you?" I asked. "Oh, you care?" he said, more listless than sarcastic. I asked him if he thought I should send him to Bellevue. "If you did that," he said, "you'd lose me. I could never trust you again." That night, I called Howard. He was out. I left a message with his service. Later, the phone rang, and when I answered there was only a dial tone. A short item appeared in the *Times* the next day. Marty DeLong had swallowed a hundred barbiturates and walked out into Central Park. Some teenagers found his body under a tree near the bear cages at the zoo, in a pool of vomit. The letter that arrived the next morning thanked me for doing the best I could.

He'd been saving up pills.

I am spinning my own wheels.

I told him that I was limited. I told myself the same. The profession is an art praying to be a science.

Rationalization or reason?

I am a bad artist.

Guilt powers all my arguments about why I should not feel guilty. With those thousands of pounds of thrust, it can power a huge cargo of excrement.

And yet the sun is full on my face, and in front of me, in Paris, a stone baby in a sculptural tableau opens its arms to the world.

For the people around me, this is the calmest of afternoons. Leaves shrug in the slight breeze. The French take for granted the orderly pleasure of being here—in the sun, near the grass, near the flowers, near the Luxembourg Palace. They look confident that they will be able to find what they search for. Or they are satisfied to search and not to find. They do not have the look of demanding the impossible. They seem content to demand the possible.

And why not demand the possible when you have the luxury of sitting in sight of the Luxembourg Palace—where, within the lifetime of that mother down the path watching her children, the swastika flew. (Perhaps when she was a child, her mother watched her play under the swastika and was also happy.) Children play as if it is their destiny to be happy. Mothers keep half an eye on them as if that were the natural order of things.

(Marion would say, Natural be damned! This is the arrangement that suits men.)

The older women read their novels, getting up once in a while to adjust their seats and keep the full force of the sun on their faces (e.g., a woman nearby, attractive, with a long straight nose, not much older than Marion, wearing a flowered frock of the sort that is no longer stylish in New York, low-cut, and a scarf tied around her neck). Light clings to the leaves.

I have a different task: to understand the uncanny—that is, what is unseen, what unnerves. To be unnerved means that your optic, auditory, etc., systems stop working. Perhaps it also means to love *[the word is crossed out]*—interesting slip—<u>lose</u> your nerve. Yet I would sooner love my nerve. Exactly. Open my eyes, receive the heat of the sun on my skin.

DeLong is finished and I am not.

I walk across the grass to inspect the statue at close range. The flowers on the hillock are lush in the strong sun. I have never been much for the names of flowers. Marion would know.

The statue is called "Joies de la Famille." Then, behind me, the piercing sound of a sharp whistle. A policeman is shouting. Faces turn toward me. I can understand only one word of his accusation: "Interdit," forbidden.

The references to Marion trigger Paul's protective instinct. A voice wells up in him: *Don't you dare talk about my mother after the way you treated her!* But this is hardly the spirit he wishes to apply to his father just now. So he lays the notebook carefully on the floor.

Noon, one o'clock, two o'clock have gone, as the earthly body of Chester Garland has gone, his forbidden acts, betrayals, epiphanies gone, while his son slumps in a chair, faint honks from the street barely audible over the rattle of his air conditioner. Was long-lost Marty DeLong the key that unlocked Chester's secrets—from his disappearance to his final leap twenty-six years later? Two deferred acts of atonement for one act of destruction?

But that can't be so. That wasn't his way—or was it? What does Paul know? He knows that he doesn't know.

Paul senses his father nearby and thinks, You're toying with me, aren't you, old man? If I guess right, does that mean you'll never leave me again? Or that you'll leave me alone forever?

Abandonment is not what Paul wants to feel. He contemplates lifting himself out of the chair—the hoisting up of his torso, the swinging of one leg onto the floor, the overall shock to his system from all this wrenching and shifting—and it occurs to him that he doesn't want to get up. He feels hot, clammy. Not owning a thermometer, he decides that the fever is probably in his mind.

He pictures his father sitting peacefully on that iron chair in the Luxembourg Garden, considers his surprising interest in the young people around him. He picks up the phone and punches up his father's—Grace's—number. Grace answers dully. Paul asks if he can stop by to consult some of his father's books. "Of course," she says, asking no questions. She *is* gracious, Paul thinks. She has that virtue. Perhaps he's been unfair all these years to think her vapid. Perhaps she's simply straightforward and trusting. The ideal second wife.

He puts on a black T-shirt, black jeans, and sandals and slouches out of his apartment without bothering to lock the deadbolt. In front of his building, a dark-skinned woman sits at the wheel of a car smoking a cigarette, appraising him with what strikes him as interest. He imagines that if he invited her out for coffee, one thing might lead to another, and these would be pleasant cross-cultural things that would broaden him as a person. But the satisfactions, he knows, would be short-lived, with a possible downside of entanglement and mess. The encounter would come to nothing. Like all his encounters. He wonders, as he starts down the street, if he is not a second-rate Marty DeLong—incapable even of suicide. So he nods at the woman, a gesture of respect, which she reciprocates with a small, sly smile. On second thought, she's probably only waiting for alternate-side parking.

Sweat starts collecting immediately on his face and arms. He begins to bake. By the time he arrives at his stepmother's apartment, he's dripping. Grace's eyes are red. Her face is still swollen, as if saturated by the humidity, although her inverted bowl of short silver hair is neatly combed. Her daughter, Susan, a few years older than Paul, sits on the sofa looking morose. Grace reaches for Paul as if he were her dead husband's most treasured possession—no, that's not fair. He never has given this tranquil soul her due. She was a shield for his father from the time they met eight or nine years ago through the Society for the Rehabilitation of Victims of Torture. A reliable office manager and a reliable wife. It isn't her fault that she isn't Paul's mother.

Now she feels tied to him by a perfectly appropriate grief that somehow eludes him. He embraces her rather mechanically, and her head sinks immediately onto his shoulder. She did not deserve this loss. Soon, she offers him a glass of cold apple juice. He stands in the living room, shamefaced, feeling convicted of unkind thoughts that seem less natural than Grace's grief, and exchanges awkward expressions with Susan. Half-full coffee cups and saucers bearing the remains of bagels are scattered around on tables. The chess game remains untouched. As to why Paul might want to rummage through his father's leavings, Grace is incurious and accepting.

Paul finds himself alone in the study, the door closed, the air conditioner *shhhh*ing—Grace must have turned it on for him. She has dusted, or brought somebody in to dust, but otherwise nothing seems to have been touched. The stillness is extreme. Paul's sense of compulsion is extreme. He runs his finger along the spines of the psychiatric journals, perfectly laid out in chronological order from 1949 on. He rips the volumes for 1973 off the shelf the moment he finds them, scatters them on the floor next to the patient's chair, sits down, opens the first journal, and is annoyed to find such titles as "The olfactory forerunner of the superego: its role in normalcy, neurosis and fetishism," and "On crying, weeping and laughing as defenses against sexual drives, with special consideration of adolescent giggling." He feels acutely offended by all this nonsense when he is in search of something else—but what? He leaves the 1973 journals in heaps on the floor and hastens back to the shelves, riffling through index volumes in search of Dr. Garland's name. Within minutes, he's yanked out ten issues and stacked them on the floor. He heaves himself into his father's chair.

From 1957 through 1974, it turns out, Dr. Garland published articles on the belief in transmigration, astrology, extrasensory perception, the psychoanalysis of Jung and Reich, the uncanny, and cults. The earlier papers are stiff going, though there are a few readable anecdotes about Dr. Garland's patients. In 1962, he published a "Note" about, of all things, funhouse mirrors, observing that patients who suffer from severe narcissistic disorders often feel a "peculiar dread" when confronted by these mirrors—because through their severe distortions, they undermine the "narcissistic pleasure" provided by ordinary mirrors and "spoil" the ideal self-image. Peculiar dread, that's exactly right for what Paul is feeling as he dumps one volume after another on the floor.

In 1969, Dr. Garland published an article about extrasensory perception, offering his observation that the female experience of telepathy seems to differ from the male: Women tend to think they can perceive the future, while men are inclined to believe that they can see over the horizon, as it were, in the present. Dr. Garland related the difference to infantile sexuality: For a little girl, the future is represented by the mother, with whom she feels an affinity, while men feel "cut off" from that future, with which they cannot identify . . . and there is more that Paul is too impatient to care about. He detects the forced reasoning in which everything depends on the ingenuity of the way in which a premise already taken for granted—infantile sexuality at the bottom of everything—turns out to be true. Big surprise. As for the question of whether telepathy actually takes place, Dr. Garland ends up citing Freud's words on the subject: "I have no opinion; I know nothing about it."

An article published in 1974, "Anxiety, Apprehension, and Prefiguration," is just as clinical as the others, though it does include some abstract remarks about the difficulty of predicting which patients will commit suicide. Paul shudders. This must be the paper Dr. Garland wrote for the Paris congress. How detached it sounds, the little that Paul can bring himself to read! The gulf between these abstractions and the man of the notebook is unfathomable. The man who could write these frigid sentences offered confident explanations for everything except why his actual life felt senseless. His faith was sliding away and he was dictating medical notes.

Paul leaps up, strides back to the bookcase, and hunts through the indexes for 1975 and later years. Not one article by Chester Garland shows up in any of the psychiatry journals; not one. But in 1975, new journals appear on the shelves like neat battalions of reinforcements: *The American Journal of Religious Studies, The Yearbook on the Psychological Study of Religion.* In the 1976 *Yearbook* there appears Chester Garland's long article "The Isaac Complex," linking the Abraham-Isaac story to both the Isaac-Ishmael and the Isaac-Esau-Jacob stories—the first intimation, evidently, of his magnum opus. In the Fall 1977 issue of *Imago,* there appears a paper of his comparing renditions of the events on Mount Moriah by Donatello, Tintoretto, and Caravaggio. In 1978, the year he published *Abraham, Isaac, Esau,* Dr. Garland starts collecting human rights journals, gathering them every year, meticulously, into cardboard boxes: *International Review of Human Rights, Index on Censorship, Article 19. Human Rights Yearbooks* come next. United Nations studies. Then, leather-bound, an annual journal called *Violations and Treatments.* Paul pulls this one out, opens it, and sees, "Editor-in-Chief: Chester Garland, M.D." The articles are about torture and imprisonment and various therapeutic techniques for treating their effects. Next to these stand books with titles like *Psychological Issues in Human Rights* and *The Aftermath of Torture: Treatment and Recovery* (this one co-edited by Chester Garland).

Desperately looking for something—what?—Paul goes to his father's desk, yanks the drawers open, rummages through the detritus of an interrupted life: paper clips, fountain pens, prescription forms, stationery. No journals, no letters. He feels frantic, like a thief who has gone to a huge amount of trouble to break into a deserted office only to crack an empty safe. He walks over to the file cabinets, finds them unlocked, yanks open one drawer, reads file titles, yanks open another, and finds an alphabetical set: patients. There is a DeLong file. Paul pulls it out and finds a painstaking list of session dates, prescriptions, amounts billed. DeLong's last visit is May 21, 1973. Book-keeping details. Could these be the only files he kept? A quick check of random patients uncovers the same skeletal records. Other files seem to contain notes for Chester Garland's books and data for his human rights work. There are files full of reviews, files with offprints of his articles. There is a file of letters from Paul at college, other correspondence, and a file called DIVORCE. Paul hasn't the heart to look through any of this. He slams the drawers shut. In an afterthought, from a shelf of reference books next to the desk, he pulls out a fat dictionary of psychiatric terms and reads about "ego-syntonic." Nothing is revealed.

Whatever he was looking for is evidently not to be found here. He's ransacked the place of places and the experience is a trashy anticlimax.

Grace taps on the door to the study. Would Paul like to stay for dinner? Rabbi Gerstein is expected. Paul is not sure he wants anyone's company, but if he does, Gerstein is not that person. No, he wants the company of his dead father's journal. He begs off.

Any other time he would have taken the express all the way to Union Square. There he would have walked upstairs and strolled about the overground world, checking out faces, making up stories about the people who own them, looking for caricature material, studying sidewalk displays, the pocketbooks, scarves, masks, dictionaries, old girlie magazines, and used paperbacks. Today, he steps out at Grand Central Station to wait for the local and lingers on the sweltering platform, staring at the uptown side where his father spent his last minutes. There is a neatly dressed boy with a Walkman, reading, of all things, *Crime and Punishment*. The station is an island of light in a great dark underground sea. He listens for the place to speak to him. He craves an answer. He will settle for a clue. The local doesn't want to come. Instead, another express does, obscuring the other platform.

On an impulse, he heads upstairs, taking two steps at a time. He strides across the concourse and walks downstairs to the uptown platform. His father must have stood just *here* and waited as the rumbling out of the tunnel got louder, more metallic. He must have stood stock-still and thought *No, not this one*, thought *I need time*, as the train rolled into the station and the doors opened, passengers emerging to resume their lives-in-progress—none of them having any reason to notice a gaunt white-haired man with a heavy look on his face—and other passengers getting on, heading for the next stations in their lives. . . .

The roar from the tunnel builds. The lights of the local bear down. Paul takes a small step toward the edge and wonders what it would be like to think *This one*, and any second now, if only you will it, tons of steel will smash into you, canceling out your feeble, leftover body. Would you wonder how fast you would lose consciousness and be done with your unpromising life? If you were Dr. Chester Garland, you would have some rough idea of the type of pain to expect and how quickly it would pass, never to return. To jump, all you would have to do is surrender, just take a step. . . . Or was that it at all?

By the time Paul is through with these thoughts, the doors are slamming open and more of the living, who mean nothing to him, are spilling out. A trickle of sweat works its way down his neck, and he decides to flee the underworld for the dwindling light.

Upstairs, the street air is full of the aromas of sugar-coated peanuts and coffee. He stops at a liquor store for a bottle of Frangelico. In his apartment, the air conditioner smells of dust. Out the window, over the electric hum, the great cataract of Manhattan is surging: the pursuit of all those happinesses, all those collisions and endings, all that bravado, grief, self-seeking, heartbreak, accident, emergency, murder. If a truck downstairs guns its engine to make the next light, will it arrive on the East Side just in time to run over a man who's now deciding to take his dog for a walk? How many old or not-so-old men are at this exact moment well into their last day on earth? He makes coffee, anoints it with a shot of the Frangelico, and reopens his father's journal.

The writing on the pages that follow looks hastier, more agitated; *m*'s, *n*'s, *i*'s blur into each other and the crossings-out are perfunctory—a few scratches, that's all.

DESPITE THE OFFICIOUS gendarme, I could have stayed in the Luxembourg Garden all afternoon, my mind sapped by jet lag, but the voice of responsibility badgered me. I was not in Paris to gaze at sublime things. I thought I had better give my paper a look, touch it up, sand it down, underline key passages for my presentation. A wind suddenly came up. Clouds were ripping across the sky where, just moments before, the sun had been holding forth. I felt a chill. A storm was on its way. I saw a sign reading "Danger: Abeilles." I heard a dark young man speaking good English with a French accent and asked him what this meant. "Bzz, bzz," he said, moving his fingers as if playing a keyboard in the air, and then thought of the word: "Bees." I thought it best to return to the hotel and joined a thin stream of people leaving the park by a back gate.

Paris: city of pastel light and radiant disappointment! My mind a dead weight. I needed to rest but wanted to drift. I walked the back streets in the general direction of the hotel and felt the comfort of Paris's stones, tawny and rose; the enormous wooden doors, beautifully varnished; the balconies with arabesque iron grillwork, potted plants, even poplars. On the stone walls, more than a few plaques. For example: "Here fell gloriously, for the liberation of Paris, the guardian of the peace François Ulmet, 24 August 1944." What exactly this guardian of the peace had been guarding one year before he fell, say, was another question, probably to be answered in German. But in 1944, the liberated city was exuberant from having thrown off its chains, and the victors could be forgiven a bit of hyperbole.

The sky darkened, and I noticed all of a sudden how many people were carrying umbrellas. Ready and easeful, as if to say, Let it rain; we have our business and pleasure to go about, and so we shall. Why complain? But I am who I am, drained, legs weak, cogency sinking fast, with a dead patient and a moribund marriage. Oh, how I would be content to be the guardian of my own peace! There was a time when Marion would have accompanied me on a trip like this, walked with me, looked at paintings with me, and that would have been close enough to peace. . . .

I strolled toward the hotel, entranced by the apartment buildings of stone, their sensuous roofs, their bulges, curves, and angles, their balconies, the slate-covered shallot shapes of the corner turrets. From one to another, continuous flow. The world is consecrated. Traffic is well-behaved. The women of Paris are composed, groomed, with light scarves of chiffon and silk around their necks, and they look me in the eye, forthright but stylized. They care about façades here. They maintain them with conviction. No wonder psychoanalysis is poorly developed in France. The French do not want to get to the depth and truth of themselves, they want to put on a convincing show. Americans want to get to the bottom of things, the French want to get to the surface, where the beauty is. Who can blame them?

This was, as best as I can reconstruct it, my train of thought at the moment when, a couple of blocks from the hotel, as I stood at a red light and a bus bore down on its way to a stop a few steps away, I felt an impulse to step off the curb—I wouldn't have had to take more than a couple of steps—directly in front of the bus. I could imagine my foot lifting, watching it come off the curb and move forward with a will of its own. The whole sequence felt, in fact, uncannily real: the wind in my hair, the whoosh of the bus careening to a stop, a burst of pain, my brain exploding, then nothing.

I was breathing rapidly, shallowly. I felt—what shall I call it?—a shudder through my consciousness. A lapse in time, a breach of continuity. I felt the urge to press my back against a building until the impulse passed. I was sweating. I was dehydrated; this was obvious. My blood sugar must have been plunging and I needed replenishment. I suspect I stood at the corner for a very long time (although I have no idea how long) because a woman my age, wearing a bright purple scarf, came up and spoke to me in an inquiring and concerned tone. Her French was rapid and I understood little of what she said but it sounded as though she was asking if I needed help and whether I knew where I was going. I nodded to show that I appreciated her goodwill and said "Non" to the offer of help and "Vous êtes très gentille" on general principles. She said, "Au revoir," in a singsong tone, formal and spirited, and walked off. My first thought was that I always know where I am going; that is the problem. My second thought was that Marion would have chastised me for my confusion. My third thought was that she might have been friendly to a stranger.

There is such a thing as the impulse of a moment that is a lifetime in the making. You have to travel years to get near the brink. Note: <u>near</u> the brink. I wasn't in danger, really, of yielding. Not then. Not yet. Desire is one thing, intention another. It was a twinge, that's all, a wish to be done with the self who suffers. My life had sent me packing. I was haggard under its weight. Haggard, laggard, staggered, weary, wary, scary, married. . . . Nothing belonged to me indisputably but my anxiety and my freedom. (But freedom for what?)

Hours since I had eaten. Beads of sweat on my brow. The physical body needed me. Crossed at the green light, stopped at a café, and ordered a large bottle of mineral water avec gaz, coffee, and a ham sandwich from a correct young waiter with a pocket watch. Drained the water, mopped away the sweat. A few drops came from the darkening sky. The waiter rolled down an awning overhead with a steel rod. The rain began pounding, in force. Across the street, sheets of water coated the slate shingles and rippled downward, a body of water, as if the wall were horizontal. The remarkable thing is that, in the street, people without umbrellas were still walking with dignity.

My consciousness was locked, seized like an engine. A wailing in my heart. More like a first-class anxiety attack than a fit of jet lag. I should have stayed with the feeling, held it, turned it around, studied it like a jewel—my jewel.

By the time I got back to the hotel to discharge my duty, I was sopping wet and without a shred of dignity.

Discharge = defuse. Discharge = ejaculate. A strange word for what one is supposed to do with one's duty.

. . .

Hotel Lutétia, striped awnings and undulating façade, where the rue de Sèvres crosses the boulevard Raspail on the Left Bank. Luxurious, charming, but human-scale: not a conventioneer's hotel, more a base for a shopping expedition. Marble steps, a heavily carpeted lobby, carved chests. Chandeliers, pillars painted faux marble. In the vestibule, a statue of romantic Diana, bow in hand, belle époque style.

Howard Spain was coming out of the elevator in an effervescent mood, nodding a staccato "Ya-ya-ya" to a thin-faced analyst from London, more or less my age, to whom he introduced me. The name Steven Holcombe rang a faint bell—one of the object-relations people. He sported a pencil mustache and slicked-back hair and needed only a silk scarf to look like Trevor Howard playing an RAF war hero. Trevor Howard, however, would not have carried a thin tan briefcase with a protruding handle. (Is it an accident that the leading theorists of early abandonment and the importance of the maternal bond are cool Englishmen?) The hotel was superb, Howard effused, the Gauloises pungent, the beer surprisingly good—the French should be better known for their beer. Howard in his blue blazer, brasher by the minute, undoubtedly reliving his college year abroad.

"Come on," he said, "we're on our way to the bar, like all intelligent analysts. By the way, did you know that German intelligence was headquartered here during the occupation? Think about that. Join us after you dry off."

I was exhausted and badly wanted to avoid a political conversation. I said I needed to nap and go over my paper, which, after all, I had to read the next afternoon.

"And we're all looking forward to that," he said, smiling, daring me to doubt his sincerity. "But you'll do better with jet lag if you stay up. Force yourself to run on Paris time."

"You might be right about that," I said, and started through the lobby.

I got into the elevator. Marty DeLong popped into my mind. He would have been appalled to know where his psychiatrist was about to rest his head—and confirmed in his view that the human race was doomed to live in its excrement. Like a fetus urinating into its own amniotic fluid. The elevator made regular clicks. There were narrow red rugs down the corridor on the seventh floor.

My little room was dark but for the bronze light of a not-half-bad reproduction of da Vinci's "Madonna of the Rocks" hanging over the bureau. Through a slightly warped window, I could see the rain driving down like nails. The da Vinci was as large as the window, its luminous flesh tones vivid against the strangely dark rocks, which in this reproduction looked like half-rotted teeth in an elderly open mouth—or a vagina dentata. Not much to the room beyond the bed, two elegant little bed tables, an antique desk.

The pastness of the past, how past is it? My life is dedicated to the proposition that human beings are indelibly marked by their original instincts. Nothing in my experience falsifies this belief. Nothing in the history of this century refutes <u>Civilization and Its Discontents</u>. Then isn't a civilization also stamped with its origins? Mustn't that be true of Hitler's demonic reign, a mere twelve years—obviously more a culmination than a starting point? But if so, a culmination of what, the creation? The expulsion? God's covenant with Abraham, or the tablets bestowed upon Moses? The chutzpah of Jesus? The origin was the scared *[he crossed out the word]* the sacred!

Scared, exactly. I slip and slide. In the beginning was fear, not love. Fear and trembling, not stillness. Abraham's fear of God, Isaac's fear of Abraham. Fear of bloody expulsion through the sacred canal, fear of bursting into the unknown, fear of the outer world with its nightmarish light and noise, fear of the father, fear of the mother, fear of fear, then fear of the mystery we call (ugly syllable) death.

My death as much as anyone's.

I ran water for a bath. Waiting for the tub to fill, I took out the text of my paper and looked it over: "Anxiety, Apprehension, and Prefiguration." Apprehension-as-learning is also apprehension-as-fear, because it suggests departing from the familiar. And so on. To my surprise, I caught sight of an actual idea. When a patient coaxes a diagnosis out of the analyst, this may be reassuring because it puts a name to the problem and promises to relieve the patient from the pressure of symptoms, but prognosis is something else. Prognosis may carry an uncanny quality, like prefiguration, in which the patient experiences a feeling as if he's experienced it before. The patient surrenders to a good prognosis and feels doomed by a not-so-good one. In either case, he regresses to a state of forgetting his will.

By the time I sketched in a paragraph to this effect, the bath was full. Brought the pages with me and took care to keep them dry. Total immersion was good for me but not for my sentences. Forced myself to keep reading, but soon the words turned wooden before my eyes: "patient experiences the feeling . . . has regressed . . . decompensation . . . must resolve . . . work through." Pure drivel. The only interesting idea: that a prognosis bears a (superficial) resemblance to supernatural intervention. Not even sure why that is interesting. Or true. Supposed to keep mining this played-out vein of an argument because the topic has become associated with my name. It sickened me.

When I got out of the bath, the last thing I wanted was to look at this paper. The next-to-last thing was to find human company. Only one thing interested me: sleep. I turned down the sheet and got in. The coolness was soothing.

Woke up thinking about DeLong. His plaintive look when, at the end of his fifty minutes, I expelled him. Good-bye, my meter is running, I'll see you next time, good-bye. Hello, you must be going. You're done when I say you're done. Until next time, you may carry around the memory of my compassionate, all-forgiving—but not all-forgetting—smile. "Am I going out of my mind?" he asked, hoping to start a last-minute conversation. "You're going into your mind," I said, pleased with myself and showing it.

4:17 A.M. in Paris. Couldn't go back to sleep.

Rolled over, tried to turn the switch on the bedside lamp. It was stuck. Got up, turned on the room light, got back into bed, and looked at the new paragraph in my paper. More garbage. The counterintelligence room. My intelligence slipping away. Quiet city, no traffic, darkness.

[Here he had sketched a garbage can.]

Death, dearth, birth, mirth.

Look here, Dr. Garland, shall we survey the situation? It seems to me, Dr. Garland, that the patient is presenting signs of, shall we say, decompensation? On second thought, let us not say "de-com-pen-sa-tion." The term sounds derived from the manual of instructions for reimbursement supplied to the physician by large insurance companies. This term is not helpful at all.

But let us try to be helpful. We need a plan.

. . .

Had a morning to kill, or—if I was lucky—bring to life. Not tempted to invest a single minute more in buffing up my paper. Not in one bone of my body was I tempted. The only question was where to go. Leafed through the convention program. Sessions started at 8 A.M., but the names of the papers looked thick, gelatinous. Surely I could find something more productive to do with myself than sit and listen to colleagues build cages out of clotted Latinate sentences. (Analysts are trained to be silent for good reason. Our skills do not lie in the realm of performance. Have always preferred to read the papers than hear them delivered. At least you can skim.) As for the discussions, they're pro forma. I could live without attending the morning session, in other words.

Museums: I could wait for the Louvre to open, or the Jeu de Paume. With a predictable, problematic outcome: (1) aesthetic frissons, followed by (2) realization that some deeper entry into the spirit of life had eluded me. And (3) there would be hours to kill first. Skimmed through my guidebook and the solution leapt out: the Cathedral of Chartres, an hour away via frequent trains from the Gare Montparnasse. Said to be one of the great buildings of the Western world. Said to feature a magnificent rose window, and acres of stupendous stained glass removed and hidden during the war to preserve it from the bombardment. (Bombardment by the Americans, but never mind.) A short walk from the Chartres train station. Open at 9:30 A.M. I consulted a Paris map. A quick, uncomplicated walk to the Gare Montparnasse. Easy enough to go to the station, check the train schedule, and see if I could fit in the round trip and still get back by two in the afternoon.

In the darkness the sky was dull, so I took an umbrella and a summer-weight tan jacket, stuffed a few hundred francs and my

sacrifice

passport into my money belt, and set off down the boulevard Raspail with hope in my heart. The air felt clean on my skin. On a day so overcast, stained glass would not be at its most glorious, but like a bombardier (strange analogy!), I couldn't choose my visiting days; who knew when I would pass this way again? What do I tell depressed patients? Take the initiative. I was cheered by all the initiative I was taking.

My stomach was growling and I badly needed coffee, so when, after turning right on the boulevard Montparnasse, I saw that I was across the street from the huge La Coupole restaurant, I crossed, stood by the door, and looked in. A few middle-of-the-night Parisians, in jackets and scarves, seemed to be drinking more than eating. They had a dissolute look, though plucky.

A woman had stopped on the sidewalk behind me, elegantly turned out, in a short blue dress that showed her excellent legs to advantage. Her silver hair was perfectly swept back—she was perhaps five years younger than I, if at all—and she was picking up a tiny shaggy brown dog. She offered a polite diminutive smile that made me want to tip my hat—had I been wearing a hat. "Bonjour, madame," I muttered, in the least embarrassing French available to me. "Bonjour, monsieur," she said briskly, passing me on her way inside to coffee and dissolution. If I had gone into the Coupole, I might have approached her. Might have tried to make conversation. One thing might have led to another. I might never have gotten on the train. But I did not go into the Coupole, and I did get on the train.

The sky was faintly lightening when I arrived at the Gare Montparnasse, which is built into the base of a slab of a skyscraper, a gargantuan tower that looms over the low-rise cafés and cinemas of the boulevard Montparnasse. An old man with a red face was lying on the floor next to the board where the schedules were posted. He reached out his

81

hand in a vague gesture of begging or an equally vague threat. I gave him nothing. He offended me. He wasn't my responsibility.

There was a train to Chartres leaving at 6:43. That was a local, extremely so. There was an express, though—or almost express; it stopped at Versailles (I must visit there some other time)—at 7:19, arriving Chartres at 8:12. Walk from the station. That would put me at the cathedral before 8:45. I could take my time touring the exterior before the doors opened at 9:30. There was a train returning to Paris at 11:45 A.M., arriving back at the Gare Montparnasse at 12:36. I could take a taxi to the conference center at the Maison de la Chimie and be there by 1:00 without trouble. Eat on the train or at the conference. This would give me at least two hours at the cathedral with time to spare. Couldn't be sweeter.

With the sense of satisfaction that comes from seeing the solution to a problem unexpectedly heave into sight, I went to a window marked "Billets" and bought my ticket. I signaled a round trip to the clerk with a little back-and-forth movement of my fingers. He was a sleepy-looking young man, prematurely bald, round-skulled, with a thick mustache to compensate. He asked a question of which I caught the word "réservation," to which I replied, "Non." He made a downward curve of disapproval with his lips, but this ritual gesture didn't keep him from passing me the ticket. Found a café within sight of the tracks, bought a double cup of bitter coffee and a passable croissant, and studied the guidebook. Around me, the late-nighters and the early-to-work. Eyes wounded but voices lilting. The pinched and unhappy faces of the people of Paris. Eyes that could rust steel. But they would never admit to unhappiness because they would assume there was nothing abnormal about it—another reason why psychoanalysis has never thrived here. A few back-packers sat, coupled up and in groups, more expectant than weary. The thump of a knife striking a cutting board as a baguette is sliced.

Everyone talks too much. Who needs a talking cure? Better a cure by silence. No danger of mistranslation. Teach us to sit, teach us to shut up.

Take a look, for example, at that infant draped over his mother's shoulder. The infant is filled with faith in a benign world. His choices are simple: comfort or discomfort. Eat, pee, shit, crawl. Once Marty DeLong had a life that pure. So did Marion. So did I. The mother is thin, with a long thin straight nose, and she offers up that competent French look. Competence is our modern substitute for faith. Know-how is what we have when we lack know-why. There is no faith like a young mother's. She has surrendered to her destiny.

When you sit in a café, you're not at home and you know it. That is what is so comforting.

I am a tourist, with time to look. But to look is not to see. Or to be young. Or to know how to live.

Like every neurotic, I am compelled to remember too many useless things, even if they are true.

I have to admit that Marion's send-off was mild, tender, nice. Nice is an overused word. Nice, in this case, means not hostile. She was sure we would benefit from this brief separation. We mouthed reassurances: Everything will be better afterward. That familiar tinsel, hope. Not hope for any particular reason, but hope on principle. Marion's reassurances had the ring of sincerity. She also required reassurance from me that her new independence wouldn't repel me. As Freud discovered, there is no move toward independence that does not require the mother to stand by, watching benevolently.

When we went to bed—how many nights or lifetimes ago was that?—she showed a tenderness that hasn't been much in evidence recently.

(I notice that, even as I write for my own edification or amusement, I stall when it comes to the subject of sex. I have never been much of a sensualist. Still, when my patients stall in their stammering efforts to talk about sex, I have no trouble telling them that sex is part of life, to get them over their embarrassment. This works well. If a middle-aged doctor nods soberly while they talk about impotence, frigidity, obsession, or various perverse fantasies, these are magically transformed into respectable ailments, like hives. . . . And then there was DeLong mouthing back to me, "Well, yes, so are eating and urinating 'parts of life,' but those parts I can manage.")

She is tender, vital. I'm the one who's dead.

Marion surprised me that last night. She came forward—she _was_ forward. She pushed away her irrational fear that Michael would hear us having sex. She put aside her usual complaints: my restless nights, her trouble falling back to sleep. It has to be said, she has kept her looks fairly well. Not so many wrinkles. Willing to wear perfume on special occasions. An attractive enough woman, comfortable with middle age. Letting her hair gray naturally. All theoretically fine with me, but it can't help reminding me of what we've lost—not only the innocent skin but the spontaneity. She the sharp-eyed graduate student researching the psychoanalytic training process, I the earnest training analyst willing to be studied. In those days we made love with wonder, without calculation—didn't just "have sex."

She swung over to my side of the bed with a ceremonial smile, as if in tribute to those days before the humiliating anatomy lessons began, as if her failure to reach climax has been my sole responsibility. Were the miscarriages my fault too? To be fair, she would not say so. (She blamed herself, in fact—obsessively, self-destructively.) She would agree that we had much bad luck. The barren months while she hoped the second pregnancy would take. Her distress after she lost each baby.

sacrifice

Her fear that she had sacrificed her best child-bearing years to her Ph.D. and the beginnings of her career. The long wait before she would risk getting pregnant again. The third pregnancy. Third drought. Depression. Third miscarriage. Worse depression. When finally Michael was born, her hormonal attention was seized by him. "You can't understand my pain." Her voice breaking. Breaking and breaking again. Too many scars.

At a table near mine, a blond backpacker leans over to a girl, also blond, and kisses her in the crook of her neck as she reaches around with her hand and cradles his head. . . . I turn away. I admit this embarrassment: I have yet to get used to watching the young brandish their sexual availability as if they were inventing it as an art form. They want the simple act of pleasure. Actually, they are confused; they don't know the difference between biology and art. This is innocence—and ignorance—that results in trouble. When Marion pointed out that in the space of a few weeks she had seen no fewer than three young women leaving my office wearing scoop-necked or otherwise low-cut tops, I couldn't make her believe that I hadn't noticed the pattern. (Of course I wasn't telling the truth.) Marion thinks dressing this way gives them a confidence that she could have used at their age, though I point out that confidence is precisely what they lack, or they wouldn't be coming to see me.

As I was saying—

That night, Marion approached me with a freshness that reminded me of what I have been missing for a very long—incalculably long—time. After we made love, she lay on the pillow and gazed at me fondly (I thought). I was absurdly grateful. We were refreshed, replenished. See, she said afterward, I had nothing to fear from her new life or her women's group. Her needs took nothing away from me. I should etch that into my brain. The group's discussions of sex were only to my advantage.

85

I would be amazed to learn—she was amazed to learn—how many of her friends, the wives of my friends, failed to reach orgasm. She forgets how many female patients tell me the same.

Then: "What's the matter? You're giving me that my-how-interesting therapeutic appraisal, the one that starts in the middle distance and never quite reaches all the way to me. That one."

I tried to play dumb. I said I didn't see the point of starting down this path at such a late hour.

She insisted. "I know what it is."

"What is it?"

"You can't forgive me for growing old, can you?"

I laughed unconvincingly. "That's not it at all, Marion."

"I'm not accusing you of being a tyrant. I'm noticing that you're human."

"Very generous of you. But that's not what's going on with me."

"OK, what is, then?"

Out with it. "Actually, I'm thinking about your word 'etch.' "

"Not actually."

"You did ask."

She gaped.

I went on. "Don't you think it's a bit hostile?"

She still gaped.

"Sharp instruments, you know," I said.

"Look who's using sharp instruments!"

But leaving aside "etch," that night was an improvement. I was relieved. Nineteen years of affection, and this is the best we can do for a farewell.

Nineteen years of affection! I make it sound like an illness—infection.

What I said was, "I'm going to miss you, Marion." She was

insipid back. She was trying. Give us credit for trying. But both of us fell far short of forgiveness.

She is going to leave me, though she doesn't know it yet.

The miscarriages are not exactly news to Paul. His mother had mentioned them when she was ill. The first miscarriage was not so unusual, the second more so, the third a curse. She blamed no one—no matter how angry she may have been at his father for other reasons. There was, after all, the miraculous Paul, who *had* come to term, the first- and only-born. She had spent the last month of her pregnancy in bed, just to reduce the danger of losing him. After his birth, she tried to conceive again, but by then she was thirty-eight. When Paul was a boy, he often wondered why he, unlike his friends, had no brothers or sisters. She had told him he was "special." To play with, he conjured an imaginary brother, Spizzy. Spizzy got a place setting at dinner. Schizzy, Marion called him. Paul would correct her indignantly. "You were a happy baby," she told him. "You had the most adorable laugh."

A "special" baby with a covenant of a sort . . . yes! And by all rights he must have been "special" in his father's eyes, too. Symbolically, at any rate—a baby with its little laugh and its chubby arms and legs reduced to a symbol! No doubt of it: In the mind of his father, *Abraham, Isaac, Esau* was already taking shape—with the father as the center of reverence, the mother and child trailing along behind. *And Marion was old when Paul was born. Chester was old. And she gave thanks.* What kind of covenant Chester had with God, the God in which he did not believe, was another question.

And then there is this other matter, of his mother's sexual dissatisfaction. This is new to Paul. His mother, of course, never spoke to him of her sexual life. It amazes Paul what women used to put up with. Women and children, whose mission was to turn themselves inside out rendering services.

A bedlam of images buzzes around in Paul's mind. He puts down Chester's notebook and takes up a sketch pad. His parents in bed: opposite sides, facing away from each other, a white sea dividing them. His father's beard pointed, a dagger; his mother's face invisible. Strong outlines, in Herb Spector's style. Next, the parents look up. An infant rises skyward from the bed, as if hurled. His father's grin a leer. A cherub ascending through a hole in the clouds. Chubby, blissful. Next page: the child on all fours, wearing a saddle labeled COVENANT, Chester riding him hard. The mother off to the side, her face elongated and creased.

Perhaps, Paul thinks, he has just stumbled into his fate: to produce a comix version of his father's masterpiece. Wouldn't you know that Chester would absorb the great themes and exhaust them, leaving Paul to perform the son's variations on the father's themes? The Further Adventures of Isaac. *Gurevitch, Gurevitch, isn't he the one who did the on-line version of his father's book? Interesting idea. Of course Garland père was the original.*

Paul shudders. For the first time in years he craves a smoke. He rummages through the drawers of his bed table, then his desk, and finally, under a jumble of single socks in his dresser, snatches up a crumpled pack containing two dried-out cigarettes. He lights one and savors the foul taste. His hand is trembling slightly. He needs to shake loose from this harebrained idea of a multimedia, audiovisual, annotated, animated, hyperlinked version of *Abraham, Isaac, Esau.*

And yet he feels drawn back to his father's Mount Moriah. He needs to know what sentence Isaac was condemned to in his father's mind.

sacrifice

WHAT OF ISAAC?

Genesis is little help. It tells us that the angel spoke to Abraham, not to his son. Isaac, on the brink of his own death, might as well have been dead wood. To him no one said a word. Nor is it recorded whether he wept, or laughed, or sorrowed, or clenched his fist. Isaac is a void. Where is his outrage? His rebellion? Does he strain to justify the man and the God who shoved him under the knife? His actions throw into question all the civilizations that trace their lineage to that moment in the desert. His justification is also the justification of Judaism, Christianity, and Islam. So we must put Isaac to the test. He must become comprehensible. What drove him?

The conventional interpretation is that Isaac was gullible, that he had to be turned to fuel so that Abraham's piety could burn. In other words, to live in devotion to God requires that you turn other people into your instruments. This is the tragedy of salvation, to which human history bears witness.

But there is a second theory about Isaac on Mount Moriah. That he leaped onto the altar with a great laugh. That he was not a child but a young man, perhaps twenty-five years of age. That he knew just what he was doing and rejoiced in the belief that what he was doing was just. That he owed this obedience to God, and to his father as well. That not to have served his father's passion would have meant he was unworthy to have been born. That he was possessed of a strong will, of his own righteous desire to enter into the embrace of the single God. This is the view of Josephus, the first-century Jew who became a Roman and was well rewarded for it—who in other words was himself a bit of a trickster. Josephus had his own reasons to celebrate willful self-sacrifice at the demand of a higher power. If Isaac had actually reached the age of consent, then he was responsible. If he was old enough to say no, he acquired nobility by saying yes. This boldness Josephus also has reasons to celebrate: He is, after all, promoting his people before Roman eyes.

Philo of Alexandria, also in the first century A.D., had a third theory: that Isaac was prematurely, remarkably wise. Isaac was "a child of great bodily beauty and excellence of soul," and "already he was showing a perfection of virtues beyond his years." He and his father, Abraham, were perfectly in agreement. "They walked with equal speed of mind." Abraham did not have to argue his son into compliance. He did not have to command him. They walked in silence because, without any need to communicate, they were fused into a single organism with a single purpose: to volunteer. Abraham's people did not sacrifice children regularly, so God was original—and so was Abraham when he chose to slaughter his son.

Philo, it is said, wrote an entire volume on Isaac, but it has been lost, so we must come to our own assessment of Isaac with only a hint of the great commentator's guidance.

The important point is that neither Josephus nor Philo is willing to accept the notion that Isaac was weak or subservient. They want to make him coequal with his father: a partner in reverence or, in more modern—possibly more damaging—terms, a collaborator. This view is certainly noble. These commentators want to believe in Isaac's freedom. They cannot accept that Abraham would offer up a helpless child just to prove he was helpless in the eyes of God. In their interpretations, Isaac trembled because he took his own life in his hands—that is, because he was fearless. This was possible, of course, even if Isaac was twelve years old at the time. Genesis says nothing about his being afraid.

Suppose, then, that Isaac was indeed a young man whose love for his father was the strongest force in his life. His submission was his freely offered gift. Having proved himself, he then *freed himself*—for the Bible does not tell us that Abraham freed him, only that he took the ram as a substitute. Sacrifice was the first measure of love, and on the altar Isaac became a man.

In other words, the son was transformed by his trauma. The Isaac who came down from the mountain was not the Isaac who had gone up. He learned to doubt, to fear, and to keep his own counsel. Or was there more? Was Isaac engaged in his own apprenticeship to God? Rather than content ourselves with notions of blind faith and reckless obedience, we should consider the question of what Isaac learned. It is at the heart of the meaning of Mount Moriah.

On the way up the mountain, Isaac trusted and obeyed. Afterward, he saw with his own eyes that God had provided. God had promised an offering and He had kept his promise. Surely Abraham would not have sacrificed his only son to this God of his! Yet Isaac was not pure in his faith. He had been tapped by doubt. His faith, if that is even the right word, had been seared on the altar. God made *him* no promises. He heard a rustle, a ripple of wind, but no angel. Not even Josephus or Philo, or for that matter Kierkegaard, maintains that Isaac with his own ears ever heard His voice. Neither did he implore God to speak to him, nor did he ask Abraham that he account for himself, for his father was a man of few words. Yet Isaac's sleep was surely troubled. Dread so intense would not dissipate so quickly. How could his father have done this to him? He labored to understand love.

Is love different from relief? he asked his mother Sarah upon his return. She was perplexed. She thought, He is a man now, but he is reticent, sobered. His silence is studied. Yet she did not ask for an account of his journey to the mountain. She did not question. She did not want to know. She did not need to know. Isaac wondered what she saw, when she gazed so intently at him, and decided that he should not volunteer any word of what he had experienced. He had learned from his father the value of secrets. He had learned that dread was his lot and he could survive it. Your father is a good man, Sarah said. Behold, he will find a wife for you, she said to him later. He always provides, Isaac said. He said no more. For years he did not speak. He retreated into the knot of his feelings.

Yes, that's it! Paul thinks. The knot of my feelings. Whenever I pull on a loose end, the knot tightens.

He is moved, then surprised, then guilty for feeling surprised—all within a few skipped heartbeats. *So my father noticed me after all, his own son, strangling in a knot of feelings.* It should not come as a complete surprise—Isaac's name, after all, appears smack in the middle of the book title—yet somehow Paul is surprised at the thought of his father trying to correct Genesis, the book that had almost erased Isaac for the greater glory of Abraham.

Trying to correct Genesis in a book. Not protecting your son in the real world.

Paul goes for more coffee, more Frangelico, more bitterness, more sweetness.

ABRAHAM DID PROVIDE. He found for his son his kinswoman Rebecca. Isaac was forty years old. When Sarah died, Abraham took other wives and produced other sons. Isaac trembled again. But Abraham sent these sons eastward, to follow in the vanished footprints of Ishmael. When Abraham died, full of years—one hundred seventy-five, to be exact—Isaac and Ishmael buried him in the cave of Machpelah which he had bought many years before.

Isaac *and Ishmael.*

Suddenly, decades after his banishment, Ishmael walks back into the story, and we step up to the edge of another mystery. We are now told that, after so many years of living apart,

Ishmael knew that his father had come to the end of his days. Why did Isaac share ceremonial rights with his illegitimate half brother, yet not with his younger half brothers, of whom we hear almost nothing? Why did he welcome Ishmael alone to the graveside? Isaac was named for joyfulness, and a name is a strong suggestion. From joyfulness comes generosity. Isaac had learned to be forgiving toward his father and toward his father's God; why not toward this half brother who had done him no wrong? *Isaac must have felt the need to atone for the deeds of his father—and his father's God.* He was willing to cradle the guilt that his father forswore when he laid Isaac on the altar. Cradle the guilt and massage it, hold it, mold it, transmute it. He was willing to feel shame and the will to justice. He knew that this half brother, who had been wronged in Isaac's name, had a claim to the soil where their father was buried. Isaac would in this way surpass his father. He would be the superior man.

Perhaps, too, Isaac, a practical man, feared the armed might of Ishmael and thought it wise to include him for that reason.

There remains another puzzle: How did Ishmael know that the time had come to bury his father? He had been banished many years before. He was a man of the desert, a wanderer. How was he located? The conclusion is irresistible. Ishmael knew of his father's passing without being told. He was brushed by an angel's wings. Genesis does not specify. The text simply relates, "His sons Isaac and Ishmael buried him in the cave of Machpelah." And yet we are not wholly surprised to learn that Ishmael, his first son, arranges to stand at his grave. Something that should be astounding does not seem astounding at all. It seems, in fact, fated. We stand in the presence of the uncanny.

After the death of Abraham, God blesses Isaac, and Ishmael falls out of the story again. He makes no claim, does not fight, respects his half brother. Isaac's gamble of generosity pays off.

God blesses Isaac, but Isaac is a man of few words and does not wish to ask anything of Him. The last thing he wants is to recapitulate the cruelties of his father. When Isaac thinks of God, he thinks of Mount Moriah and trembles. As the years go by and Rebecca remains without child, he fears that he is doomed to repeat a life he still fails to understand. He is becoming a connoisseur of doom. To win his freedom again, he must become the first analyst and, long before Freud, analyze himself first.

Isaac now considers his journey to Mount Moriah from many angles. He imagines that his father had been jealous of God, that he must have wanted to be the One. But if man was created in the image of God, then he must resemble the whole God! God, Who created man and brought forth Isaac from Sarah, was also the destroyer of Sodom. Abraham had brought forth children, and in this he was like God the creator. What remained for him was to be become like God the destroyer.

Isaac wondered whether he had been born to be one of a sequence of interchangeable sons. Suppose that Abraham had actually gone through with God's design and sacrificed him. Would God have sent a replacement son to console the inconsolable Sarah? Would ninety-year-old Sarah have forfeited her one and only chance to bring forth life because God had made a private arrangement with Abraham? And was Isaac's Rebecca now to prove barren precisely because Sarah had been spared— that is, precisely because Isaac had come into the world? Did this God bring children into the world only to drive them into the wilderness and prepare them for slaughter, just as He pleased? Must an absolute King of Kings be served absolutely?

Thus did Isaac strive—and fail—to make sense of the sacrifice that had not taken place. His mind was troubled down to its roots. This God of his father was incomprehensible. He could not love Him beyond measure. He knew dread, and his wife was barren. So he reached the limit of his analysis. Although the thought of his father and his father's God filled him with anguish, he put aside his doubt, took his freedom into his hands, and prayed to the God of his father that his wife might conceive. And she did conceive. Isaac was sixty years old.

Paul feels lost—trapped in this impenetrable allegory—and, suddenly, bone-weary. Without getting up from his chair, he closes his eyes . . . and jolts awake to the ring of the phone, without any idea how much time has passed. He picks up the receiver and hears a dial tone, nothing more.

Again, the uncanny.

Awake now, he reaches not for his father's published words but for his journal. He needs access to the actual Chester Garland who lived an actual life. He rediscovers his father still in the Gare Montparnasse.

THE LIGHT OF the rising sun was seeping through the enormous, steel-ribbed train shed when I left the café. The darkness slowly turned the color of a bruise. All around, echoing slightly, the twittering of the French language, softer and higher in pitch than English—an appealing and incomprehensible murmur. There was a ceremonial feeling, an active anticipation. The passengers-to-be were watchful—looking at their watches, in fact. How similar we are everywhere, we humans! My stock-in-trade is suspicion too, suspicion of the conscious—that is, the deceitful—mind. If I were content with what I could see and hear, where would I be? I was full of eagerness for the cathedral.

I saw the sign posted, "Versailles Chartres," walked down the track, got on board a second-class car, and easily found a seat in an empty nonsmoking compartment. There was clearly no great rush for this crack-of-dawn train. It always pleases me to arrive early for trains and planes, just as it does to settle into my seat at the theater long before the last-minute arrivals push in and make pests of themselves. The dark wood of the compartment wall had the look of age and care, like certain Paris doors. Brown seats, pallid yellow trim—some kind of vinyl, I think. I faced forward. I dislike facing rearward in a train, seeing only where I've already been. A psychiatrist believes that people should learn to see backward in order to face forward. The look back is supposed to be a prologue, albeit a fascinating one. But a train is a different matter. As if to prove the variety of human desires, an elderly man with rheumy eyes and lumpy skin peered into the compartment, hesitated, and sat down catty-corner from me, facing the end of the train. As for me, I badly wanted to be propelled ahead.

There was a rapid clicking of heels, and then a short dark-haired woman holding a young child by the hand poked her head in—I had the impression of a sundress, high leather boots, an attractive body, and a rapid intake of breath, for she had apparently been rushing. She looked around with disapproval and withdrew. She must have wanted a smoking compartment or an unoccupied one. There was an umbrella handle sticking out of her open-topped handbag.

A long bell sounded and the train eased forward. How I relish this sensation of freedom and grace! When a plane takes off with a roar from a standstill, the great engine noise is the sign that you are accelerating, accelerating, and then—the moment of truth—you're ripped from the ground. You <u>take off</u>—it's a process of harsh removal, a wrench, a gamble, sudden movement from zero to high speed. In a train, you inch ahead, and it's as if the station releases you into the movement that is the train's natural state, as the nature of man is to breathe—in, out—in continuous motion. In a train, forward motion is a deliverance. I was, needless to say, a man in search of deliverance.

sacrifice

The sky was bluing up as the train slipped through outlying Paris, squeaking each time it crossed another track, easing again and again onto the right one. I had the sense of a vast organization at work, successful civilization, a chain of intelligence directing the switches, all so that millions of individuals might go on about their business—a tremendous achievement when you think about it! A rumble started, low moans, as if the train were swallowing hard, and so it went: slight lurches followed by smooth passages. There wasn't much to see. Nothing to write home about, as they say. Too many of the new apartment buildings have the look of cheap afterthoughts slapped up overnight to cut Paris's reputation down to size. Suburbs of stone and stucco houses cramped together. The train's mild clacking soothed me. Let the suburbs, the warehouses with their corrugated siding, the mechanical expanses of railroad yards, be undistinguished! What did it matter to me? They had their weariness, I had mine.

I had been musing for some minutes in this manner when the conductor, a short man in a blue coat with a leather bag over his shoulder, appeared and emitted an efficient and rapid burst of French from which I caught the words "billets" and "messieurs" and nothing more. My compartment mate pulled out his ticket and offered it to be punched. The conductor then reached for my own ticket, which I passed over. He studied it as if he had never seen a ticket before, frowned, pushed the ticket back at me, said "Alors," and another flock of words flew from his mouth. His tone was one of supreme indignation, although he was not yelling. The French have the habit of speaking the most routine words in a tone of remonstrance, as if the addressee were an insulting bastard, a moron, or a small child who must be firmly taught the elements of civilized conduct. The civilized thing is that they remonstrate with gestures, not loudness.

My first thought was that the sleepy ticket agent must have

sold me a ticket at the wrong rate, invalid on this particular train. I was humiliated. I struggled for the right French words. All I could muster was "Je . . . ne . . . comprends . . . pas."

The conductor repeated himself more emphatically and a little more slowly, so that I could make out not only "billet" but "Chartres," "train," and "pas," but still I hadn't a clear idea what he was trying to tell me, and I was starting to feel wronged. The elderly man was looking on disapprovingly—not only had I committed some offense but I was incapable of explaining myself! There then appeared at the compartment door a young man in a light suede jacket and wearing rimless glasses, with long reddish hair, rather handsome, who said in accented but lucid English, "May I help?"

"Please." I invited him in with some relief. He asked a question of the conductor, who replied elaborately, though still indignantly.

"He tells you that there is an error," he said to me. "Actually two errors. You have a ticket for Chartres."

"Yes, that's right."

"But, you see, this train does not go to Chartres."

There is such a thing as a sinking feeling. I felt it. I plunged. I had fallen through a trapdoor and there was no bottom. Life was a free fall into doom. My life was suddenly, fatefully, forever wrong. The elderly man was staring at me with distaste, as if my distress were an insult to the orderly course of the universe.

"This is the train to Dreux."

"Dreux?" (Of course, I didn't yet know how this name was spelled. It sounded like a sharp swallow, a sort of glug.)

"Well, that is . . . another town, you know. Dreux. It is"— He turned to the conductor. "Avez-vous une carte, monsieur?"

"Oui, mais—" The conductor, shedding his irritation, decided to be helpful, for he had apparently reclassified me as needy, like the war-wounded who are entitled to convenient seats on the Métro. He pulled out a fat book of maps and leafed through it until he came to the one he was looking for, which he placed on the seat next to me. Paris, a dense asterisk of rail lines, appeared at the upper right-hand side. With a tobacco-stained finger the conductor stabbed at a point in the center of the map and explained, with a flicker of triumph, as if he had just concluded an elegant mathematical proof, "Voilà! Dreux." He then moved his finger down a bit and said, "Voilà! Chartres."

"But the sign at the station said Chartres!" I protested, as if a protest would change the facts. "It said Versailles and Chartres! I saw it very clearly!" I was innocent! This could not be happening to me! But it <u>was</u> happening to me. What <u>had</u> I seen? What had I done wrong? Something—some self-sabotage. I was a stumbling fool who would always botch his choices. No, be honest. "Sterile fool" was the phrase that came all too quickly to mind.

The conductor, his lower lip pressed against the upper into a grunt of sadness at the ways of the world, shrugged minutely. An American lands on the wrong train and acts as though this were someone else's fault. Les américains with their air of privilege!

"Alors. Well, evidently," said the young man in suede, "there is a mistake. Maybe the train to Chartres left on the other track. But this one"—he pointed down to the floor—"unfortunately, this is the train to Dreux." He said something to the conductor, causing him to soften his expression a bit, but this afforded me very limited pleasure.

"I took the wrong train!" I declared, not brilliantly. How could I have done such a stupid thing? With all the time in the world to kill at the station, I jump on the wrong train! Stupid! But I am not (especially) stupid. I must have meant to botch my little adventure. Yes! That was it! I <u>wanted</u> to blow this trip to smithereens. "I took the wrong train! Holy God! What do I do now?" The train was every second taking me farther from Paris, farther from Chartres, closer to some godforsaken place I had never heard of before.

"Well," said the young man, who was still trying to help, "you can—maybe you can depart at Dreux. Let me see. Yes, why not?" He turned to the conductor. I heard the word "horaire"—schedule. The conductor shrugged again and then emitted a burst of language. The young man said, "Maybe, you know, there is a train from Dreux to Chartres. I will be right back," and he rushed off. The conductor moved on to punch more tickets. The elderly man took a look at me sidelong, disgusted. Shame poured over me. I was horrified. The young man must have gone for the police. . . . A crazy thought. I had nothing to fear. Nothing so terrible had happened. This was amusing. Yes! And correctable. I patted my jacket pocket frantically, as if a potential thief had just brushed past me. But there was no need to worry. I had the text of my paper. I patted my money belt; I had money. I had my passport. I was fully accounted for.

I had. I have. I was.

My heartbeat had gone off-rhythm. Sweat tickled my forehead and dripped.

But there was no need to be so disturbed. It wasn't <u>necessary</u>.

A textbook case, this astonishment that sets a person reeling. I should not feel as I <u>am</u> feeling. I thought I knew what was what: who I was, where I was going.

But nothing irrevocable had happened. This was a comical setback and nothing more. A mistake, that's all. No harm done in the end. Sometimes a mistake is only a mistake. Why wasn't I laughing?

The young man came back and said, "I have it," and brandished a thick book, which evidently listed all the train schedules in France or Europe or, for all I knew, the world. He sat down next to me, leafed through, and found Dreux. I peered where he was pointing. We would arrive in Dreux at 8:03. And look! Fortunately, there was a train from Dreux to Chartres at 10:32! All I had to do was kill two and a half hours in Dreux, and I would get to Chartres in less than an hour. With no harm done.

"You are in luck, monsieur!" the young man said triumphantly. His pleasure in my reprieve was infectious. It was as if the blood had started to flow again in my veins, and my heart resumed beating evenly. I looked out the window and, ridiculously, we were passing through a little station marked "Plaisir-Grignon."

Smile, Chester! There's going to be a happy ending for you yet, my man. And yet something was seriously wrong— something wrong—something. What? I looked at the book more closely.

He passed it over to me, his finger marking the page. Dreux was on the line that ran from Paris to a place called G——. Beneath the Paris–G—— schedule were listed the Chartres–Dreux trains. I checked the Dreux–Chartres schedule again. Yes, arrive Chartres 11:25—in good time to catch the 11:45 back to Paris, exactly the train I would have taken if I hadn't made my careless mistake at Montparnasse! But I would have to skip the cathedral.

Well then, Chester, you'll have to find another time! That's what adults do. Where id was, there shall better planning be. Twenty-four hours ago, the glories of Chartres had not even entered my mind. I had managed forty-nine years in ignorance of these splendors. They would remain splendid. This was what I would have said to my son. This is what I would have said to a patient in the grip of an obsession.

And then, as I contemplated the map, the solution came to me. Why hadn't I seen it before? Dreux was almost due north of Chartres and only 45 kilometers away. I could take a taxi, arrive in Chartres by nine at the outside, say, and still have two hours to spare at the cathedral. I <u>was</u> lucky. Taking the wrong train would prove to be a laughable little episode, a story to tell on myself when I might need a humility lesson. Ridiculous to be chastising myself over an error of no consequence. A taxi, yes!

We sped through a station whose name I didn't catch. Long lines of tall, spindly trees rushed by close to the track. In the background, some woods, a cone-shaped steeple, and then bright green fields slid by. Left to itself, this train would have lunged on unceasingly. I have never loved—this thought burst into my mind. Never in my life had I loved. No, that was absurd. I was coming apart. I was getting what I deserved. I was going to die. In thirty-one minutes, this train would stop in Dreux. After four minutes, at 8:07, it would depart again, and stop at a series of towns whose names meant nothing to me. G—— was the end of the line. A point on the sea. Arrive G—— at 11:43, just the time when, otherwise, I would be leaving Chartres for Paris, my conference, and my life.

"I must go," said the young man in suede, "but you may return this to the conductor when you are finished with it. OK?"

"Of course. Thank you so much. You are very kind." You are talking to a man who has never loved. But who keeps his appointments.

"Not at all. Oh, there is another problem about your ticket."

"What?"

"It must be composted." He explained the French system. Before getting on the train, you are supposed to insert the ticket into a device that stamps the time of departure. "This is not serious." He smiled and left the compartment. I sank into a reverie. The adrenaline surge had left me feeling clear and strangely peaceful. Whitish-gray concrete slabs of housing, some tall, some short, like matchboxes, rushed by the side of the tracks. They were bleak, and I should have felt bleak, but I didn't. I felt relieved. Perhaps I loved Marion enough. I cared for a child and patients well enough. I had enough respect. I had a worthy place in the world.

The elderly man continued to regard me with disgust as he stood up and prepared to leave.

We eased by the projects and began to slow past stucco houses and some stone. The public address system went into a monotone ending with a word that might have been Dreux. There were warehouses with corrugated iron siding starting to rust. When we slid into the station, the sky was still leaden but I felt a curious warmth on my skin. There was that little bustle of restlessness as passengers made ready to alight, and the train came to a stop noiselessly, as men come to decisions. I saw the young man in the suede jacket stride off purposefully toward the nondescript terminal, and behind him a lean couple older than I, the two of them marching off as if in close-order drill, their bodies not touching.

The young man turned and gazed in my direction, but I could not read his expression or even be sure I was what he was looking at. The couple passed him. The young man turned and followed them toward the terminal and the remainder of his day.

I knew with a click of certainty that I could have been striding off behind this young man to resume my formulaic life, via the taxi and the cathedral, via the train, via Paris, to the psychoanalytic congress, the reading of the paper, the colleagues; then the plane, the wife, the child, the practice. Via all the known quantities. Chester Garland comfortable, a little foolish, a lot relieved, reconciled to his highly sensible, decidedly adequate existence. Chester Garland, adept at getting back on track after a brief escape attempt. Schedules and maps. Minor successes and major safeguards. The good-enough life. Ticking. Until the good-enough end.

I did not believe anything I felt.

But I believed this: Good enough was not good enough.
Just like that, jump. Don't look for a safe landing. Jump.
Out of a trap.

Here, a thick double line crossed the page, and below it
Chester resumed in a slighter but more careful, settled hand.

Paul has long since finished another cup of coffee and
Frangelico. He considers pouring one more but cannot bring
himself to move.

I DO NOT know whether what I wanted was to manage my destiny or throw it away. Very likely it is not for me to know.

A man faced forward in a train compartment. The man was
alone, his face relaxed. His mind was released from many bur-
dens and words. He felt the way he sometimes felt after a successful fifty minutes dispensing insight from his leather chair.
He leaned back heavily and breathed. He had dodged an arrow.
The train edged ahead. Trees and houses alongside the tracks
blurred. The town of Dreux receded. Recent events receded. He
could inspect his life from a great distance, or, when it pleased
him, come closer, hold up the parts, and turn them around
and around, like artifacts from an archaeological dig. There was
a bright black flint of thought in the mind of the man. He
scraped at it, hoping to work up a spark. The train picked up
speed. He watched warehouses pour by, houses with surfaces
of cracked stone, vines cut back to tiny stubs, backyards
with casual gardens. The man stared into the middle distance
(where had he heard that phrase recently?) and summoned up a
mildly pleasing image of his wife, soon deciding that he had
thought enough for one morning about his not-good-enough
marriage.

A witness, had there been one, might have seen the man
wince. The man was pained to own up to the pile of waste called

his life. The man was Chester Garland, was I, was Chester Garland I, the First.

I will know what I need, thought the man, when I have left everything behind. I could start by leaving behind—

Yes? Yes?

—leaving behind the bitterness, which violates my oath. A good physician expects this of himself even against all odds: to look everything dead in the eye and keep ambivalence in its place.

Let the click of the train on the rails go on forever. Let the stations dissolve. In the unconscious, as is well known, there are no stations, only journeys.

I wonder whether my own son will grow into a man like that one in the suede jacket, a guide to the lost. One thing I will say for myself, I have tried to put my limited talents to work to relieve suffering. Whatever my failings, I have accomplished some of that.

I have probably not been the best father, though I am probably *[something is crossed out]* enough.

Enough. Paul's hand, clutching the notebook, is trembling. Gently, as if it were a live bomb, he sets the notebook down. A rancid taste fills his mouth.

He had a girlfriend once, Jenn, a philosophy graduate student turned aerobics instructor, who taught him self-hypnosis. Lie down, loosen your limbs, clench and release every part of the body in sequence. Then imagine you're taking one step at a time down a dark staircase. At each step it gets darker, and you tell yourself that you're closer to what you want. What is it you want, Michael Paul?

He wants his father back, dragging himself out of a subway tunnel to beg forgiveness—no, to kneel before him, so that Paul can accuse him of . . . of what? Of everything.

Enough! Paul would love to stop the accusations. He slogs into the bathroom and stands before the mirror. His eyes are shiny, the pouches below heavy and dark. Coming attractions. These pouches are going to grow, the neck is going to thicken. In a few more years, it may be Chester Garland's sad, distant eyes that stare back at him from the mirror to prove whose son he is, and that tight smile, further proof that the men of the line don't give anything away for nothing. One of his old girlfriends—Abby the dancer—used to say, "Your lips won't crack if you smile, you know." But they felt as though they would. "All unhappiness is a failure of gratitude," she said.

It crosses his mind to call Jenn, downgraded after she dumped him to a transient comfort—exactly what he needs now. No, he needs a new girlfriend. He can live without either. He needs to get out of the apartment.

He slips on a pair of moccasins and a plain white T-shirt without a logo, and in a stupor starts downstairs, a sketch pad and pen in hand. The city is a tank of humidity. He's tired of all the rings and studs jabbed into eyebrows, lips, and chins. Flesh not of his flesh. Losers should keep their metal out of sight. Fleets of taxis nose up Second Avenue. He makes his way across town to SoHo and stops by a new upscale café with black steel sidewalk tables. Tall women with sculpted cheekbones—they can't all be models, can they?—stroll in with the grace that comes of years of effort. Paul is perhaps ten years their senior and feels ancient.

The loose black curls of the waitress trickle down her cheeks. Ripe lips, a Eurasian look. He orders a Black Russian and admires the delicate curvature of her waist as she turns. He picks up a pen and sketches rows of women's waists; he turns the page and draws a young man with a fashionable stubble of hair, bulging eyes, a single loop earring, looking into a mirror, and scribbles under it. *Question: What is the dif-*

ference between Paul Gurevitch and a dead man? Answer: One generation.

The waitress brings the Black Russian. She stands to his left, trying to read his caption. "Cool," she says. "You draw." Her voice is a kind of mist.

He sips the drink and lets his mind go. Her apartment, a nearby studio. His hands tour her waist, her smooth thighs. . . . Hard as he tries, he can't force his way farther into the fantasy. Even his fantasy life lacks conviction.

The waitress returns, asking if everything is all right. Paul looks at her in disbelief—*everything* all right? I'm an orphan, he thinks. "It could be worse," he says.

"Let me know if you need anything," she replies sympathetically. He can see it, though: She's embarrassed for him. He walks slowly home. What does he need? He needs a model who needs nothing, a cover girl, a heart-shaped face, a crust of personality on top. . . . Perhaps two! He's ready for one of those king-size porn body triangles where no fluid goes to waste, a sort of eco-efficient symmetry of moist and intense sucking. He needs a new friend—not the lucky ones who are relocating, not the hypochondriacs, not the ones whining about their crummy jobs.

When he has climbed upstairs, he picks up the remote and starts "Switched-On Bach," the electronic version recorded by Walter Carlos before he made himself over into Wendy Carlos—now there was a man without fear of transformation!—and listens to a few minutes of a Brandenburg Concerto. He needs a project, something to keep him busy for weeks, months—and not *Abraham, Isaac, Esau,* in multimedia. A name comes to him: HIP GNOSIS. He goes to his bookcase, plucks out the tales of Edgar Allan Poe, and reads, for the ninth or tenth time, what has been his favorite story since childhood, "The Facts in the Case of M. Valdemar." He picks up his sketch pad and draws an old bony man stretched out in bed: gaunt, with whiskers and big staring eyes. During his dying moments M. Valdemar has been hypnotized, only to be brought out of his trance after he's dead. . . . Paul has known for years what the final frame will show: "a nearly liquid mass of loathsome—of detestable putrescence." Putrescence—beautiful, almost onomatopoetic word. He smears lines, draws puddles, little outward-pointing arrows to suggest that liquid is in the process of spreading, but he can't get M. Valdemar's dissolution right. He lets the page float to the floor, picks up a different pen, and with a flourish writes on a new page, "The Facts in the Case of M. Garland." That one he crumples and tosses.

A breeze has come up, rattling his window blinds. A blue light is flickering across the street. He's been sweating profusely, and there's a chill on his skin. He pads over to the bed table, pulls out a half-smoked joint, and lights it. The smoke scorches his throat and he begins to cough, but when he stops there's a mild, pleasant buzz somewhere in his brain. He's relieved to find himself, as ever, alone. There's no one to whom he has to explain himself. He turns off the light. He could coast and go on coasting, in the warm and fluid night, in the random darkness, out beyond land, beyond knowledge, beyond pattern, beyond need—

On second thought, he switches on the lamp and submerges himself in his father's journal.

Little by little, Chester's handwriting is degenerating—melting down—into a fever chart of ripples and bumps. Paul finds he must scramble along, skipping a word or a phrase, retracing his steps, studying context, and still it's all he can do to make sense of what he's reading. All these pages of anti-climax. . . . But there is always a chance that the next section might be the one.

sacrifice

THE CONDUCTOR SLID open the glass door, poker-faced but indignant as he fired a string of words at me—something about "supplement." "Plus lentement," I pleaded. This time I could make out the word "destination." I said "G——" and he used a word I didn't understand. I opened my wallet and held out all my money. He took a hundred-franc note, wrote out a new ticket, and dropped coins into my hand that I didn't bother to count.

As the conductor moved on, the roof of the sky darkened while the area near the horizon grew brighter and there was a voluptuous glow in the landscape. Images sharpened. Clumps of trees slipped past the window, and culverts, concrete abutments, railings. In the distance, a village of pale yellow stone held the light. We flew through brilliant green fields piled with haystacks.

I leaned back and canceled my debt to the past. Just like that, I wrote it off. Just like that, it released me. What did it matter that I had made mistakes? That was my nature, and so what? Not all my mistakes were mistaken. I was alone. There was a shine on the heavy sky, as if it were a bowl of polished lead, and I was suspended inside the moving train, speeding along with it, shuddering when it shuddered. I felt at risk, but smarter and, after a while, for unaccountable reasons, comforted. A village of weathered gray stone flowed by. Everything in my mind converged. I closed my eyes, I do not know for how long, and swayed with the train. I heard the clacking of the rails and then nothing—the positive presence of nothing—as if there were high pressure in my ears and then the suspension that comes when you speed into a tunnel: no distinct sound, only a nothingness within and around me, a nothingness that was full. This makes no sense. I am a modern man. Illusion is insubstantial. Nothingness is not full. What this nothingness was full of I cannot say: lightness or—not lightness. I have no words. I stopped longing for words. Now I sit transcribing that full, fine nothing-ness into words, but at the time the words fell away and left me with a feeling without a name. It makes no sense to say it, but I am saying it—I was not thinking in words at all. I was in the world; the world was in the compartment and in me; this world was all I required. My senses were content. I heard the soothing hush of the current of time, unrelenting, and the world was luxuriant. I heard my passionate blood circulate through my inner ear. I heard all these sensations, but somehow without language. I was liquid, and it was my destiny to move, not to arrive, never to arrive, but to be the conduit of this motion.

I heard the words "God is here."

I heard that sentence exactly. The voice that spoke wasn't mine, exactly, or anyone else's exactly, and it wasn't that God was speaking to me—I have my foolish side, but I'm not a raving idiot—and still I heard "God is here," as if those words amounted to a substance, not <u>signaling</u> the presence of God, but <u>being</u> that presence. I am not explaining this well. How can words be other than words? "God" is a word, "is" is a word, "here" is a word. Yet those words in that order at that time in that place were not symptoms and not signs. They did not refer elsewhere. They did not indicate anything beyond themselves. They did not command me to do x or y. They <u>were</u>. They were radiant, an emanation from some other dimension that had fallen into my world.

These words made no sense at the time, and they make no sense as I set them down. I have kicked away my lexicon, my phrases—all the nicely worn furniture that my career consists of. . . . Why, after all, should words make sense? Don't I know well enough the tricks the unconscious will play? I am highly suggestible, the good Dr. Resnikoff once said with a chuckle, and she only had to say it once for me to remember. And yes, yes, nature suggests repose, and oceanic experience stems from a need to dissolve ego-boundaries and settle into the all-engulfing womb, into the mother, but still. . . .

There was no doubt that I had heard those words that didn't sound precisely like words. They resounded. A power in the third person, the more-than-personal person, revealed itself in this way: <u>God-is-here</u>. Wherever this power was, whatever it was, I had been in its presence. Why those words, and why radiant? I cannot say I was capable of thinking anything organized or lucid until the words "What does that mean?" formed, like foam, on the surface of my joy, and I thought, I don't know, but God is in the compartment. Listen to me! I am not making sense, and I didn't and don't care. I was on vacation from making sense. Sense made me.

I rose and floated above doubt. Doubt was tiny and diminishing, like rooftops seen from an airplane that's just taken off. There were no visitations from angels, no heavenly chorales, no auras or glows, and the cosmos failed to shudder. That didn't matter. Those are dead figures of speech. I thought, God is not this, God is not that, God is not words or concepts. God is the essence. The rest is details.

I relished a sensation that felt as much like a certitude as I have ever felt, and I was not willing—I am not willing—to dismiss it. Oh, I tried, I did try. I asked myself what interpretations I would suggest, were I my own patient: What is this? Enough of this self-serving absurdity. Your joy is performing a hoax upon your senses! Or, more gently: What blithe, harmless megalomania! Analytically: You might want to consider the possibility that you are momentarily overcome by a desire to shed your superego. You see how you have projected that desire into the all-enfolding and all-forgiving mother? Quizzically: Can there be a God that demands nothing of you?

To which I argued back: Bury your punitive supergod! The true God is nothing of which you have any idea. The word "God" is an ash of the original Holiness.

To which I argued back against the arguing back: Chester Garland self-dramatizing as usual, making much too much of a moment of joy, of which, God knows—aha!—God knows he has little enough experience. Take this moment of happiness for what it is. Lean back and breathe in this animal joy just as it comes to you without dragging worn-out old God into it. . . .

But there was nothing worn out about what I knew: that God, the First Cause, the Ground of All Being, the Bottom of Things, was with me.

I opened my eyes, and the internal arguments broke up. The horizon had brightened and a streak of blue appeared. Brown cows grazed in the distance, oblivious. Then, on my side of the train, the sky suddenly emerged a crystalline blue, while the view through the corridor window remained darkened, as if the other side of the train had reverted to black-and-white. The shine in the air was momentary. As I watched, the blue was smudged by gray. Crumpled clouds were heaped on the horizon in every direction. Out the window, another succession of fences and plain houses, warehouses, telephone poles, a cement factory. I would not look at my watch. I was thirsty and my mouth was dry, my lower lip was cracked, and I did not want to get up and go searching for water. I felt I could hold my joy as long as I liked.

Far down below me were shouts, accusations, like anti-aircraft fire that had no power to hurt me: <u>You have no power to declare your life null and void. You are a lost man, in flight. A family man. A deserter with a fancy rationalization. Your weightlessness, if that's what it is, is a product of the fact that you've run away. It won't last.</u> I waited and then, after a while—I don't know how long, because I still hadn't looked at my watch—I felt a rustle of something else, as if there were still another presence in the compartment.

The train trembled slightly, but my trembling was internal and distinct. Some tremor was moving through my autonomic nervous system. . . . Yes, doctor, I feel a quivering, the likes of which I have never felt before. <u>Where do you feel it?</u> That's the funny thing, I'm not sure where. Here in my chest . . . or here in the back of the head . . . or perhaps here . . . a sensation of onrushing . . . exhilaration. <u>So you are not certain where this sensation arises?</u> I know this sounds bizarre. <u>Interesting.</u> Do you have any ideas? <u>I wonder about an infection of the inner ear. You know that presents a variety of symptoms. How long have you been feeling this way?</u>

Words made flesh. Sensations without place. An infection of the inner soul. I closed my eyes again. I was plunged, of course, into a classic anxiety attack. It took a while to recognize what I was feeling now—dread—and I felt acutely the loss of that useless God who had barely made himself known to me. Well, let's take a look at this . . . dread. Dread must be dread of something. Of death, then? Not death in the abstract, but my personal ending? Why should death frighten me? Because life is so superb that to lose it would be a dreadful waste? Far from it. To cease existing would be a mild relief. Not to exist is also something of which I know nothing, and therefore I have no reason to fear it. No, fear of my death isn't the trouble. What I fear is my life. Stark, raving normality. Death by rations. My wife is going to make me pay for my hypothetical crimes, my son will grow up to despise me. I will be in moral arrears forever. My life is a foreign country and I pass through in a sealed train, and to make matters more pathetic, I am the one who sealed it.

Twenty or thirty more years of this.

God, is this what You want? If You want anything from me,

speak up! If You want nothing, why do I find myself on a god-forsaken train heading nowhere in particular?

I am still alone. Nothing has changed except that the light seems soiled. Beyond, a row of poplars, tidy fields, a fragment of a square tower, and a blackened, scorched tank car on a siding. A steeple of pale gray stone comes into view and momentarily lifts my heart. A steeple does wonders—there it is. Centuries ago, life was organized around the uncanny. Having no other name for what they believed, they called their superstition by the name Jesus Christ and told themselves a peculiar story about sheer power, which they called God, and about helplessness, which they called the Church, and hunger, which they called resurrection; and even if this story worked wonders for them only once or twice in a lifetime, they heard about such wonders, and those were as many wonders as they needed.

I hear the purposeful click of heels, that characteristically uplifting sound of our era. Down the corridor from behind me strides the young woman who had looked into the compartment before, her face visible in the mirror above the seat facing me. She has short dark hair and turns neither left nor right. As she passes, I see she is wearing slender calf-high boots and holds a toddler by the hand. The corridor is narrow and so she is half pulling him behind her, a blond boy in short pants, white shirt, and suspenders, in some distress, waddling along uncomfortably. The woman's dress is made of a light material, rust brown, clinging nicely to the round of her hip. Her legs are trim, but it is more than this that reminds me of Marion—Marion as she was. The tenderness of this woman makes an impression on me: the tenderness of her hand guiding her son, the lightness of her touch as they pass out of my sight. A woman who has not been battered by life. How much I enjoy observing people when I am not obliged to patch them up!

Absorbed in his father's journal, Paul hasn't noticed the way he's been picking at the little abrasions by his fingernails. He's scratched them raw. Now he's disgusted with himself, a familiar feeling. At dinner one night, his father noticed similar abrasions and exclaimed, "Michael, holy—my God, you're butchering yourself! You're a glutton for self-abuse!"

"What's a gerlutton?" Michael had asked. Marion thought this adorable. Later, she bought a bottle of bitter medicine for painting children's nails and spread the liquid on Michael's fingertips with a glass applicator that made him shudder. *Detestable putrescence.* The chemical burned and turned the rims of his fingers red, but he learned to leave them alone, "learned the hard way, which is the effective way," said Chester. To compensate for the loss, he took up the habit of ripping the corners off book pages and absentmindedly chewing on them. He came to savor his father's labels: *butcher, glutton for self-abuse.* He was somebody.

Now he is somebody else, wondering at this God who visited Chester Garland so generously but failed to order him home to comfort his family. He doesn't know whom to disbelieve in more, his father or his father's God. What kind of journey had Chester taken, Paul wonders, from the God of the train to the implacable Yahweh of Mount Moriah? The God of the compartment made no demands or promises, issued no covenants, did not make a ninety-year-old woman pregnant. He, or She, or It was by no stretch of the imagination the God Who performed His little experiment on Isaac, or Who sent His only begotten son to be nailed on the cross right down the road from Mount Moriah, or Who tolerated a world filled with torturers and their victims. Chester was certainly aware of the differences. Why, then, didn't he write his book on the all-forgiving, all-enveloping God of the train?

Never once did his father utter a word about any God—not

in *his* hearing—or set foot in a synagogue (but for the occasional bar mitzvah or memorial service). Never did he express the slightest interest in religious life, any religious life. Yet after a peculiar experience on a French train while in flight from his family, he took it upon himself to rewrite substantial portions of the Book of Genesis. As if no one had ever produced such a commentary before. As if the great rabbis had remained silent for hundreds of years.

It's too weird. But still, to Paul's surprise, for the first time in his memory, he feels a slight edge of affinity with his father—another lost man. The one thing he's never imagined is that Chester Garland, too, could think of himself as a failure.

Paul picks up his sketch pad, remembering the term for the direct knowledge of God: Gnosticism. That's something Paul can believe in, something an artist practices. Paul scrawls the words HIP GNOSIS and considers the anagrammatic possibilities. Perhaps he can make something of SING. O SHIP, SING? The plea of the sirens. Or POSING. There's a solution: HIS POSING. Chester Garland making a getaway in his rolling chapel posing as a man of God? He didn't mean to skip out on his family. God made him do it! The same God Who seduced Abraham, that psycho. Who shoved Sarah, Hagar, Ishmael, and Isaac around.

Stop. Paul is ungenerous again and knows it. Whose posing? he wonders.

I THINK OF Marion, big-boned and striding, in slacks. Marion with her neatly parted dirty-blond hair that she has decided to let go silver. Marion betrayed by her body, Marion "failing at her womanly mission." Those were her own words! It wasn't that I was to blame for the lost pregnancies or the missing orgasms, but for failing to grasp what she was going through. For not understanding deeply enough that the reason she withdrew from me was that she despised herself.

Carrying Michael to term should have made the difference. But her habit of self-blame turned into self-protection. She built up a fortress around herself and the baby. Fair enough, that she should be protective. But she grew into her habit of withdrawing from me. After eleven years of marriage, he was the proof of her womanliness. She is right about one thing: After he was born, she found she was eligible only for part-time teaching positions. She had sacrificed her work for her womanhood, and then her body had betrayed her. But everyone makes sacrifices in the name of the reality principle. (Didn't I give up the pleasure of writing to make a focused career as a psychiatrist?) <u>Yes, I wanted a family. I wanted a child more than anything. But you could be more sympathetic, Chet. You didn't have to give up your career altogether. I didn't choose my choices. And I'm one of the lucky ones.</u>

First sullenness, then rage: violent, displaced, disproportionate. Taking pride in her wounds. Picking at them to keep them fresh. She doesn't appreciate my pointing this out. Her tears make her righteous—and it would be unwise for me to lecture her on the theory of female masochism. In her circle, such suffering is a badge of merit. She is betrayed, therefore she exists. She burned up the best years of her life trying to have children, failing to have children, needing so badly to have children. <u>I know this isn't your fault</u>; she protests too much. <u>We did it together. We're creatures of a patriarchal society.</u> Except that in her melodrama, I'm cast as a Turkish pasha, or at least a southern sheriff! She wants a wife too! Well, I can see (some of) her point. I'm inclined to think she may be right, too, that the theory of penis envy is retrograde, "chauvinist," and probably wrong.

Her therapist encourages her to act out. The day I walked in and her group turned toward me, aggressive and embarrassed, like cats caught in the act of chewing up little birds, I had to tiptoe through my own apartment. She gave up her career

TODO GITLIN

willingly, I reminded her. Michael needed her, I pointed out. She'd said it herself, many times. She replied that "willingly" was the wrong word when you're the prisoner of an "oppressive system." A little smile at the word "oppressive"—she knew how crude it sounded. But still she used it and still she meant it. I asked her to consider the possibility that she was projecting onto me her own ambivalence about choosing Michael over her career. Just consider, that's all. She: <u>What's wrong with you is that you always have to win.</u> I: Nonsense, and do you notice you're just repeating a formula? Don't you wonder why you're doing this? She: <u>You want to know my secret for getting by? Oblivion, Dr. Garland, but I'm finished with that, do you hear me? I'm tired of blaming myself.</u>

And then, of course, the rant began. I could see it approaching, hear the thunder boom, a force of nature, but to see and hear the force—I could even admire it—was not to stop it. I would find myself gasping for breath long after the downpour was over. The more I defended myself, the more vigorously she attacked, and I found myself saying things I didn't wholly believe (or did I?).

Once, I loved her deeply. Once I was young and (yes, why not use the appropriate word) potent enough to overlook the barb in her tongue, not to speak of the one in my own. Now I have only hazy memories of a time when she wasn't a difficult woman. Now that she is fortified by an ideological fixation, her defenses will not be easily broken through. Not by me, anyway. Penis envy, Howard laughs, when we discuss this. Knitting needles! Balls of yarn! Howard is a purist about the canonical works of Freud. He is not the only one of my colleagues who utterly fails to understand what is happening among women. They have much to be angry about, legitimately, but in the meantime they can be hell to live with.

I have to face the fact: I no longer know how to handle this

118

woman. She smells my weakness. One might as soon blame a shark for being a shark. But the blood is in the water, and if we stay together one of us will surely swim in for the kill.

If the elderly French gentleman with the bumpy skin had heard my whole laughable saga, he would probably say, "I had a wife like that. Let them forget who wears the pants, they walk all over you. If you ask me, sounds like you've made your bed. . . ."

But God was here, in this compartment, as neither prosecutor nor judge. My superego is mine alone with its whips, its blisters and white heat. I myself am the flames of hell.

God came not to guide or bless me, and certainly not to judge. Guilt is my bondage, my shrine, and my lollipop. Show me a tragedy, I call it a crime and rush to the scene to volunteer for responsibilities I don't deserve or need. As if my marriage were mine to control! (As if DeLong had been mine to control!) I think of Hillman, the distinguished (as they say) foundation executive who spent months in my office trying to work through the damage he'd suffered after a taxi plowed into him on Madison Avenue and broke his leg in four places. He kept cursing himself: If only he'd looked! He savored his self-accusations. It didn't matter to him that the driver (drunk, it turned out) ran the light and hadn't the least interest in whether anyone was standing in his way. It didn't matter that Hillman had the Walk light, that he was inside the crosswalk, and that witnesses told the police they hadn't seen the taxi coming either until too late. No, Hillman was convinced he should have noticed. Thought it was his duty to notice, just the way he thought it had been his duty to notice that it was time to leave Warsaw in '38, when his parents didn't. He was ten years old then, and he was supposed to understand the power of human evil! After nine years in analysis, Hillman thought he knew a lot about denial. But he lived for his self-reproaches.

Then you agree that it just might have been possible for me

to anticipate that taxi, he would say to me. I would look at him calmly, refusing to play his game. Your refusal to answer speaks eloquently, he would say. Why is it so important to you for me to condemn you? I would say. And so on.

Here, a large X slashes across the rest of the page, and the first volume of the journal ends. Paul immediately picks up volume two, which has a black fleur-de-lis design on its yellow cloth cover. The pages are larger, the lines more closely spaced. His father was writing more fluidly now, more legibly, with a thinner nib.

ENOUGH GUILT! THE presence that filled my compartment, whatever it might have been, felt like a blessing. The memory blesses me still.

The light improved with my capacity to forget. I had a view of green hills in the distance and animals that might have been sheep. The woman with the toddler in short pants approached down the corridor. Half rising, I sidled toward the compartment door and without much thought, to use an old-fashioned word for an old-fashioned occasion, accosted her. "Pardon, pardonnez-moi—bonjour, madame."

She stopped and gazed at me, her right eyebrow up in a sort of ironic greeting. She might have been twenty-five, thirty, or anywhere in between. Her skin was smooth and pale, with the slightest crow's-feet beginning to fan out from her eyes. Her short hair was tossed, full of flows and eddies. Spiky bangs fell just over her eyes, framing her face, which was round, so that the overall impression was of compactness as well as a certain turbulence. Her eyes were large and audacious, of an indeterminate dark color, and the left had a slight cast, so that she seemed to be observing from two vantage points at once. Her mouth was large, her lips broad, and she wore red lipstick of a brightness unusual for American women her age. I confess that what made the greatest impression on me was her sundress, which was cut low with a scoop and gathered pleasingly at the bosom. There was a silver cross dangling around her neck. She was lush—not strikingly beautiful in any conventional sense, but she looked like the kind of woman about whom people say, "She can look out for herself." She had the boy by her left hand and there was a cigarette in her right.

[My father loathed cigarettes, Paul thinks.]

"Bonjour, m'sieur," she replied, in a contralto voice and a tone both firm and polite, at the same time pointing the cigarette away from me. A whiff of pleasantly acrid smoke reached my nostrils anyway.

"S'il vous plaît . . . je voudrais . . . vous demander une question." I parceled out phrases one at a time.

"Bien sûr," she replied briskly, and then called out, "André!" to the little boy, who had gone on ahead. Andrej—the correct spelling of his name, I was later to learn—came back, shy and giggly, snuggling his head against her hip and hiding his face. Her eyes loomed up at me. "Yes, how can I help you?" she said, in perfect English and an accent that I couldn't place except that it wasn't French. Little creases tilted upward like parentheses at the corners of her mouth. She gave off a scent of something floral—gardenia, perhaps.

"I was wondering . . . can you tell me . . . uh, what can you tell me about—about G——?"

Something has been itching at the back of Paul's mind. He's wondering what's so mysterious about this town, G——, why his father didn't come right out and name it. Why this nineteenth-century coyness? Paul thinks about getting the atlas, seeing if he can figure out which town his father was heading for—but he doesn't want to interrupt his reading.

A MIDDLE-AGED MAN out of the blue asks her a stupid and ill-formed question, almost stammering, and what does she do? Is she put off? No, I interest her. Her face gives nothing away. Her expression is solemn. She must be embarrassed for a stranger so ill at ease to stagger about under the burden of his own question.

"Excuse me," I added unhelpfully. "I realize this is a strange question."

It is the middle-aged man who is uncomfortable. Once she realizes this, she smiles, formally, as if to put him at his ease. Little dimples appear in her cheeks. "It's quite all right. As a matter of fact, I am going there. I am living near the town." She studies his face and waits. "You are American"—making a scientific statement about the nature of things. This woman makes her discoveries and says what she thinks. There is none of that soft American doubt that I see in many of my patients: the statements that sound like questions, the need to talk even if one has nothing to say, in order to be assured that one exists. The woman shoots a narrow stream of smoke into the air and, standing a couple of feet from me, with her head tilted back, watches me with utter confidence that she has the right to do so. Her look outlasts mine. I cannot help but smile. I clear my throat. Just then, an elderly man in a double-breasted suit and an ascot approaches down the corridor and looks at me inquiringly. The woman with the child steps into the doorway of the compartment to let him by. When he has passed, I cannot help but invite the young woman with the boots and the accent to take a seat with her son in my compartment.

She must think two things: one, that I am old enough to be her father, and two, that I am harmless. (Later she will admit that she thought both.) I slide back toward the window, so she can sit on the opposite side and keep her distance. She stubs out her cigarette on her boot sole, and bearing the stub upright like a bouquet utters, "Come," to little Andrej, steps around me, deposits the stub in the steel ashtray beneath the window, leaving a trace of gardenia in my nostrils, and takes the seat opposite me, crossing her legs. Her boots are of a light leather—not, perhaps, very sensible for the season—and their height and texture naturally call attention to the flesh that emerges there, with a softness and shape that make a vivid impression. The boy squeezes up next to her, on the door side, fixing on me his large eyes, more distinctly green than his mother's. He has frown lines streaking his brow but makes no sound. She gazes at her son with a benign, supervisory half smile. There is a certain fullness under her chin. The boy leans against his mother and closes his eyes.

"I am American, yes."

"I know that."

"I suppose it is obvious—"

"You could not be English. You are not polite enough."

"I'm sorry—"

"Don't be sorry, I am not paying them a compliment. English politeness is like English summer, brief and chilly."

This brings a laugh out of me. "You see, the reason I stopped you is that I have never been to G—— and I'm wondering what sort of place it is. And where to stay. What to eat. That's all."

"Oh, it is, you know, one of those charming French towns on the sea, charming in an ordinary way, if you know what I mean. If it were any more charming, there would be too many tourists. If you prefer to talk to tourists about other touristic sites, as many tourists do, it is not far to Mont-Saint-Michel. It is bad

enough that there is lighthouse and casino. You will find G——
a little quiet, a little—mmm, boring. The beach is rather good,
you know. The crêpes are excellent and the apple . . . apple—
mmm—you know, cidre"—pronouncing it "see-dra," making a
glass of her hand and pulling it up toward her mouth. Her "r"s
are softened, she says "tuck" for "talk," and since she occasion-
ally drops her articles, I wonder if she might be Russian.

"Cider."

"Cider, yes, excuse me, my English is not very good." She
says this briskly, as if she has nothing to be ashamed of and does
not really require any excuses.

"Your English is excellent, much better than my. . . ." I stop.

Her plucked, precisely sculpted eyebrows pop up for a second, and then she opens up a last-minute smile that is worth the
wait, showing even upper teeth with a small gap in the middle.
Her lips are thicker on the left than on the right. The light has
faded. Her eyes look brownish and warm now, the pupils soft.
"Czech. My—mmm—mother tongue is Czech." She adds, to be
helpful: "From Czechoslovakia."

"Yes," I say awkwardly.

"So, you know, here they have also Calvados," she goes on.
"They are very proud of their Calvados in Normandy. You know
Calvados? Eau-de-vie from apples. Very tart and rich. So, it is
perfectly agreeable place. Practical." She gives a little laugh.

"If I had a clear idea of what I wanted, that would probably
be exactly it."

"Well, you will be happy there."

Her right foot swings like a metronome, but she makes no
move to get up. Tick-tock goes her boot. She turns to peer out
the window at the landscape she is leaving behind. There is a
small round birthmark at the top of the valley above her collarbone. I think again the banal and necessary thought that I am
old enough to be her father. But of course I am not her father.

"I can tell you, G—— is excellent place to recuperate"— and she is off into her story, turning her great searchlight eyes on me just often enough to ensure that I am paying attention. The truth is, I do not take my eyes off her face the entire time. It changes frequently as she speaks. At some moments, when she gazes at me head on, her face seems almost flat. At other moments, when she turns to the side, a slight unevenness, the very hint of a bump at the top of her nose. There is no point in recording every detail. Perhaps after a time I am no longer listening to her words. I do not know. There is a good deal about the course of my life that I do not begin to understand. (Do not care to understand?) Let us leave the question of understanding to the philosophers, the question of intention to more credulous psychoanalysts, the question of inevitability to the astrologers. Let us say that a wave crashed over me. Let us say that I was immersed. Let us say that I was willing.

So Milena—for that was her name—Milena of the sundress tells me that she grew up in a small town in western Bohemia, the youngest of seven children—Catholic, of course. At school, she demonstrated impressive proficiency in the English language, won a scholarship to Charles University in Prague, and in her final term—this was unusual for a university student— found part-time work writing subtitles for the English and American movies that were suddenly pouring into Czechoslovakia. For that spring term was the spring of all springs; it was Prague Spring, a splendid time to be young and freedom-loving. "False spring," she called it. "You do not know how good it smells, false spring, when you have grown up in such a rotten system, a system that is built on fear, and you have to bear the shame of it, always, always. Every day, the humiliation of acting as if the lies are the truth." She takes a drag from her freshly lit cigarette and shakes off the ash. "But listen to me, I am telling you much more than you want to know," she interposes. "Please, I am very sorry."

"No, no, not at all," I say. "Please go on."

She searches my face for a clue and decides to go on.

She was "rather good" in her studies, and so she was admitted to the University of London for the fall term with a full scholarship. As it came time to leave, she feared that, once overseas, she would miss out on the liberation breaking out all over the country—all over the world! But her parents, factory workers both, were adamant that London was the opportunity of a lifetime (and God knows, they must have had their apprehensions, though they never quite said in so many words that they thought she should get out while the getting was good). Anyway, since the English language had cast its spell on her, and since she convinced herself that the Spring would still be in force when she returned, and since she imagined that after a time-out in London she would go back to her homeland better trained to be of service to the democratic socialism of the future, she departed from Czechoslovakia calmly. As it happened, she departed several weeks before the start of the fall term in order to get herself well settled in London. So it came to pass that when the Russian tanks rolled into Prague in August, she was not hurling cobblestones at them, not screaming at soldiers or spray-painting slogans, not rushing around Wenceslas Square with her friends one step ahead of the curfew, not going to jail, but sitting up all night in a small furnished room in Bloomsbury like any girl from the provinces, and listening to the BBC, and trying and failing to get through to her friends on the phone (her parents had none), and weeping.

"We believed that the more we shouted, the more we made noise, the less they will be able to do anything against us. We thought they would not dare. We were not practical," she says definitively.

sacrifice

She thought of going back, but what sense would that have made? To add one more depression to the homeland? In London she would find a way to be useful. So she dried her eyes, and went to protest meetings, and carried petitions to tube stations, and picketed the Czechoslovakian embassy, and slept little, and caught cold, and tore herself out of bed, and went to more meetings, and got sicker, and kept up this pace until she felt better. Because her English was good and quickly improved, and her credentials were convincing, she became a bit of a television personage and a liaison with English students, the most passionate of whom refused to believe that Che Guevara communism committed them to Leonid Brezhnev communism, good-hearted people who couldn't work up any enthusiasm for Brezhnev's tanks however little they thought of American imperialism. Nothing helped, but results were not the point of doing what had to be done.

The emergency hardened into the status quo. Messages came filtering from home, all saying: For everyone's sake, don't come back, not now. New scholarship money was raised to help Czech students stranded in Britain thanks to the Soviet tanks, so she stayed on in London for another year, keeping useful and busy by translating for the émigré movement— English-language documents into Czech to be smuggled home, and documents of the Czech resistance into English for the émigré Czech press in London—accounts of secret police interrogations, solitary confinement, freezing temperatures, beatings, broken bones badly set. Milena's life felt useful, connected to the struggle. The news from home did not improve.

At meetings, she would run into an Englishman she referred to as Tom. "You do not need to know his last name," she said. He was Labour and Oxford, a comforting combination. He was "politician, important politician, very committed to our cause, you know." He was eloquent, gracious, and married. He had a usable extra flat at his disposal. He was discreet, but not always careful. The next thing she knew, she was pregnant. He never said he loved her, but he was nothing if not a gentleman. He offered the quick, sure solution, all expenses paid, but she would not consider an abortion. "I was devout Catholic. I am still, not in all ways, but in this way," she told me with a defiant set of her chin. Resourceful Tom had a second-best way to demonstrate his generosity. He was of an old—that is to say, transnational—extended family, and one of his great-uncles had acquired a seventeenth-century farmhouse near G—— on the Normandy coast, that had, in turn, come down the line to Tom, who had never gotten around to fixing it up sufficiently to his wife's liking. Not that it was falling down. During the war, the Germans had commandeered the place to house some of their military intelligence group and kept it up rather nicely, until they abandoned it just before the Americans dropped in after D-Day, leaving a few mines under the road nearby as calling cards. If Milena insisted on having her baby, why not go there? Tom would see to a midwife, provide continuing funds, take care of everything. With his connections, he even saw to her temporary withdrawal from university for "illness," with guaranteed readmittance when she was ready.

Tom kept his promises. The baby was healthy, cheerful, a lively distraction for Milena. Her country had died, but her baby would live. She would keep him out of her parents' sight and spare them the shame. Andrej was growing up without want. He was growing up without a father as well, but that was not the worst thing in the world. She had visits from fellow exiles. Tom, with his cross-channel contacts, was able to arrange for her resident papers in France and provided a small but adequate stipend. He bought her a used car. Her bank account filled up automatically on the first day of every month. Living was inexpensive. The French state provided Andrej with an excellent crèche half the day. She gardened (although evidently not that much, for, as I said, her skin was pale). She went on translating for the movement. Tom made no demands and it was just as well, for she fell out of love with him soon enough. She had as many friends as she needed, most of them fellow refugees from the workers' paradise who had made their way to the Paris suburbs. At this moment, she was just returning from a visit to them. In the winter, she would take her son back to London and there resume her studies toward a literature degree. Someday she would go home. This was not the time.

She spoke evenly and precisely, with a lilt. I was transfixed. I sympathized with this woman, of course—admired her, actually—that goes without saying. But somewhere in the course of Milena's soliloquy I passed from sympathy and admiration to something more intense. I entered her. Let it sound abrupt, sexual. What do I care? Do I have to report back to Ida Resnikoff in her old age or the entire psychoanalytic association? I mean that I identified with her, with her losses and (not least) her confidence. And I mean more. What I do not mean is countertransference, against which we are so strenuously warned during psychoanalytic training. Leave aside the analyst's unresolved conflicts for once! This wasn't analysis, this was a story told on a train to a man trying to make up his life as he went along. Milena's composure passed directly to me. She was hurt and resolute, but more resolute than hurt. When she was ironic, it was not the self-loathing I have seen in patients (cf. Marty DeLong) masquerading as sarcasm. She suffered but she did not cherish her misery or wallow in an identity crisis. This woman was who she was wherever she found herself, and she had the audacity to hope that the world might take her just as she was. If not—well, that was no fault of her own, and she would carry on as best she could.

It was one of the findings of my training analysis that I suffer from an essential lack of trust, stemming from inconsistent mothering on the part of a woman who had lost her father at the age of six and had herself suffered from the unsteady attentions of a narcissistic mother—and so it goes back in an unbroken line, the endless begats of neurosis. Generations of ambivalence have poured into my character. "Well," as Ida Resnikoff said, not long before my termination, "it is better to know the hole in yourself than to stuff it full of rationalizations." Deep self-confidence, therefore, always makes a strong first impression on me. I am not talking about the automatic self-confidence that comes of a successful professional life, and certainly not about the obstinacy that runs in my family—one grab for power after another—let alone the neurotic rigidities I encounter in the obsessive-compulsive characters I have treated. I mean the authentic self-trust that radiates from within. I sensed this power in Marion when she was young. (Evidently I can be mistaken, too.)

Self-possessed Milena possessed me. She held my attention so tightly that some time went by before I noticed that the train had passed into a long stretch of enclosing fog, through which I could only faintly and intermittently see patches of pine forest and meadows with occasional farmhouses. As she approached the end of her story, we emerged from the fog into another domain of sharp blue sky. The country was rolling now, with tidy fields divided by hedgerows. We were approaching a village of stucco houses. There, people were going on about their lives, lives in which the predicaments of Czechoslovakia and psychiatry were equally remote. The train stopped at the station—there was a sand-colored Hôtel des Voyageurs across the street—and an older woman carrying an ugly little gray poodle walked by our compartment, heard Milena's voice, glanced at me dubiously, and passed on, leaving a mist of acrid perfume behind her. The two of us, Milena and I, were the foreigners. The train resumed its reassuring movement. More fields slipped past, casual hills, more hedgerows, a farmhouse with its roof fallen in, various shades of green. Spheres of thick vines grew around treetops.

Anyone with his wits about him would ask why this woman was confiding in a stranger on a train. I wondered more than once. Possibly I amused her, or she classified me as a minor and fleeting peculiarity in a life full of more significant surprises. But she would never have admitted anything so boorish. "There was something—I don't know, something about your manner," she said later. It was not a very satisfactory explanation, and although I could bring up her strong defenses, absence of childhood trauma, supportive parents, etc., I do not have a better one. She did not yet know I was a man whose profession was to listen to stories. She did not even know my name. Perhaps she had told this story so many times it had become routine and what she was confiding was, in her eyes, only a trifle. Whatever the case, the story was hers by inalienable right, and she asked nothing of me. Unlike Marion, whose every statement seemed to conceal an implacable demand, Milena evidently did not expect anyone to work out her destiny for her. Like my patients, she needed help to live her life, but unlike them, she already had her life.

"Something about your manner"—this is as good an explanation as any. I did not know (I still do not know) whether she knew what power she had over me (what power I had given her) at that moment. Later, if I probed, she said she could not explain or had already explained. She said I was too curious, naive, "so American."

"You have known other Americans?" I asked.

She blushed. "At the cinema." She smiled and danced away with a toss of her hair and a flash of knowingness.

The more I heard of her past, the faster I fled my own. "Yet you sound hopeful," I said.

"I am resigned to my hopes," she said casually, closing off further questions. "And you?" she asked, resting her gaze for more than a casual moment on my wedding band, which I had made no attempt to conceal. "You are on holiday?"

"In a—in a way, you could say that. I am—"

She interrupted for the first time. "Believe me, there is no need to say any more. I understand what it is to be accidental. You are so-to-say on holiday." She showed her dimples. Her eyes seemed greener now, and glittered.

"You could put it that way." I was (as much as I ever grin) grinning, pleased with myself, like a man free-associating in another language for the first time.

We passed a small windmill and, at an intersection outside a village, a tall sculpted cross and the slumped body of Christ. There were propane tanks in the backyards. Then we were slowing into the outskirts of G——, the train squeaking across the converging rails through the railyard, some white smokestacks visible out the window, a few high-rise apartments, nothing remarkable. The conductor walked briskly through, making an announcement about G——. Passengers began lining up in the corridor. Milena uncrossed her legs, stood up, and stretched—

No, that's not it, exactly. Milena stood up and <u>time</u> stretched. She was leaning away from me, shaking her hair, and time sagged and split open. She lifted out of time. She was impossibly vivid; time was a husk. None of this makes any sense—this I do not need to be told—but at that moment nothing felt like a metaphor. This woman felt more real than the rest of my life. She had another dimension. I could say that I recovered some lost felicity, but when had I ever known such felicity? To write these foolish sentences only states the problem and clarifies nothing. I am speaking of poise, not allure. I do not mean to be vulgar. I am not speaking simply of the dark cylindrical openings where her high, sleek, soft boots made space for her legs. The shadows around her legs—yes, something to do with that. Softness, but that was not all of it, possibly hardly any of it. I am not speaking simply about shapeliness, about fine substantial breasts or, to put it less clinically, her bosom, her outright bounty, conceding to gravity, swelling and half emerging at the rim of her dress as she bent down to help her son onto his feet. . . . All this I noticed, and not indifferently. But I am trying to speak here of something else.

This something was the opposite of uncanny, for instead of dread I felt a flood of joy.

I thought, I am going to take my newfound freedom into my hands and lay it at this woman's feet.

And why not? Was my freedom not mine? Was it not my life to wreck?

She left Andrej in my care while she went back to her original compartment for her belongings. Andrej, a little Buddha, sat with his open smile—his mother's full lips and exuberant cheeks—and studied me. He pointed at my watch and said something that had the cadence of a sentence, rising and falling, but in his own private language, incomprehensible to me. He squeaked and jammed his right fist into his mouth. I had no idea what he wanted, but I felt a twist of hunger, a sympathetic hollowness in my stomach. How many hours had it been since I had eaten? What time was my muddled stomach keeping? I showed Andrej my watch, which read 11:45 in the morning, just the time when—if my original plan had worked out—I would have been leaving Chartres to return to Paris, and if I had been in New York, I would have been—what? Winding down my working day and thinking ahead to dinner . . . no, from

France you don't add six hours, you subtract them. I would have been asleep in my bed with my wife. But I was in G——, watching over a little blond boy in short pants who grabbed for my watch with moist fingers.

Milena came back with a small, boxy, battered suitcase, tan with white bands, surely a family hand-me-down. Her silver cross caught the brightening light. I could see that the cross had a finely tooled border—probably an heirloom. We stood in line in the corridor, rocking slightly as the train lurched and eased its way to a halt in the station. A few expectant-looking middle-aged French ladies were in front of us, ready to disembark, and a smooth-shaven young man in a denim jacket with a tiny dog peering out from between his buttons, along with two exultant teenage girls with reddish hair, a fervent young blond long-haired couple who might have been German or Dutch, the girl wearing a long turquoise dress spangled with sequins, the boy with a scraggly beard and backpack. The man in the double-breasted suit and ascot who had gazed at me from the corridor was glowering at them. Behind me, a swarthy young man had, contrary to regulations, started to smoke in the corridor. Andrej reached for me, but when I held his shoulder to steady him, he started to wail. Milena took the boy, saying to me, "I am sorry. You are strange to him." Then she asked abruptly, as if suddenly catching herself being a bad host, "Where is your baggage?"

I sheepishly held out my umbrella. The hollowness in my stomach was going to my head. "This is it. Well, you know, I didn't plan on staying overnight. I intended to go to Chartres." As if that explained anything.

"Oh?" was all she said.

Journey's end, a sharp edge in time. I took her suitcase and stepped down the metal stairs onto solid ground, set down the suitcase, turned, and offered my hand to Milena, who reached out and deposited her hand in mine, like a lady under the escort conditions of an earlier century. This was one of many times when I was not to know whether she was satirizing an attitude or indulging it.

The lady smiled, put on her sunglasses, put Andrej down, took his hand, and spoke firmly to him in Czech. The sun was strong, yet there was also a trace of moisture in the air, producing a tang on the skin, and the smell of the sea was pungent and surprising. (I am, I realize, hardly ever aware of the sea on the island of Manhattan.) A gust of wind sent my hair spilling down over my eyes. I stood under a fresh, unfamiliar sky full of swiftly skidding clouds and felt hopeful and hungry.

I took up her suitcase again. Planted across the final inches of track was a short hedge: a lovely touch. She led me into the station. If I am not mistaken, an admiring glance or two shot our way: the gray man out for a holiday with his "young niece." Then we walked past car rental and information offices and out to the parking area, where passengers just arrived were watching taxi drivers in jackets and ties lay their suitcases neatly into the trunks. There was a traveling circus set up across the street, with a carousel and a bumper-car rink. In the distance, past a ravine, loomed a chateau. G—— is a resort town, a place for careless joy, as placid as a lake after a fish has leapt and then vanished beneath the surface. Such was my liquid state of mind.

I set Milena's suitcase down on the sidewalk and Andrej plunked himself down on it, wearing a grin of high achievement. I turned to Milena, whose bangs were blowing in front of her eyes. Her eyes showed green in the glare for a moment before she put on her dark glasses.

"I was wondering," I said, "if you could recommend a hotel."

She knew of a decent one in the lower town, on the beach, and would be happy to take me there.

"No, no, you don't have to do that. Please. I'll take a taxi. Thank you for everything."

"Actually, please, it is not a bother, it is on my way." Because of her dark glasses, I could not read her expression. She put a cigarette between her lips and started to rummage around for her lighter. The sunlight was strong. A cathedral bell somewhere chimed heavily. The carousel across the street spun. Abruptly, in a state of delight, Andrej started tramping toward the carousel, picking up speed as he headed for the curb and the area where the taxis were picking up customers. Milena sprinted after him, knocking over her suitcase and dropping the cigarette from her hand in her haste. She caught him just before he ran out of sidewalk, grabbed his hand, and yanked it down, like a lever, to stop him cold.

Andrej's little face crumpled and the sound of his wail followed a moment behind, blasting through the plaza, while Milena crouched almost level with him and scolded him in Czech. She was remarkably cool. From the quickness with which she regained her composure, I judged that she had been through this sort of situation before.

An elderly French lady dressed in a suit looked on with a frown, wondering what children were coming to these days.

Freud describes how common it is for children to test the limits of their autonomy.

Soon enough, Andrej subsided. Milena ran her hand softly over the crown of his head, stroked his hair, wiped his face, blew his nose. A few seconds later, he was all smiles again. Milena took his hand, I picked up her suitcase, and we stepped into the parking lot.

The car was bright blue with a rounded top, squat and ungainly like a goose, but it was not called a goose—rather, a 2CV, or Deux Chevaux, two horses. She raised the trunk; I placed her suitcase inside. She opened the passenger's front door for Andrej (he made a delighted noise) and the back door for me and drove out of the lot. A strange beast of a car, with its gearshift

sticking straight out of the dashboard. It shook like a contrap-
tion from some earlier century. Traffic was sparse. Milena rolled
down her window. There were dormer roofs, Tudor façades,
bakeries, antique shops, hunting and fishing shops, pharmacies
with their reliable neon crosses. "You see, it is perfectly typical
Normandy town." She pointed to a clump of modern buildings,
of nondescript cement, in colors that had faded under the
burden of a brilliant light. She fell comfortably into the tour-
guide role.

"I don't see what you mean," I said. "I see nothing
interesting."

"That is what I mean. There was forced renovation by the
Allies," she said dryly. "From bombs, in 1944, after invasion,
during the days when you were driving the Germans out of their
positions."

"I didn't get here myself."

"Don't take it personally." She laughed. "The people do not
care that the bombs were American. They know whose fault was
the war. Anyway, they blame everything on the war, only 'the
war' in inverted commas, that impersonal thing, you know. Outside town, you can see where the German mines destroyed the
old coastal road." The events sounded recent, the way she talked
about them.

Pulling and twisting the gearshift with impressive dexterity,
she slowed through a multiple intersection and turned onto a
one-way street, at the end of which the gray stone wall of an
upper town came into view. She pointed out the spire of the
cathedral. "On this side, medieval," she said, with a little smile I
could see in the rearview mirror. She drove quite a bit faster
than seemed necessary or wise in a town whose streets were so
narrow. The car rattled but she was unfazed. She turned at the
last possible second onto a street called rue des Juifs—"This
is the street of the Jews, you know"—and made a right turn

confidently onto one cobblestone street and then another, but then suddenly braked, tossed her cigarette out the window, and shifted into reverse. She may have been momentarily lost. After several more turns, we passed a stone building marked, in neon, "Casino." Past a wall lay the wide beach. Colorful umbrellas were dotted here and there. The water was green, vast and ruffled with whitecaps. In the distance, a long, flat island. People come to a place like this not so much to bathe as to slip away from the world they know. I have not had a conventional vacation in six or seven years. My composure has come from work for as long as I can remember. Composure is next to godliness. Marion will be off at the Cape for the full month of August, with Michael.

It occurred to me that I had better call Paris and explain that the psychoanalytic congress would have to get along without me.

The hotel Milena had in mind could not have been on her way. It stood on a small promontory into the English Channel, or, as the French call it, la Manche.

"They say this is the highest tide in Europe," Milena said, turning into a driveway between stone pillars. The sign read Hôtel de la Manche, with three stars and a pattern of waves, and the word "Thalassothérapie." She pulled into the small parking lot and stopped. The hotel had a blotchy pinkish stucco surface and a steep slate roof with three gables. The sea air was pungent. Andrej was squirming.

There was that pleasantly unhurried air of a resort town. A couple of guests in bathing suits sauntered past the car, perhaps toward lunch. (My own stomach was growling again.) Potted cypresses stood erect to either side of the entrance, and there was a sign in the door: Complet. "Oh"—Milena threw up her hands—"look at that. Completely full! Terrible. I am surprised." She swiveled to face me, pushing her dark glasses up onto her forehead. She was genuinely apologetic. Her gardenia scent was strong in the salt air. "Really, I am surprised."

"It serves me right for delaying my plans till the last minute."

"August is big season for, how do you say, healing baths. People reserve."

"I suppose France is not a good country for spontaneous decisions. But surely there are other hotels. If you don't mind waiting, I'll go inside and ask—"

"No, that will not be necessary," she said definitively. "I know where they are." She paused, resting her right arm on the back of the seat and her chin on the back of her hand. She had all the time in the world. She fixed me in her gaze. "Tell me, once you are settled, what is your program?"

"My program?"

"You know, your—your plan, your activities. If I may ask. How many days you will be here."

My program! A comical notion. My program had ceased to exist. I was without props. But what is my freedom if it is not freedom to yield? And why not? What was I waiting for?

I gave out one of my therapeutic "mmm" sounds, the ones Marion calls remote. Milena said back, "I'm sorry?"

"You'll have to pardon me, but the idea of a plan seems a bit far-fetched to me at this moment." The car shook in a gust. I felt light-headed from all the salt air and gardenia, and yet grave as sin. "I should explain something to you. I didn't come to France for a holiday. I came to deliver a paper at a psychoanalytic congress in Paris."

"Oh!?" she exclaimed, with a combination of exclamation point and question mark, as in the notation for a chess gambit at once brilliant and dubious. (It occurs to me here that we need a wider range of punctuation marks for the more interesting moments in our lives.)

"That surprises you?"

"No—no, not really." She folded her arms on the back of the seat and rested her head on them.

"I am a psychoanalyst by profession. I should be presenting my paper this afternoon." I checked my watch. "A little less than three hours from now." I laughed. I had the sensation that the dark glasses resting upon her head were a second set of eyes, watching me as I watched her watching me. A single plunging gaze, its origins lost, slid back and forth between us.

"I intended to go sightseeing in Chartres in my spare time," I explained. "I ended up on the wrong train."

"But that's a shame!" she said. Not such a shame, I thought. She added, "Now you are a displaced person, like me." The wind was at her hair again, and when it faded she pushed her bangs away from her eyes. Interesting—she chooses a short hairdo that is more practical than the long hair now in fashion, and then, having gone to that trouble, leaves it long enough so the wind drives it into her eyes, which is hardly practical. After thirty years of experience at dredging the human psyche, I still do not know what goes on behind a face. Interesting how psychoanalysis teaches us to listen to words—that is, to distrust them—but has painfully little to offer about how people look. Freud, averse to the gaze, devised a form of treatment conducive to the analyst's concealment. Even when psychiatry reached the upright stage, it was marked by its beginnings, like Homo sapiens himself, and failed to develop attention to faces unless they displayed symptoms, like tics.

Psychoanalysis for me began as a credo. It is ending as a forgivable error.

"It's all a mistake, you see. I'm not supposed to be here." I temporized. How many times I've heard lines like this from patients! A wife or a husband talked them into analysis. The neurosis made them do it. They want to lie down and have me pass my hand over their heads and produce a diagnosis, make some adjustments, scrape off some dead skin, while all they have to do is say "Aha!" and repeat a formula after me. They are paying me to introduce them to the self who was buried alive. Not even God has such powers. Half the work is done when they realize that their parents may have ruined them but not even their parents have the power to fix them. So, I wanted Milena to tell me what I was doing in G——, in front of the Hôtel de la Manche, lost in her eyes, doing wrong and feeling no pain.

She didn't.

"This must sound strange to you," I said.

"Not so strange, in my interpretation. I know many displaced persons." Cheerily, she flipped the sunglasses back over her eyes, faced forward again, turned back as if to say something else, thought better of it, smiled, shifted into reverse, glancing past me as she backed down the driveway from the hotel, and headed off the promontory on one-way streets toward the thick, bleak wall of the upper town. Just after turning left to parallel the wall, she lurched a bit to the right as if she were going to ride up onto the sidewalk and park there, in the French manner, but she slowed only momentarily and then picked up speed again. Around the other side of the upper town, the harbor came into view, gleaming with small yachts and fishing boats. The street was deserted. At the crest of a small hill, Milena suddenly downshifted, pulled to the side of the road, stopped, engaged the emergency brake, and swiveled to face me. "You will want to see."

The car trembled in the gusts. I opened the door and stepped out. For a moment, it was so bright—I want to say unnaturally bright—that I, too, had to put on dark glasses. On the one side, the stone wall, with a drawbridge into the medieval town. On the other, the sea, deep dark green with brownish bands. The low flat channel island heaved up like a splendid mistake. The wind was hurling white clouds across the sky from the sea side, with slate-gray clouds massing in their midst. The gusts made ripping sounds, as if we were out on the waves, blown about in a flimsy boat. The slate clouds passed over the sun, and darkness coated us. A few seconds later, the sunlight was fierce again. The weather was toying with us.

Milena sat in the car watching me. I stepped over to her open window. She looked up. With her right hand she was stroking Andrej's hair. "The weather is as on an island," she said. Her forearm, a little plump, rested on the window frame, the cigarette smoke curling into the air. Her dangling wrist was graceful and slender. "I come from a landlocked country," she said, and tossed her cigarette down the road. I encircled her wrist like a bracelet. The wristbone is a delicate nub. Without lifting her head she raised her eyes. I was light-headed. I let go of her wrist. With two fingers of her left hand, she reached up and touched me on the lips. Just like that, she pressed my lips in a sort of blessing. "I am not supposed to be here either," she said quietly. "No one is supposed to be anywhere."

I took her two fingers deep into my mouth. That is how it began—my detour.

There was no more talk of hotels.

I was in the back seat again. She was back inside her composure. She made a U-turn and paralleled the wall of the old town. My life would never again be the same. She left her window open, and her hair tossed about. There were fine hairs at the top of her spine. We passed a drawbridge into the old town, a granite gatehouse, clumps of tourists. The town thinned out quickly. The light now brightened, now dimmed, as clouds the color of tarnished silver plunged below the sparkling cumulus for minutes at a time. It felt as though the same wind were driving us forward as drove the clouds, and when she turned north onto the coast road, the car lurched as the wind slammed broadside into us. My heart was slamming into my chest.

"They say this is the place where the mines blew," she said.

"Mines?"

"German mines after Normandy landing. They blew—blew up American lorries. There is a monument somewhere. Look, over there." She pointed toward a clearing, where a granite pillar stood.

I said nothing.

"But they were destroyed," she said brightly, as if taking personal pride.

We were enraptured. I suppose that is the proper word for it. Enraptured, why not? Captured. Captivated. The Deux Chevaux might as well have been flying a white flag from its antenna. Andrej seemed to pick up the high excitement and gurgled a sort of conversation with himself—sentences, almost, with a definite arc, as though he was asking himself questions and answering them in a private language. I loved that child. I loved the wind and the aroma of apples. I loved falling in love.

Paul stops, goes back to the beginning of the paragraph, and reads it again. I loved that child. I loved that child. Not him, not an allegorical Isaac, but another child, an Andrej.

I loved that child.

Child love entered my father's life here, he thinks.

No angels hovered over Paul, no last-minute rams. Yet the angel came to his father, and delivered unto him a son who was not Paul. A well of tears forms behind his eyes, but he quells it.

From the furnace of his bones, Chester Garland has offered Paul an inheritance that turns out, unsurprisingly enough, to be ashes. And yet, against his will, Paul feels a flicker of admiration for his father. To pick up a young woman on a train!

He closes his eyes in disgust. What is he thinking? A son admires the betrayal of his own mother? And for what?

He walks to the window and looks out onto the street. There's a burst of laughter, an indecipherable shout; a boom box sprays the street with salsa, then subsides. Behind the impressive silence, all the noise of the city merges into a single dull rumble that passes for the abandonment New Yorkers call peace.

A car alarm suddenly wails: *screek!—da-da-da-da, screek!—da-da-da-da, screek!* Dogs begin to bark. Paul goes to his desk, picks up a pad and a stick of charcoal, and sketches an aged man wearing an eye patch, flies buzzing around his head. After some reflection, he names it "The Joy of Contempt (But with Faith in Self-Improvement)." He takes colored pencils and sketch pad to the bathroom and, with the pad propped up on his knee, his foot on the sink, works up a self-portrait, adding, alongside his face, a fist gripping a hammer that drives a nail straight down into his chin. His imagination scares him. He roughs in a bright yellow border. "Portrait of the Artist as Guilt-Edged," he would call this one, if he were to finish it, but he tears it in two—perhaps he will do something with the halves some other day—and goes back to the easy chair, where he draws a modernist skyline of Great Depression vintage, with two slender skyscrapers left of center, like shorter World Trade Towers displaced into Midtown. The two are buckling halfway up and about to crash, probably into each other. He starts filling in the outlines of the buildings with some purposeful smudging and sees that there is blood in the corner of his right thumb where he has been picking away at the skin. He is giving himself stigmata. He smudges a bit of blood onto the chin in "Guilt-Edged" and the lips of the figure in "The Joy of Contempt."

The car alarm ceases. The great cataract of the city roars on. Revelations are nigh! The end is at hand! His father listened to silences and heard extremities—edge time, the hot and holy days when the wind roared out of the desert and men were banished, damned, fearing infinite death, left to their fantasies of damnation, their wars and diseases, but there were no car horns, no phone trills or screeches of subway brakes. Chester Garland longed to live like these crazy people, on the lip of the sacred. This made him feel like a man of consequence.

The taste for edge time—it runs in the family.

A supermarket shopping cart rattles by, the bottles clinking, slow and metallic, beneath Paul's window, like the noise of a train sliding across one rail junction after another on its way into a terminus. When the car passes, the city's indistinct noise is back at low volume—rumbling like a tunnel without end.

WE DROVE FOR a few miles beyond a charming sign with a diagonal slash through the word G——, passing apple and pear orchards, small farmhouses with propane tanks, and a hand-lettered sign advertising a farmer's private stock of Calvados. A car approached from the direction we were heading; after it was gone a car that had been tailgating passed us. Then we had the road to ourselves. The hedgerows came right out to the road, sometimes blocking the views beyond, but behind them I could see bright green fields rolling up mild inclines. No one was visible. We passed between two perfectly planted columns of trees that made up a long cool canopy in the sunlight.

Just beyond, the road curved to the left, dipped, and widened into a paved courtyard. There were two small stone buildings on the right-hand side and, on the left, a somewhat longer house, the wings on either side recently added or refurbished. Several walls bulged a bit, with black iron braces, cross-shaped, to keep them from cracking further. The stone was reddish and sponged up the light. The slanting roofs were of black slate; the one over the left wing was partly dismantled down to the tarpaper. No windows faced the road, only a couple of small square holes. On the left were two perpendicular parking spaces, one of them occupied by an ancient wooden wagon. Milena downshifted, turned in next to the wagon, and switched off the ignition. The engine sputtered. There were no other cars in sight, no people.

"Here we are," she said. "Your shelter. Very . . . rustic, yes?"

The gasoline fumes dissipated and a light fragrance of apples filled the air. I heard the wind whistling somewhere—offstage, as it were—but the air outside the car was perfectly still, and warmth radiated from the stone walls. She pointed left— "There was the barn"—and right—"There was—mmm—pour les chevaux." "The stable." "Yes." There was her small hand in mine. There was Andrej wobbling happily toward the lacquered wooden door into the farmhouse. There was a long old-fashioned iron key, like a jailer's—forgive the romantic thought and never mind who was the jailer here. As Milena maneuvered the key, I pressed my lips into the crook of her neck. Giggling, she dropped the key and it clanged on the stone. "Your beard, it—oh, what do you—"

"Tickles."

"Tickles, tickles—yes."

I picked up the key and presented it to her. "You are an impatient man," she said. I have waited a long time to be impatient, I thought. She led the way inside. The temperature immediately dropped. The roof soared. The room was a warehouse smelling of sunlight and warm dust. She strode through it, pushing aside heavy drapes, twisting knobs, pulling windows open, flinging shutters wide. Breezes entered. Objects were crowded together, as if in a child's room or an attic, though somehow the whole was not disordered: a stuffed sofa, several small antique chairs of leather and wicker, old lamps, tables, and shelves full of bric-a-brac, seashells, vases, masks, framed photographs, all set on a thick, elliptical cotton rug worn so that its pattern was barely discernible. In the wall facing the road was a fireplace, one stack of thin logs inside and another on the hearth. Above were scenic cracks in the plaster almost but not quite covered by a print of van Gogh's sunflowers. The wall to the left was sheathed in a light blue fabric, on which were tacked miniature paintings. Bundles of dried flowers hung upside down from hooks here and there. In one corner, there was an old spinning wheel; in another, facing a large window, a smallish turn-of-the-century secretary, barely large enough for the portable typewriter and the pile of manuscript pages piled next to it. A shelf featured a chipped vase of dried blue flowers next to a clumsy black telephone. To one side of the shelf was a large black-and-white poster, young people waving "V" signs at a tank with a lost-looking soldier of the same age riding on top. The window gave onto a vegetable garden in back, next to which were a sandbox, a plastic train, heaps of building blocks, and small toys. Behind, past an apple tree, the meadow rose to a line of evergreens a hundred feet away. A second door led out to the back. There was a borrowed look—a woman improvising a life in somebody else's house.

When this woman with bare shoulders, eyes that didn't match, and lips that were not symmetrical opened the back door, her son toddled out to his toys without needing to be told. She kept lookout, her arms folded over her chest, her breasts flattening and bulging upward. She turned to me with a smile and said, "Please make yourself at home. Would you like tea?" Before I could answer, she was through the doorway. I heard water running and the whoosh of a flame catching. From the kitchen: "I will go to market. I was not expecting company." When she came back into the room, she was holding a dish of chocolate and biting her lower lip.

"I have only chocolate," she said, but chocolate was not what I smelled. I smelled her gardenia, and something else—oddly, something like pepper. "You are hungry."

I kissed her as if the world might end. The chocolate dish clattered as she set it down on a small table. She was in my arms, improbable, solid, absolute. As she pressed against my chest, the strap of her dress slipped over her left shoulder. The fingers of my left hand slid into the smooth cavity next to her collarbone, the fingers of my right slid under her bra strap. Her skin was cool satin. Her lips were warm satin. My arms wanted to encircle her waist, my lips wanted to encircle her nipples. I wanted to devour her. I was drunk on gardenia and pepper. I wanted to be everywhere at once. She undid the top button of my shirt and with her palm and outstretched fingers made circles on my chest.

A piercing alarm sounded from the kettle in the kitchen. "Wait," she said, easing away after a little bite on my lip.

This is a girl of the faith. I wanted to take her cross in my mouth, too. Regression in the service of the ego.

Is it you for whom I have waited? You who have come to me at last, and not a moment too soon?

But first, in the spirit of the reality principle, she would drive Andrej to his crèche in town and stop at the market on the way back. Of course, in the meantime, I was welcome to use the phone (she explained how the operator was reached), drink more tea, make myself otherwise at home. (Postponing gratification: a means to prepare for gratification.) The kiss, the imprint of her body, the smile she flashed in leaving would hold me. After she closed the door behind her she unlocked it again. An afterthought: Would I mind picking three or four apples from the tree out back?

I was alone for the first time in what seemed like a very long while. I took off my jacket and stood in the rear doorway amid the scent of apples, watching the clouds cluster up. I felt hungry again but did not want to eat; I wanted to stay with the hunger. A motorcycle buzzed in the distance, got louder, then slowed as it passed the farm buildings, and when the buzz dissipated I could hear even more keenly my remoteness from the world I *[Chester has half obliterated a word here and substituted the word]* knew. Birds twittered. The occasional whistle of wind was the only other sound.

I picked four bright apples and carried them inside, sat down at Milena's desk, dialed the operator in Paris, and asked for the number of the Maison de la Chimie. The operator, in that tone of French protest and indignation I was getting to enjoy, asked something of which I caught a word that sounded like "repeat." I repeated. She rattled off numerals. I dialed and heard on the other end words that sound nothing like "Maison" or "Chimie." I hung up and repeated the information farce with a more helpful operator, getting a completely different number. This time I could make out "Chimie." I asked for Dr. Howard Spain. More farce. The receptionist said something, to which I eked out, "Je ne comprends pas." "I only take messages, I am sorry," she said in English, with real sorrow. I asked her to write down the following words: "I cannot be there to read my paper today. I will call back. There is nothing to worry about." I asked her to read back the message. I thanked her and enjoyed the singsong "Au revoir, monsieur," in return.

There is nothing to worry about. By the way, Howard, in case anyone asks, you can say that there are logs in the fireplace and the aroma of apples in the breeze; that I too am borrowing a room that is not my own; that this morning (could it have been just this morning?) I borrowed a presence that called itself God; that if I were a praying man I would pray to be worthy of this blessed peace; and that my prick is stiff, sweet, and attentive. Since the day I began my training, I've always known exactly where I was going. I'm off the track now. Call it reckless abandon or middle-aged acting out, as you wish. Find a new category of psychiatric disorder. Throw a dart at the Diagnostic and Statistical Manual. If you're not going to do your middle-aged acting out when you're middle-aged, what are you waiting for?

I will pay for this, I thought, feeling lighthearted.

I pulled off my wedding ring and dropped it into my pocket.

I walked around the room inspecting paintings and objets d'art, the skin of Milena's room. One of the miniatures featured the low flat island I had seen from the heights of G——; others, islands with castles, fields with peasants and hedgerows, women sewing and cooking. On the hearth there were dolls in satin gowns, two tiny scarecrows, little lacquered boxes. A woman's room of petite things and inner spaces. I sat by the fireplace and began to write in this notebook.

Will I be worthy of this silence and peace? And why not? Who says no, Dr. Ida? The unforgiving father, of course. The God Who damns, the harsh punitive Old Testament superego. The fearful Laius, tossing the infant Oedipus into the wilderness to prevent his only begotten son from growing up to slaughter him. The scheming mother reckless for power. Get thee behind me, Satan, and stay away from my hind parts. How literary we are today. But this was not a moment to indulge doubts. This was a moment for indulgences. This was a moment for beauty and borrowing. As many of these dusty objects must have been collected by persons whom Milena never knew, so might I borrow their presence.

A roomful of transitional objects for my own transition. Adult toys to make us familiar with something. That is what we are for each other: objects in transit, floating passions. We grasp for these things outside ourselves as once we grasped for the breast and the connection it offered. What is the romantic feeling if not nostalgia for that luminous promise? To bask in the plenitude of bric-a-brac is to long for the contentment of our beginnings. Psychoanalysis is right about this, if not about everything. We never leave the warehouses of childhood. We only shuffle and reshuffle our antique possessions, possessions that comfort us because, like us, they exist in time and survive. We strip them, repaint and rearrange them, sell off some and substitute their equivalents, replace transitional objects with other transitional objects until that glorious day dawns when we recognize that we actually have nothing and this is acceptable. Others will live in our rooms.

The thought that Milena will return here, to her house and to me, makes me happier than I have ever been. I long to make this room my own, too. And yet I know this is a ridiculous hope— she is not mine, and this taste for miniatures is not mine (and may not be hers). But my own acquisitions at home have nothing to recommend them, either. Their familiarity I can live without.

Can it be true? That I am free? As true as that the wrong train was the right train, and that as a result I am writing these ruminations in a wicker chair by a fireplace in a refurbished farmhouse on the Normandy coast.

I no longer see Marion or Michael or my couch, my desk or my letter opener, my bills or my phone, my back issues of journals, my books, my masks (Freud's masks, let it be said!). I see my Milena walking through the big oak door, standing before me, her skin radiant, sundress bunched at her feet. . . . Come, woman. Improvise with me.

A man who has just arrived is always young.

I was arranging the apples in the shape of a pyramid on the kitchen counter when Milena walked in carrying a string bag of leeks, turnips, zucchini, pears, a small melon, a cluster of elephant garlic, a thick slab of butter, two wedges of cheese, two bottles of wine, and in her other hand a shopping bag that she offered to me. "For you," she said.

"What?"

"For you. Take." There was a soft cotton white shirt, a pair of men's briefs, and black socks. "I didn't know your exact size but I hope this will do."

"I am more grateful than you—"

"Please. You are my guest."

"You have to let me—" I pulled out my wallet.

"Don't be silly. Please!"

"You are an extraordinary hostess."

"Thank you. You are kind. I do not often have chance to entertain."

The butter was already beginning to melt in an iron saucepan. She peeled a garlic clove and rapidly diced the vegetables and apples on a chopping board.

"May I help?"

She tossed her hair and her eyes widened.

"I'm sorry?"

"May I help?"

"You help already. Wait."

Sauté vegetables with apples and pears in sweet butter, to the browning point exactly, and the results will be sweet. Wash it all down with warm fermented cider on an empty stomach, and effervescence is unavoidable. The woman in charge has the large, absorbing eyes of a figure in a Russian icon. Her lips are thick, pagan. Everything frozen in me begins to thaw and move; I hear the ice cracking—

The empty stomach is not the point. Surely, Dr. Garland, as you head over the falls, you are not fundamentally surprised, are you? The observing ego is not surprised. In the cauldron of the id there is no surprise.

Did there come a point when I was no longer watching myself watching her? I'd like to think so.

We ate and drank in silence, and when we were done she traced the circumference of my ring finger where my wedding band had been. "Don't say anything," I said. She stood up and put out her hand, and I kissed it, kissed up to the crook of her elbow and then up to the tuft of hair in her armpit. She beckoned me back through the living room and into her bedroom, making me feel I was leading her to her own bed. I laid her down on the duvet and dove into her kiss. She picked up my hand and examined it again. She took my ring finger into her mouth, as before, but this time she bit it—gently, at first, then less gently. Then she took the finger and plunged it into her bodice. Her breasts were cool, but a rivulet of sweat trickled between them.

She opened me like a melon. She tore into my flesh and found it sweet.

"You are still hungry?" she asked later.

"As you are." I lay between her breasts, with her cross, and listened to the dynamo of her heart. She brushed my face with her hair. I was unsalvageable.

It was as if we had invented a new color.

"You keep your eyes open," she said. "Why?"

"I want to see you every possible second."

I stared at her cross, silver and shining, in my hand.

"Tell me about this."

Her eyes glittered but her mouth was solemn. "I am—
mmm—Catholic, of course."

"You believe, then?"

"This is normal—to wear the crucifix in a Communist
country—but usually it is worn, you know, inside, underneath
clothing." She laughed. "So we should remember that there is
suffering in the world."

When I saw she was laughing, I laughed too.

Her laugh ended before mine did.

"Next to my town, you know, is a Russian army base now.
They have turned it into a dump. The people cannot swim in
the river. The birds are dying. The trees have no leaves. You have
no idea. The crucifix is a sign to ourselves that we have not surrendered. . . . I am sorry. I should not be talking about such terrible things."

"It's all right. Then you are not a believer, really?"

"I was raised Catholic. Now"—she shrugged and her voice
trailed off—"now it is not easy to say. I am Catholic, but outside
the Church. I no longer have the heart to confess to a man in a
dark box. But I believe in Jesus Christ, who lived in the world,
not in a box. I believe that from suffering will come good. This is
practical truth. From labor pains comes a child. It is confusing,
isn't it? You think so, Chester; I know I am right. You think, this
girl had a child with a married man who is not married to her,
and yet she believes, and yet she does not stand with the other
believers—"

"I am coming to think that confusion is a natural state
of grace."

"That is generous, more generous than the Church. The
Church does not tolerate confusion. They are like Communist
bullies. They want to clean up the world."

"And don't you, Milena? Don't we all?"

She raised my fingers to her lips and didn't answer the question. "I don't care what the Church thinks. The Church does not make children. It is normal to make children."

I still did not understand how a Catholic girl from a small town in Czechoslovakia knew what she knew about a man's anatomy—specifically, what happens when a woman encircles a man's balls in her hand and presses her fingers gently and firmly through the tenderest skin of the scrotum to the hard root of his penis. The depth that is reached that way, the sensation that all your striving is over and life is unendurably sublime.

"It is normal that things be simple," she said.

"Is this simple?"

"It is now." She swallowed me whole.

Sex kidnaps time, holds it hostage. Sex cancels everything that was less than sex.

Days passed, days of appetite, sweet breezes, lunacy. I bought new shirts, and another notebook, and a new fountain pen. Fragrant, extravagant days. Serpentine, scented, apple days. Freely flowing days of bounty and curvature. They were simple enough, my apple days. I ache for them. They came to feel almost normal.

The nights were another country. Sometimes we stepped into the backyard in our bare feet. The grass was cool in the moonlight. Birds nested in the apple trees. One night I teared up for no reason. "You are the apple of my garden," I said to her. "It is an expression we have."

Milena said, "It's only sex. You were starving."

I said, "For you."

Absolute presence.

. . .

Late the night before Howard and I were due to fly home from Paris, I called the Hotel Lutétia and asked for him. Milena was reading Proust in the bedroom, Andrej was asleep in his own bed. Howard's phone rang three, four, five times before I heard his noncommittal "Yes."

"Dr. Spain, I presume."

"Chet, for Christ's sake, where are you?"

"Did I wake you?"

"No, no, I'm packing. As you should be. We're leaving in the morning, you may remember."

I gave a therapeutic "mmm."

"After the psychoanalytic convention, as you may recall. The event that brought you to Paris. France. Where are you?"

Note for a history I will never write of the psychoanalytic profession: Joshing as professional reaction-formation. Concern about one's patients has to be felt but disguised. Beneath the banter, Howard Spain is a patient, caring, domestic man—as I had been thought to be myself.

Further note: Patience (adj.) = persevering. Patient (n.) = sufferer under treatment. The connection between these terms is evident. I am neither.

I watched an ant cross Milena's desk toward the phone.

"Would you like to clarify?" Howard went on.

"I'd like to, yes."

"Chet? Are you there?"

"Howard, that's why I called, to clarify."

"Are you in your right mind?"

"Fine. I'm fine."

"Where in God's green hell are you?"

"Well you may ask, Howard. Well you may ask."

"I'm asking."

"I took a spontaneous holiday."

"Spontaneous holiday. That's an interesting concept." Suddenly he was receptive, analytical. "Are you really all right? You sound—disconnected. Chet? You there?"

"I'm more than all right. But I owe you an apology. I didn't mean to give you a scare."

"Chet, what is going on?"

The ant made its way up onto the phone wire. For the ant, it was a long way down. "It's not like me to skip out on my responsibilities, is it?"

"I'm glad you're amusing yourself. You're not amusing me."

"I'm sorry."

"You might be interested to know that I told the audience you'd been taken ill."

"Thank you. I am sincerely sorry. And I'm quite certain I haven't been taken ill."

"Where are you?"

He was testing me and I was going to submit to the test and I was going to pass it. I looked up at the grim, frightened eyes of the Russian soldier on top of his tank in Milena's poster.

"Hello? Where?" Howard repeated.

"I'm—in France, Howard, and just where I want to be," I said, and felt, in my secrecy, superior to this devoted man who was excellent in all the professional ways, a couple of years younger than I but steadier, with his adventures behind him, married to another distinguished analyst, with three fine kids.

"You're in France. All right, it's not that big a country. And may I ask what you're doing somewhere in France?"

"You may ask. I may not answer. No, I will answer. I'm living my life as you are living yours."

"Are you in trouble?"

"Trouble is where I am not."

"Then you're telling me that you've gone around the bend."

157

"That's one interpretation. My own is that, as a sensible man, I'm taking a holiday. That means a holy day, as you know."

He wasn't about to let me spin off an etymological lecture. "You're too calm. Where's your affect, Chet? Where are you putting it?" He tried analytic temporizing, therapeutic condescension. "You've been under a lot of stress. You should be home."

"I'm fine, Howard. I need some time, that's all."

"You need time."

"That's right. I need time."

"May I be blunt, Chester, my friend? Will you forgive me for speculating that you're acting out?"

"I'd probably think the same in your place if I were in a clinical situation, which I'm not. But I'm in my place, not your place, and I think I'm doing quite well, thank you."

"You're distressing me. Have you talked to Marion? Marion, your wife?"

"I'm going to do just that, Howard, my friend." As if on cue, Andrej began to wail from the back bedroom, a lusty wail, stopping for an intake of breath and then resuming with a lustier wail, and Howard said, "Good God, what's that? Is that an infant you've got there, Chester? Where are you?"

I heard Milena pad into Andrej's room, heard her calming him with sweet assurances.

"Howard, I can't stay on much longer. Everything will be revealed, I promise you. But I need to know if I can still count on you to cover for me. My patients, I mean. Not that I'm expecting any emergencies." For years, we had served as back-up for each other's patients, Howard and I; I was responsible for his patient load in July, he took mine in August.

"Except yourself."

"I can see why you would say that, Howard, but I'm not an emergency." Neither was Andrej, who had subsided.

"Chester, Chester. Get some perspective, man. What would

you think if I were the one who didn't show up to read his paper? And disappeared? And then called from God knows where with a baby screaming in the background? What would you think, man?"

"I'd think, you've always been reliable, but—"

"You've always been reliable too. The concept of mania would cross your mind, I'm quite sure. The concept of acting out."

The words floated above the receiver, balloons bouncing along the ceiling. The poor shriveled vocabulary of the profession! Never had these terms seemed so meager to me. How can one speak of acting out when the ego and the instincts are in alignment? When feelings are intelligent and the ego is at peace?

"Chester?"

"Right here, Howard." Milena padded to the edge of the room, wearing her purple dressing gown and looking quizzical. Why was this conversation taking so long? I blew her a kiss and waved her over, but she smiled demurely—respecting my privacy—shook her head, and went back to the bedroom.

"May I ask how long this holiday of yours is going to last?"

"I don't know. I'm asking you to cover for me this month. As usual."

"Of course I'll cover for you, Chester. That's not the issue."

"Thank you." Just then, I suffered a sudden attack of practicality. "And may I ask another favor?"

"Why stop now?" he said, resigned.

"Did I ask for that?"

"Go ahead, Chet. I'm sorry. Go on."

"You see, when I left the hotel, I didn't pack. My room—"

"Your room?"

"My belongings, they're still in my valise. I think. Most of them, anyway. It's hard to explain. I left in a hurry—"

"Chet, you're worrying me again."

"It's not the way it sounds. I left most of my things in my room, that's all. Can you pack them up and ship them, or—"

"I'll take them home. Chester, how long have we known one another?"

"Twenty-two years? Twenty-three?"

"Listen to me, then. You're burned out. You had a suicide in your practice. That's as hard to take as a death in the family. Worse. Marriage is no picnic, and neither is this profession. It's all right if you burn out, happens to the best of us, which is you. Take a leave, Chet. It's honorable. It's been done. Don't do anything you're going to regret later. Promise me?"

I promised, knowing that a promise of that sort is so empty it could float up to the ceiling along with the jargon.

"And by the way," he said, after pausing, "why don't you tell me about her?"

Predictable. Howard is no fool. "I'm not ready and I'm not manic, that's all you have to know. Thank you for everything, and I'll talk to you later."

I hung up, released. I felt as if I were lifting away from a heavy gravitational field. This was not the meager epiphany of the analytic insight, not the buttoned-down pleasure of shop talk, not the orderly tick of the scheduled day and the equally scheduled night. I was looking down upon my dwindling and measured past, my crabbed, unhappy consciousness, and upon reliable Howard, plodding toward professional distinction. Good-bye, good-bye down there! Keep your self-scrutiny!

But why, when I rejoice, am I always breaking up and away? Why upward and not inward?

For the first time since the train, I felt a rumble of apprehension, but it passed before I was back in Milena's bed.

Reliable Howard. Paul replays the phrase in his mind. Spain, the man his father would call on for help, the man he trusted to take care of his patients, might just be the man to throw some light through the murk.

Cryptographers need help, too. He looks up Spain, Howard, M.D., in the telephone book, dials his number, and listens to one ring before he casts his eyes on the alarm clock, notices that it's just past five in the morning, and hangs up in embarrassment. *Crazy, Paul. You think the whole world's stopped because your father's dead?* On second thought, the number Spain's listed must be his office number. He presses redial, waits for the machine message to kick in, identifies himself—and what should he say now? That he's groping his way through his father's confessions? That he's desperate? It's too late to hang up. He's committed, and so he says, lamely, "I have a question I'd like to ask you. I'd appreciate your calling me back as soon as possible."

How long has it been since he has heard the voice of a living human being? Even Howard Spain on tape is a contact of sorts, a reprieve from the isolation that seems to have chosen him. Yet no one has sealed Paul in with his father's remains. He's done that himself, climbed in.

SHE HAD LIT a candle next to the bed and lay in a white silk nightgown, deep-breasted, reading the Penguin edition of <u>Swann's Way</u>. She inserted a bookmark and laid the book on the floor beside her.

"Your friend, you enjoyed speaking to him?"

"Yes. My friend is a good man."

"And you are not a good man?"

"I am a good enough man. For a lost man."

The flame of the candle reflected bronze in her eyes. "You are a found man."

Words, words. What we cannot speak, speaks us. Her mouth receiving my tongue. The weight of her breasts against my chest. Her flesh the only voice in my inner ear.

.   .   .

Andrej was taking a shine to me. Early the next morning, he took my hand as he toddled around the house, pitching forward, waddling on his chubby legs, committing his body just ahead of his feet until—boom!—he was about to fall back on his puffy diaper. I yanked him up. The little stoic didn't cry. A sturdy child. His mother's child.

"Is he giving you trouble?" Milena called from the bedroom. She was reading. Her relief at such moments spent with herself was palpable.

"All is well." I picked him up and swept him in an arc over my head. He burbled. "Outside, Andrej?" I asked. "Do you want to go outside?"

He shouted his eager syllables. His golden curls were like turbulent water ruffled by the wind. Once I had golden curls. Once my boy did.

Finally, for the first time in my life, perhaps, was I ready to be a father?

A father's love. For most of my life, I thought this was the cost of tending to your inheritance, a price to be paid for the passage of genes. The narcissism of paternity furthers the species, but that does not make for love. This I learned, as one learns such things, early. I imbibed it as my father's sour milk. "My son, you are my future," he would intone, with sentimental impersonality, as he might speak of one of his investments. How many hours did Ida Resnikoff hear me devote to this theme? The whine and rumble of my father's possessive longing; was that love? The hours added up to days. I lay on the Resnikoff couch, wondering where to put my hands—folded upon my chest? dangling on the carpet?—and carped about his distance. I carped long enough to come into contact with my longing for him. I had a nightmare. I was looking into a display window on Fifth Avenue. A trophy

sacrifice

statuette inside burst out, showering me with slivers of glass.
Oh, she was pleased, was Dr. Ida. I wanted my father near; I
didn't want him at all. He was my prize and my enemy. I felt my
ambivalence like a pair of scissors. (Dr. Oedipus, I could spend
an hour to two writing on that theme.) I wished politely that he
would become someone he wasn't. Analysis had me. My tears
were my reward. This was how I struck psychoanalytic gold.

Ridiculous to flagellate myself with these self-reproaches. I
loved—enjoyed—no, loved Michael when he was cherubic.
I can love him when he is not. But I am entitled to a life. As
Marion is to hers, with a child she needed relentlessly.

I feel guilty about being away from him now. I ought to feel
guiltier.

I do miss his audacity, the way he goes on about his life as an
autonomous, uncontrollable little person. His earnestness at the
piano. His high, rebellious voice. It is like missing familiar surroundings. One is content to be elsewhere but still feels the
absence, like the faint ringing of a bell carried a long way in the
breeze. Somewhere he and his mother are going about their
lives, attached to me for reasons that defy understanding. He
has what he needs.

Truth time, Chester. You can live without them. Happily.

Andrej, whom I have known for a few days, sends me
incandescent smiles. My son is sullen, preoccupied. Sometimes
it seems he was born with a furrowed brow.

I was ready to trade in my old set of illusions for a new set.

Phoned Marion. Placid afternoon in G——, just after eight A.M.
on the Cape. She didn't answer until the sixth ring. Sounded
like a static storm howling through the transatlantic connection.
The disturbance suited me. Through the static, I told her I
would be staying in Paris a few more days "for consultations."

163

I heard the sleep in her voice, the perplexity, and, soon enough, the suspicion.

Asked about Michael. "It's been raining, and he's stir-crazy from playing Monopoly with his friends, but otherwise fine," she said. "Are you all right?"

I said I was fine.

"What's wrong?"

"Nothing. You sound sleepy."

"I'm wide awake. It's good to be at the Cape, Chet, but I miss you."

"Miss you too," I said.

"Michael misses you."

"Well, it's mutual."

"He wants to know when you're coming back." A little curl of eagerness.

"A few days. I'll call you when I know exactly."

She hesitated. "OK."

"It's OK," I lied.

Every morning Milena drove to the market in G——, dropping Andrej off at his crèche. We sat in the garden and fed each other the pieces we tore off butter-soaked croissants. She cooked apples and pears and made soup, which we ate cold. She diced pears and sautéed them with cubes of chicken. She made compotes and pies that we washed down with Calvados. Several hours a day, she translated. The pile of her manuscript grew. We walked in the woods nearby. We lay in bed and listened to rainbursts drum on the roof. Days passed.

"Chester. Chess-ter. This is a common name in America?"

"No. My parents thought it sounded American."

"What was your father's name?"

"Louis."

"Louis Garland." She sounded it out.

"Louis Gurevitch."

"Gurevitch! You are Russian!"

I felt a twinge of guilt, as if I were occupying her. "Russian-Jewish," I said.

"Chester Gurevitch."

"Only for my first nineteen years."

"I do not understand."

"My father thought that if I had a more American name it would help me in my career. Because America was an anti-Semitic country then. Gurevitch was good enough if I were a cutter in a garment factory, but for a doctor, no; he thought it was not American enough."

Frowning, she looked as though she had swallowed a rotten fruit.

"Chester, I have a confession."

"I thought you didn't believe in confession."

"Seriously."

"What is it?"

"My parents do not like Jews."

"Fortunately for them, there are probably none left in their neighborhood."

"You are making a joke, but it is not funny."

"No, I don't think it's funny, either."

"Chester?"

"What?"

"I want you to have your own name for me."

"Why?"

"I don't know. I want to belong to you."

"But I like your name, and I like the way you belong to yourself."

"I like my name also, but I could have two names."

"Milena. Milena. All right, you'll be Millie. But only for me."

. . .

She was translating a Czech philosopher named Hrasek who wrote about the conflict between moral principles and the idea of "the nation." I sat one afternoon under her apple tree and picked through the manuscript while Milena, barefoot, cut back the plants, picked beans and squash. The text read fluidly but was rather abstract. I was surprised that she was devoting herself to translating such a rarefied book when, I would have thought, surely there were pamphlets to publish on more immediate topics.

"They are trying to kill our ability to think," she said. "What is urgent is to defend ourselves."

If I followed him, Hrasek maintained that people who spoke different languages could still share a decent life within the same national boundaries. He was arguing against those he referred to as "so-called realists," who said that peoples and nations have no permanent allies, only permanent interests. This principle, he claimed, turned everyone into an immoralist, as well as an informer, and produced war. The alternative was to milk realism for all it was worth and then some—to make realism more deeply realistic. All nations had to transcend their interests. There were things they simply were not morally permitted to do to anyone else.

"If I understand this," I said, like a bright student, "it's similar to what Freud said: Where id was, there shall ego be."

She looked perplexed. I explained that Freud meant we could tame our blind instincts if we learned where they came from.

She had a twinkle in her eye. "Everyone in the Austro-Hungarian empire could foresee disaster, so they all became realists. The Czechs specialized in the stupidity of nations."

"Are you a realist, Millie?"

She smiled. "I am the mother of a small boy. Does that answer your question?"

"And what has become of Hrasek?"

"Of course he is known to be against the regime. Once he was beaten badly—a warning. He was dismissed from the university and works tending a furnace."

I shook my head.

"That is a good job in my country," she said. "He has time to read."

"Like us," I said, trying to joke.

"No, not like us at all."

"You must think I am incredibly naive," I said to her. We were sipping Calvados under the apple tree. Andrej was taking a nap in his room.

She had her sober look on. "I think it is a question of experience."

Inside is where I wanted to go. The sweat in the shadow between her breasts. Great rolling waves. I was a man upended, toppling in the swells. Marion could be right: I may not have cared enough, before.

When I called Marion for the second time, the circuit was not howling, there was no storm between us, and she could hear me perfectly well when I said with a dry mouth that I didn't know when I'd be home.

She assumed a schoolmarm tone. "What do you mean, you don't know?"

"I'm trying to—"

"What are you telling me? You're suddenly inarticulate, Chester. Why is that?"

"This is hard to articulate."

"I've talked to Howard. He thinks you're ill. Really, you're ill. We're worried sick about you."

"There's nothing to worry—"

"Do you think what you're doing is—is appropriate behavior?" She had been talking to Howard.

"I doubt that's the question."

"Oh, and what's the question, then? Should I ask a question you feel like answering? What would that be? You're out of your mind."

"I doubt it."

There was a long, expensive transatlantic hush until she said, "Who's the woman?"

"What?"

"You heard me. Who is she?"

"I'm not going to get into that now, Marion."

"When are you going to get into it, then?" Her voice was rising, but she was straining to tamp it down. "You have a wife! You have a family! What do you think you're doing? You—"

"Good-bye, Marion." I hung up, pleased at my own self-control. I thought later, If I pass any more tests I set for myself, I will graduate some day. I will terminate my interminable self-analysis. I will reach childhood's end. And then I will fall off the couch, or the edge of the earth. But I have done that already, into Milena.

"Chess-ter. Do you play chess?"

"I do. Why? Do you?"

"It is discouraged for girls to play. But my older brother taught me. He is much older than me. Twelve years."

She spoke to me—a man who himself had a few years on her—so easily, I cannot say I was surprised to hear about the brother. "What does he do?"

"He is the manager of a factory. He has a good life. For a bad life."

Milena was not half bad at chess. She got better.

Some days we walked through the countryside, rented bicycles, bathed at the beach.

"What are you thinking?"

"What I am thinking is, You are ravishing."

"Ra-vish-ing." She rolled it on her tongue. "That is a beautiful word. But I do not know what it means."

"Ravishing. It means beautiful to the point of devastation."

"Ah, ravissante."

"Ravissante. Tu es ravissante."

"You must roll the 'r.' R-ravissante."

"R-ravissante."

"Good! But still untrue. And I thought you were a wise man."

"And I thought you were more perceptive than that."

"You mustn't think that. You look wise."

"Yes, I've been told that. It is good for my work."

"I do not understand."

"I mean it can be useful in the transference."

"What is that?"

"It's something that happens in analysis—one of Freud's great discoveries. The patient transfers onto the analyst the feelings he had about his parents when he was a child."

"I see. But you <u>do</u> look wise."

"Don't be fooled. It's the eyebrows."

She licked them. She licked my closed eyelids. I was saved.

．　．　．

Everything about my situation is absurd. I am a grown man with a wife who would be better off without me and a child who gets very little from me. To look at their situation as objectively as possible, I would have to say that in the long term this is a bad bargain for them. They suffer in my presence and they will suffer more in my absence—for a while. Then they will get over it. As for me, familiarity with my family breeds contempt for myself. The only thing required of me, with them, is to go on suffering—and toward what end? Meanwhile, here is Milena, my Millie, who does not merely tolerate me, she wants exactly what I can give her. I cannot believe my good fortune. Exactly, I cannot believe it will last.

O ye of little faith, I said to myself.

There were old candy boxes on the dresser in the bedroom, and a black-and-red lacquered box on a doily on the bedstand, next to a black-and-white photograph of her family posed in front of a curtain: a short, stocky man with thick white hair, a woman with wide shoulders and Milena's large, widely spaced eyes, herself, three brothers, four sisters. Everyone was solemn. Her father looked to be in his sixties but was, in fact, younger than I. The cross around her mother's neck looked like the one Milena wore.

She enfolded my hand as I held the photo. I asked, "Millie, are they believers?"

"Of course! They go to church. People of their generation, they go."

"What I mean is, do they believe deeply? Do they think that God gave his only son?"

"I don't know. I have never asked." She stared at the photo as if she had just noticed it for the first time, and a sob burst from her throat.

"You miss them," I said stupidly.

"They have a grandchild they have never seen."

I put down the photo and held her shaking in my arms as she wept. She had said she did not have the heart to confess to a man in a dark box. I was the next best thing. She confessed her anguish at being separated from her family and her country, and her guilt at raising her child without a father, and her guilt and anguish that she was not doing enough for anyone. Uprooting was not freedom. She did not know, or care, that I was a man in a dark box too, though lacking a gospel.

When her tears subsided she wiped her eyes and said, "Make love to me," and I did.

I sat down one morning to write to Marion. "I apologize, I apologize, I apologize again. I know this must ring hollow to you. But don't you see that this is your chance for your own freedom? You have told me that I am remote, that you feel imprisoned in my self-analysis. This is your chance to break out."

I ripped up the letter.

Inside Milena, I traveled deep. The rest of the day, the feeling of her lingered on my skin, inside my skin. I carried her imprint like an unmade bed.

One afternoon, I was leafing through Milena's Proust when she walked in with Andrej. "Oh," she said lightly, "you have discovered my treasure!"

"I kept your place," I said.

"Never mind. You should like Proust. It is really a man's book."

In a split second I realized this was not an insult coming from her. She was not Marion. "Do you think so?"

"Don't you identify with M. Swann?"

"I can't tell," I said. "The writing is so lush, I can hardly understand what is happening."

"That is a very diplomatic answer, but I think you don't want to say that you think of me as Odile."

"I don't know enough of the plot to say."

"Will you watch Andrej for a moment?"

"Of course." He took an unsteady step after her as she went to the bedroom, but I caught him up, lifted and tossed him a few inches into the air, and caught him. He reached for my nose. I did something I had done with my own son. I held his nose in my thumb and two fingers, then withdrew, sticking my thumb between the fingers, saying, "Look! I've got your nose!" He felt my thumb, then his nose, and was still looking perplexed when Milena came back wearing blue jeans. He squirmed and I let him down.

"I will leave you to Odile for a moment," she said, tossing her hair. "Excuse me." She took up Andrej and held him fast, then turned to me and asked, "Do you think Swann would have loved her if she had had a small child?"

"Of course he would," I said, "or it wouldn't have been love."

She let him down and sent him outside to his sandbox while she went to the garden and picked some yellow squash. The sky was cloudless. She came back inside and dumped the squash on the counter with two apples and an onion and began dicing them with a clove of garlic. I stood on the other side of the chopping block.

"You are distant now," she said. "You have gone back to Odile."

"Oh?"

"Yes. Chester, is it Andrej? You are upset that we cannot be alone?"

"What? No, no, not that. I'm not jealous." I meant it, mostly.

"Then where are you?"

She scrutinized my face. I marveled that she seemed to trust me when she had so little reason.

"Sometimes I think you really see me as a character in a fairy tale who works in the garden without a care in the world and comes inside with her dirty hands and makes love."

"If this is a fairy tale, it's more that I'm the psychoanalyst frog who's transformed into a human by the kiss of the princess."

"Perhaps. But I think you are avoiding something. I think you are running away from your family."

"Not running away, but running toward, Milena. My world is full."

"No, it isn't." She smiled. "But you will have to wait."

The next morning, when I awoke, she was studying me. "I want to ask you a professional question. Is that all right?"

"I am at your service."

"Good. Here is my question. Is this what normal feels like? Happy? Do you think so?"

"Sometimes it seems that way. Of course, Freud says that all that is possible is common unhappiness."

She was contemplative, her lips open. "I have been thinking, Chester. You know, Freud was a Jew."

"Well"—what is this? I was thinking—"but so am I."

"I know. I mean you are both dark in spirit. Look, I know that Jews understand things deeply. Jesus was a Jew. I am not supposed to think that, but it cannot be denied. Even so, Freud is wrong. Even if the Communists said he was wrong, he is still wrong."

173

"Freud was right about many things, but it is also true—"

With her damp fingers she anointed my lips. "I don't care about Freud. Come here."

On a cool, overcast day, the clouds blowing in from the sea like crumpled carbon paper, we drove into town together to drop Andrej off at his crèche. Milena lifted him out of the car, held him like a gift, set him down, and took him in. Then we drove uphill and walked on the promenade around the old city wall, above the harbor. Her hand lightly gripped my upper arm. She trusted me, as if the two of us had walked this way many times, and I wondered if she had walked this way with other lovers, and whether they had been well-groomed professional men wearing ascots or melancholy youths in denim jackets, and whether she had kept her self-possession with them, too, and where they had failed her. After a while, rain started to leak through the salt air. My glasses were quickly coated, and the harbor disappeared as if it had been sealed off by cement. "We should have brought an umbrella," I said. She pursed her lips and gave back a skeptical little French pop of air. I took off my glasses, and hand in hand we ran over a drawbridge to take refuge in the archway that passed through the old wall. Milena's boot heels clicked on the cobblestones and rain ran down her arms in sheets. "I love to get wet," she said. A man older than I, on a bicycle, wearing a dark cap and a plaid shirt, had taken shelter on the opposite side of the tunnel.

Milena lit a Gauloise and inhaled deeply. "This is a perfect place for a swim, don't you think?"

"Absolutely."

"The quiet. Listen." The rain drummed on the drawbridge, drops splashed into a puddle in the street, and the sounds of the storm cascaded through the tunnel. We waited in silence. Lovers had walked here for centuries, rumpled each other, kissed, quarreled, made furtive love. Contented Christian tradesmen sauntered here, vengeful Englishmen, neurotics, believers in astrology, German soldiers. "Oh, God, I will hate to leave," she said. "I have now fallen in love twice here, once with Normandy and once with you." She expelled a stream of smoke and gazed off at the rain, which was slanting away from the sea. "Chester, promise me. Don't fall in love with this place and think it is Milena you are falling in love with."

Her words were poignant, and they pierced me, but I was certain I was in love, as certain as the rain. "When you get to my age, you've seen many lovely places. Many."

"Oh, you sound ancient now. But I am serious!"

"I used to be ancient. Now, I don't know." There were times when she seemed the older one, in fact. That was one reason why I didn't intimidate her.

Behind her, the man with the bicycle watched us with narrow eyes. A couple of women my age, in tan raincoats with little umbrellas, walked through the arch into the old town. Time idled. The smell of sweet earth was pungent in the air. When the rain had diminished to a drizzle, the man mounted his bicycle and rode off. Milena said she was hungry, so we walked into the old town and stopped at a restaurant with an easel board in front advertising crêpes.

The place was rather full, but the tall, polite waiter was able to seat us in front of the fireplace, which dissipated the strange August chill. Ladies in scarves inspected us. The two who had passed us at the wall were among them, and another whose glance lingered, une femme d'un certain âge, with a pageboy parted in the middle and a long jaw, reminding me, disconcertingly, of Marion. To these tidy women, we might as well have been rare fish just swimming into sight behind aquarium plate glass.

"You must try the galettes," Milena said, "a kind of crêpe, but not sweet—I cannot explain, you'll see." We ordered them with ratatouille, for me, and ham, for her, and a carafe of fermented cider to warm us. It was our first time in a restaurant—after a week together, or was it two weeks, or three? (The days did not stand still to be counted. In love, as in the unconscious, there is no sense of the passage of time. That is why classic psychoanalysis is interrupted when the patient falls in love. The poor unconscious is, for a while, stripped bare of all information. Nothing but passion remains, a blazing light that washes out all the contrast.)

With her lower lip extended, Milena shook her head from side to side, like a wet dog. Her damp bangs clung to her forehead like little darts. Her smile was ablaze. Yet the pleasure I felt at being the object of that smile turned into a kind of embarrassment.

"Chester, are you sad?" she asked me.

"Sad? I'm wet. Why, do I seem sad?"

"Isn't this an agreeable place?"

"Agreeable, yes. Seriously, am I sad?" I was on the verge of tears. I put my hand over hers on the table. "I want this to last—"

"You miss your family."

I hesitated. "You want me to say that I do."

"I only want you to say the truth."

"The truth is not easy. It takes time to find the truth."

"I think that you avoid telling me about your wife," Milena said firmly.

"Oh? Why do you think so?"

"It is obvious. But it is not fair that you know so much more about me than I know about you."

I had a sudden desire, which I suppressed, to ask for one of her cigarettes. "You're not telling me that you have no secrets left of your own, are you?" I temporized.

"No, Chester, I have not said that, but in fact it is true."

"My wife—" The word sounded comfortable but empty, like analytical categories. "I don't feel I have a wife anymore, Milena. That's the truth. It is all very far away."

"Only an ocean away."

"More."

"I don't know whether to believe you. Tell me, at least. Tell me about the woman who bore your child."

The waiter arrived with our galettes, which he placed in front of us with a warning that they were "chaudes." In all of England there was nothing like the aroma that filled my nostrils, as there was no one like Milena. How could she seriously doubt that I had left my life for good? I leaned over my plate, keeping my elbows clear. Milena stubbed out her cigarette and started to eat.

"She is a good mother," I said. "That is who she is, fundamentally. That is the main thing she cares about."

"What could be more important?"

"We were married in another world at another time, and that world no longer exists. It was so hard for her to have children. She was deeply hurt. She suffered. We suffered together. A lot of things were wrecked." I didn't see any need to go into details. I mentioned Marion's abandoned career and her women's group. Milena pursed her lips disapprovingly.

"She feels stifled," I said, feeling strangely defensive. "The plain truth is that I don't love her. I ceased to love her. That's what matters. That's why I am released to love you."

I thought she would be pleased to hear those words, but she looked at me quizzically.

"Oh, you speak like such a young person, Chester." As if she were herself ancient and envious. "Nothing is so simple, I do not believe. You may say that you do not love. That is easy to say. I think it is as easy to say that you do not love as that you love, but that doesn't make it true."

She had put down her utensils and was gesturing passionately. I leaned toward her and spoke over the bistro murmur. "Let me put it this way. The longer we live, the more garbage we accumulate in our lives. My wife disappeared underneath her pile of garbage. The person I loved is buried in history. And so was love. And so was my life. The lucky thing is that I met you when I was ready to live again."

I said such things and believed them.

She sipped at her cider. Her eyes were fixed on me. Her scent, something of fruit and smoke, drifted across the table. "You are naive, Chester. You are a good man but you are very naive. Someday, I will be surrounded by my own pile of garbage. Perhaps it has started to grow already."

"It's a little late to chase me away, Millie."

"Perhaps your profession is escape artist and you will make your escape from me too." With her outstretched fingers she touched the back of my hand, and then her fingers skittered away like a mouse. It was the sort of game she played with Andrej. She did not smile, but her voice softened. "Already I have diapers in my life, you know, Chester. I am not a free woman." But I did not take this as a no. I took it as yes, and.

She held up her glass and smiled through the cider, and, crazily, I had no doubts. I had plucked her and the whole world was right at hand; I could touch it, it was rounded—her eyes, her bosom, my luck. There were no sharp corners. She was with me, in more than a geographical sense, of her own free will— not out of duty or habit, not out of forethought or calculation, not because I happened to be the one who for years had shared her furniture and her suffering.

I stepped through my fear and imagined Marion. I saw her as if through the wrong end of a telescope, diminished and angular—a good mother no longer content to be that, a woman shopping for purposes, hoping for injections of vitality. I could hear her screaming, "You're walking away from me? After a fourteen-year marriage, just like that, because you're tired of living with a real-life woman and you're ready for someone younger and more exotic? And you think I'm just going to turn my back and say, 'OK, whatever you like, dear'? You think you can just walk away with a snap of your fingers?" But that is exactly what I did. The space between us is the sum of our marriage. I walked away a long time ago.

I could also envision her differently. She has just come upstairs with the mail. Seeing my handwriting on the envelope, she carries it into the kitchen. The room is bright. Water comes to a boil for a pot of afternoon tea. She holds a butter knife in her hand to open my letter. She is serene and poised in time and space like a Vermeer lady.

"You should write to your wife," Milena said, as we drove back to the farmhouse. "You should be fair, you know, and tell her if you are not going back."

I am not going back.

Later, after making love to Milena, I lay with an arm thrown over her hip and wrote and rewrote that letter to my wife in my head.

Paul rereads the last two pages, then imagines his mother— the actual Marion, not the "diminished and angular" creature his father imagined. She didn't scream, not in his presence. She cherished order. He can't hear her bite off a phrase like "snap of your fingers." She was no harpy. She was composed, though not the placid pushover of his father's Vermeer fantasy, either. (Peculiar, how Vermeer fantasies run in the family.) She had her resentments—who could blame her? Her goodness got her short-changed. She was an adult woman who wanted more out of life than cooking or guarding her husband against intruders. When he deserted and humiliated her, even then she didn't denigrate him—not in Paul's hearing, anyway. She wanted him to have a father he could respect. It wasn't her fault that Paul grew so estranged from him. She deserved incomparably more than an afterthought letter from a runaway husband.

He's churning in these thoughts when the telephone jolts him. An eerily calm voice at the other end of the line, says, "Paul? This is Howard Spain. Am I calling too early?"

"What time—?" But Paul can see for himself: It's just after eight in the morning. "No, no, I'm glad you called. Thank you. Really."

"I'm an early riser. The older I get, the earlier."

"It's kind of you to return my call."

"Don't mention it. How are you feeling?"

"I guess as well as can be expected." *As you doctors say.*

"I understand. It's a tremendous loss. You know how much I cared about him. You have all my sympathy."

Paul says, "Thank you," and waits.

"Well. What can I do for you?"

"Yes, I—I wanted to ask you—well, you know—I'm thinking a lot about my father's life."

"Yes, of course. That's appropriate." Does Paul imagine the slightest of hesitations?

"And—about my parents' divorce. The time that led up to it."

With professional reticence, Spain says, "Yes."

"My father kept a diary."

"Yes." This is filler. Spain is noncommittal.

"He left it to me."

"I see." Spain is not surprised. From his father's description, Paul doubts Spain is the surprisable type. Paul can't even tell whether Spain knew the journal existed.

"That's why I'm up at this hour."

"I see."

"I don't really have a specific question—or it's more that everything is a question for me, if that makes any sense. About him." *About me,* Paul doesn't say. *His feelings about me.* "Who he was. I don't know. I'm trying to—"

"Yes."

"—to understand."

"Of course."

"You know, he wasn't always easy to know."

"No, I wouldn't think so. It takes our whole lives to get to know our parents."

Spain's tone tells Paul everything: He is going to stay loyal to Chester. Like Cavender. Like his mother, even.

"So now you've undertaken your own search," Spain temporizes.

"Yes, right."

"That makes sense. We are open to learning a great deal in the midst of these crises."

"Yes. I'm finding—a lot of surprises."

"That goes with the territory, doesn't it, Paul? Things not turning out as we project?"

This conversation is going nowhere fast.

"Do you have a specific question?" Spain asks, precise and competent.

With a sinking feeling, Paul says, "Not really. I just wondered . . . what else you can tell me about what happened in France, when he—you know—he didn't deliver his paper at that conference."

Spain skips another beat. "I don't know what I can tell you, Paul."

"About this woman, Milena."

Spain hesitates but recovers quickly. "I'm not sure I follow. You have his diary—"

"I'm still reading."

"Yes. Well, I expect, knowing your father, that it will be self-explanatory."

"I don't see—"

"Let me say this, Paul." Spain is deliberate. "You're very fortunate to have his own words. Many children don't ever have those. They're the closest you can get to him. Closer than friends, closer than colleagues."

In other words, I'm on my own. Marooned in my own sealed room.

He thanks Dr. Spain and goes back to the yellow notebook.

FREUD SAYS SOMEWHERE that when two people go to bed, six people go to bed. All the parents are there. But why stop at six? There are lovers and wives, mothers and fathers of mothers and fathers. There are long chains of begats, an orgy of predestinations, mistresses, and curses. We go to bed with ghosts. And we are already populating the future, branding it. We are already spawning consequences.

The next morning, I awoke in the thick of a crowded dream. A crowd was drifting toward me in slow motion, a crowd of impassive faces. People I thought I recognized at first: Michael, Marion with her hair in a ponytail, Howard Spain, Jerome Rosenfeld, Alicia Kornreich, and other psychoanalysts, but as they came closer they metamorphosed into people I no longer knew, people who, in fact, were vaguely hostile or at least indifferent, and bumping into me in a way that didn't hurt, exactly, though it made me extremely uncomfortable. They looked straight ahead as they passed. They seemed not to see me. I shouted, "It's Chester!"

It was almost seven and light was diffusing through the morning haze. Milena and I lay back to back, tangent at our shoulders and buttocks. I rotated myself toward her and reached down along the soft skin of her rump. Her skin was warm, domestic. She murmured and reached for me blindly. I could smell night sex. I thought, My love is enough for her. But I am a compulsive man. In my head I was still rewriting my letter to Marion. I pulled on my pants, went to the kitchen, poured myself a glass of grapefruit juice—jus de pamplemousse, a more delectable way of putting it—went to the living room, sat down at Milena's desk, picked up a pad of onionskin paper, and wrote the postponed letter straight through.

"I do apologize, Marion," I wrote, "which is easy, but I do it anyway and I do it sincerely. I had to resort to radical means to start up my life again. I needed distance to overcome my fear. What has happened now cannot be revoked. I did not exactly intend this to happen—it started with a mistake—but, you know, the deep unconscious is poetry and it is as Rilke wrote, 'You must change your life.' The only way out of a trap is to leap. This is what you have found in your women's group, and it is what I have learned, belatedly, in my own life. Our marriage is the past. I am convinced that you had already come to the same realization, but it has worked out peculiarly so that I am the one who comes bearing the old news. We both already knew we were finished. What we once had was deep—but is now dead, the corpse of a marriage. We should respect it and lay it to rest.

"I do not expect you to understand or approve, but I want you to know that what I have done I have not done lightly. I will not change my mind; too much has happened to propel me into this decision. I shall meet my obligations to you and Michael. This is the least I can do. It is for the best. In any event, as you have been trying to tell me, there are times when one must strike out for a new life—"

And so on, honest, blunt, but not brutal, I hoped, though she would take it as brutal, and there was nothing I could do about that. About Milena I simply said I had met a woman and fallen in love with her, although she was not the reason I was leaving our marriage. Our marriage was fossilized. She thought so herself. I wrote four pages, crossed out nothing, and numbered each page in the upper right-hand corner when I was done. This was a letter made to be crumpled, balled up, and thrown at the wall—but it was the best I could do.

I went back to the last page and added, "I hope in years to come you can forgive me and we can remember the better times." It was the truth, but I didn't need her forgiveness. She would never forgive me, and I could live with that.

I addressed the onionskin envelope, leaving no return address. Now, I am a man who likes to leave a mark on his envelopes. Call it caution or vanity, but even on business-reply envelopes I have always written out my address. It bothers me to entrust even the most inconsequential letter to the postal system. My letter would go through the hands of two systems, in fact. But I knew it would get through. It was not destined to come back to me. Truth be told, I relished the furtive feeling.

Marion might have said that I was always furtive without knowing it.

Andrej came waddling out of his room, and a bleary-eyed Milena came padding along behind him in her dressing gown. She started to lift him into his high chair, but he began to wail, so she carried him over to me, bent down, nuzzled my cheek, and let him reach for my nose, which he found an acceptable plaything to squeeze. "Did you sleep well?" she asked.

"Well enough. Well enough. Give him to me." Andrej snuggled onto my lap and squealed with incomprehensible joy.

"Thank you." She wreathed her arms around my neck, then kissed the top of my head and headed back to the kitchen. "I think, from the way you sit, you did not sleep well enough. You are burdened."

I straightened up. "If I'm not mistaken, Millie, I've just written the hardest letter of my life."

Her eyes opened wide, her forehead creased. She started peeling an onion. "Perhaps it is too hard for you, Chester, and you should not send this letter. Maybe it is too hard for you to give up your wife, you know? Something so hard maybe should not be done at all."

She called out something to Andrej in Czech—I caught the word "omeleta"—and proceeded to dice the onion. Then she started on a green pepper. Andrej bounced up and down and made little whoops.

"Something so hard is exactly what has to be done," I said. I stood up and carried Andrej over to her. Her eyes were tearing from onion fumes. "Let me do this, all right?"

"No, no, it is fine." She chopped. "It will wake me up." When she was done with the pepper, she took out a chunk of ham and started dicing that.

"You leave me nothing to do but look," I said.

"Then that is your job: to look!"

I filled a kettle with water, lit a small wax match, and turned on the gas. Milena placed on the counter a porcelain crock of apple butter with a flower design, then cracked four eggs into a bowl and whipped them. The previous day's baguette sat in a blue cloth on a serving dish. How shall I say this and have it make sense? Everything was impossibly vivid. The sun was burning away the haze, a crow cawed nearby, and the kitchen glistened with color—the pink of the ham, the silken purple of Milena's robe. I could live on this kind of commonplace joy, I thought. I could live _for_ it. As a child, I would experience such moments of ordinary enchantment in my mother's kitchen, with the smell of fresh apple pie, or after a thunderstorm, when stillness was an event. Not many such moments since.

The water came to a boil. I measured out coffee in the glass

cylinder, poured water on top, adjusted the plunger, and asked
Milena if I could borrow the car to drive into town to mail
my letter, because I didn't want to wait for the mailman to arrive
on his rounds. I was too excited to wait. I wanted one less
middleman.

"Of course." Her smile lit up the room. "And Chester,
will you stop and pick up a fresh baguette? Et trois pains au
chocolat aussi?"

"I can't tell you how much pleasure that would give me." I
made a flourish with an invisible cape.

"Your omelet will be ready for you when you return, Lord
Chester. And your fresh coffee, of course." She held out her
gown and made a mock curtsy.

The envelope was upright in my pocket, a sort of badge. I
headed for the door.

"You are forgetting something, darling," she called out.

"What's that?" The "darling" was not lost on me.

She picked up the car key from the counter and dangled it
like a bell from her finger.

Thresholds after thresholds. Did I blow her a kiss? I don't
remember. I was happy enough. I was young. I was Errol Flynn,
secure in the knowledge that I would return later that day, my
derring-do done, to bed the lady. I might have been grinning
foolishly, and why not? I took the key and went out to the car.
There was a tang in the air, sea moisture, the scent of apples. I
filled my lungs. I had the sense that the day was going to blaze.
The world tingled on my skin. Was it Kierkegaard who wrote,
"Anxiety is the dizziness of freedom"? I was a man on my
own, choosing a life. If I had rewritten my letter to Marion, I
might have added, You, who have decided to jump the track of a
life that no longer felt like your own, ought to understand me,
who now picks himself up in his hands—picks up everything
he has, his one and only life—and jumps.

I got into the driver's seat—the steering wheel was a little close—and practiced maneuvering the strange Deux Chevaux gearshift, a rod sticking straight out from the dashboard at a right angle. I sat for a while pulling the rod, twisting the handle, shifting, getting the hang of it. Then I let out the brake, shifted into reverse, and fed the gas. The car lurched back, and I heard to the rear—I had better say it directly—I can hardly stand to think it—a sickening thump and a scream. The scream lasted forever. I jammed on the brake and there was a screech. A screech and dead silence.

I think I screamed, "No!" I knew before I jumped out of the car what I was going to see. I have never wanted more to be wrong, but I wasn't wrong. The boy lay sprawled on the pavement, his face down and twisted to the side, inert. Nothing moved. I raced to him, reached his side, fell to my knees, and went for his left wrist. His pulse was tangible and it was rapid. There was a purple blur as Milena flung the front door open and came running, screaming, "Andrej!"

I watched her bear down and said sharply, "Milena, no!" but she did not stop and I had to reach up and grab her by both wrists and bark out, "Wait!"

She started to wrestle with me, then froze. I turned back to Andrej. No, no, no, no, this could not be happening. Yes, yes, yes, yes, it happened. With my hands I made it happen. I had to retract it. I could not, ever. I rested my head on the pavement next to the little face and said, "Andrej? Andrej? Talk to me. Talk to me, Andrej." His eyes were closed. Nothing; he said nothing. "I didn't see you, I swear I didn't, forgive me," I thought, stupidly, or said aloud, I don't know which. He lay there, damaged, and I lay on the pavement breathing on him and watched his blood spread on the pavement under his head, spilling out of some wound in his face that was not visible. But his nostrils, thank God, moved. They moved very faintly, but they moved nevertheless.

"He's alive," I called, without taking my eyes off the boy. "We can't move him, not at all, not one inch, all right? All right?"

"All right."

"Now get me a towel, please." I don't know if I was screaming or whispering. Milena shuddered. I tried not to.

In a case like this, one has to fear that the neck is broken.

In this precise case, I had to fear that Andrej's neck was broken. I had to fear that I—no one else—had broken his neck.

God, help the boy. Useless God, give me another life. But this was the life I had chosen. Once you start down a track and you pick up speed, you do not switch onto another track just as you please.

From somewhere nearby, a bird trilled, its song swooping down the scale and then rising again, gliding down and up that way achingly, a gift for no reason at all, on that senselessly beautiful day when I smashed up three lives. I remember a bird singing while Andrej lay unconscious and bleeding on the pavement, and I watched my life tumble over a cliff.

To notice the song of a bird at such a moment! If a patient were to tell me such a story, I would think denial or, to use a clearer word, self-deception. I might think about the self-serving idiocy of our species. But I couldn't help myself. That is the kind of human being I am, or all of us are.

She avoided my eyes as she held out a towel. I wedged it under Andrej's head and applied pressure to the place where the wound must have been. "Call an ambulance," I said.

"Is he all right?" she demanded.

"He's alive. Please, Millie, call the ambulance. And Millie?"

Black sparks flew out of her eyes but quickly she jerked her gaze away, and then she was on her way into the house.

. . .

Life is glass. What shatters, stays shattered.

I replay these events in my mind ten thousand times and it is always the same. The events replay my mind. My mind becomes the events. It is like a scar gradually joining the body. When the scar is fresh, it screams. Eventually, from the inside, it is lost in the rest of your flesh. The wounded becomes the wound. You have nothing else. You are nothing else. You cannot even tell why you are alive, or why you have the right to stand in the sunlight.

Breathe. Tremble, nostrils. Beat, little heart. No change.

Her clogs clattered away on the pavement and she ran back wearing a shift and—anticipating my next instruction—carrying a blanket. "They will be here soon," she said. Her face was hardening over. "Cover him, Millie," I said, and she did. Then she sat on the pavement, her hand encircling his right ankle.

When the ambulance came, the attendants—two young men in white tunics and short hair—jumped out bearing a stretcher. By now, an old woman from one of the other buildings was standing not far away, staring at the spectacle.

"Milena," I said, "tell them to be careful not to move his head."

She rattled off a translation.

"Bien sûr!" the shorter attendant replied.

They lifted him gently and expertly onto the stretcher and into the back of the ambulance. In the moment before they readjusted the towel over the wound, I could see a long gash running down his forehead alongside his right eye. He must have been hit by the bumper, I don't know. I started toward the back of the ambulance behind the boy, but Milena interposed herself and said simply, "No." Her eyes were scorching.

"I ought to stay with him, Milena," I said. "I am a physician."

She kept the fierce look but after a hesitation nodded briskly. She climbed in, then I did. Andrej lay between us.

Everyone was professional.

Eee-aaa, eee-aaa, went the siren on the way into town. Milena held Andrej's hand. There was nothing else to do. Nothing. Do no more harm. You've done enough. I rehearsed statements, discarded them, and said nothing. Let me explain. No, not that. We have to wait. Wait. You have to wait. That's all you can do. I do not know if he will be all right. Nobody knows. When the ambulance swerved and Milena had no choice but to look up at me, I said, "Milena, it was an accident."

"Yes, I am sure." Her mouth was tight. Only when she had talked about the Russians had I seen her mouth tighten.

"He ran behind the car. I was backing up. I—"

"You didn't see him," she said, in a voice like a heavy door slamming. Then she took her silver cross in her mouth.

God laughs at prayer. My mind, my enemy, lash, lash at me, bitter, futile remorse. On the road to a new life there are many hairpin turns, washed-out sections, detours.

Excuse 1: It had been a long time since I had driven a car, any car at all, and an even longer time since I had had to contend with a stick shift.

Excuse 1.1: Let alone such an unusual gear stick.

Self-accusation 1: It was inexcusably reckless to get behind that steering wheel without any experience.

Extenuating circumstance 1: I am a good-hearted man. I didn't want to put Milena to the extra trouble of giving me lessons.

Return to the beginning and repeat.

My knees stung. My pants were torn through at the knees from kneeling on the pavement. Blood smears on my skin, on the pant legs. Grains of sand in my wounds. Andrej looked peaceful. How fast could the car have been going? Not very fast. So not much damage. I thought, Don't jump to conclusions.

We headed into town at a steady speed. I had nothing to do but interrogate myself. I stood over myself with avenging eyes and a court reporter at hand:

Leading question 1: Why such a hurry?

Non-answer answer 1: To mail the most important letter of my life, that's all.

Leading question 2: What was so all-fired important about making a special trip to town to mail it?

Self-accusation 2: I should have turned in the driver's seat and made sure no one was behind me.

Self-accusation 3: I should have reminded Milena to keep Andrej inside.

Excuse 2: Milena didn't think of that herself.

Self-accusation 4: She was sleepy. I knew that. I should have known that. I had been awake long enough not to have that excuse myself.

Excuse 3: Andrej was rash and rambunctious, that was already established.

Self-accusation 5: A good reason for me to be exquisitely careful. I should have looked in the rearview mirror. Or did I? If I did—I honestly do not remember—if I did look, I should have

191

looked longer; I should have looked a second and a third time; I should not have been born.

Bare fact 1: The God, or god, of the railroad compartment was not with Andrej or with me. He was a firefly god.

Bare fact 2: More than a ton of steel smashed into the little boy.

Bare fact 3: This did not have to happen.

Bare facts 4, 5, and on to infinity: I was the one, the only one, and forever will be the only one who could have kept this from happening.

Gibberish. Temporizing. Unbearable self-disgust. But my desire is pure: Let him live.

It could have been worse. X rays showed no fractures. Young bone is soft and does not break easily. The young brain is a plastic and wondrous organ.

The ward was freshly painted, a hospital gray tone, with lace curtains at the windows. Given the fact that a ceiling fan was spinning and five of the eight beds were occupied, the room was rather quiet. In the far corner, behind a curtain, Andrej lay in a coma, eyes closed, his chest lightly rising and falling. An IV fed fluids into his arm. There was a bandage over the vertical gash next to and above his right eye where his head had cracked on the pavement and the doctor had taken twenty-six stitches. The skin around the eye was blackened. Intracranial bleeding, I explained to Milena. Blood inside the skull.

The nurses, in gray like the walls, wore headdresses with little wings and looked like awkward angels. There was a wooden crucifix over each bed and a plain wooden chair on either side of Andrej. The attending physician was stocky and short, almost elderly, with a soft voice—weary, or all too comfortable with irreparable damage and death. He spoke some English, slowly, with a slight British accent, and said to Milena and me jointly, as if I were Andrej's father, "He is stable."

"How long can this go on?" or something like that, is what Milena asked him in French.

He had somber brown eyes and a small scar at the crown of his forehead. "He can go on this way for days, or weeks." Months, he might as well have said. Or years. There is no knowing.

"And then?"

The doctor considered and shrugged, not with French superiority but humility. Then, for some reason, he switched to English. "Anything, madame. There is bleeding inside his skull. He may be perfectly normal when he recovers. He may not. All you can do is wait." Seeing the red-stained rips in my pants at the knees, he pointed and said sympathetically, "I should look at that."

I shook my head. He did not look up at the crucifix as he parted the curtain and moved on.

Milena gazed toward the opening in the curtain, as if the doctor might return to say that it was all a mistake, he was terribly sorry, he had confused Andrej with a different patient who was in serious danger, but as for Andrej, there was evidence that he would return to consciousness any minute now. The curtain rippled in the fan's breeze. The skin beneath her red, raw eyes was dark and moist. She opened her mouth to speak, but no words emerged. I turned away, toward Andrej. By the time I looked back, her face had hardened into a mirror of stone and she uttered one word.

"How?"

The word drifted away and the silence around her surrounded me like a verdict.

"This is horrible," I said in a monotone, idiotically.

"I trusted you."

My mouth was bone dry. "It was an accident." I swallowed. "He ran out—I don't know. I love you—you have no idea how sorry I am."

"It does not matter," she said. "You should go."

"No, I should stay."

"I want you to go."

"I don't want—"

"Do you want me to condemn you?" she snapped. "Will you go then?"

I wanted a miracle, but it was no day for miracles. "I would give anything to take this day back. If I could press a button and exchange places with Andrej, I would do that. You know this."

She gazed at me as if from across a canyon. What I was saying was simply of no interest. This was a woman I did not know, but she acted as if she knew everything she needed to know about me.

"Is there nothing else you want to say?" I said.

"Nothing. Just go."

I could not move. I stared at Andrej: the slow, regular movement of his chest, the pallor, the bruise. What kind of attachment could I claim to him? Or to Milena, for that matter? She had every right to want me gone, but still I could not move.

"I want you away from my son. It is not right, Chester! How can you—?" She stopped herself. I took a tentative step toward her, but it was a step too far, and she put up her hands as if she were warding off a blow and started to shake. Her voice was a hoarse command. "I mean it. Get away. Now. Leave!"

It was as if her hands in the air were against my chest, shoving, so persuasively did she repel me. I went to the bathroom, took off my pants, washed out the wounds on my knees. The floor of the bathroom was filthy. I went to a musty waiting room and sat in a peeling leather chair. She could not keep me out of a public waiting room. I had a right to wait! I got up, went to the window, and studied the parking lot. I reviewed my leading questions, excuses, extenuations, and self-accusations. I got to know them by heart. When I got to the end of the list, I sat and started again. But what I had done was inexcusable. I bathed in abjection. I was loathsome. I had squandered the best hope of my life. I raked myself for itemizing excuses. I battered myself silly for having gotten in over my head. I told myself I should have known that infatuation is dangerous. I told myself that what I had with Milena was not infatuation. I told myself there was no way to know what I had with this woman except to give it time, and now there was no time to give. I told myself that if anyone should know whether my feelings were real, I should know. I blamed myself for not knowing. I heard a shrill voice inside my skull: You have no one to blame but yourself! I whimpered back, Blaming is a primitive ritual—internalized punitive superego. The whimper was not convincing. I closed my eyes. I asked myself what I would do if I were in Milena's place. I knew she was right to want me out of her life. I admired her sheltering impulse, her devotion to her child. I had no such devotion. But I did care deeply for Andrej; I would do anything to help. I was careless, not evil. So what? Carelessness is culpable where a child is concerned. My main desire was to punish myself. I stitched up my wounds. Then I tore out the stitches and gouged into the wounds again. I stared at balls of dust on the far side of the waiting room. I studied the cracks in the wall but couldn't find any pattern. I tried to open the windows, but they were painted shut. It was then I realized that my letter to Marion was still in my pocket.

Realized and rejoiced—with only a twist of guilt. After all that I had been through, here was my chance for a reprieve.

Deserving or not, a reprieve! My luck was not always bad. Admit your mistake, Chester! Your real life, suspended, awaits you! Your only home, the shelter where imperfect love truly dwells. Perfection is a pipe dream, an infantile hangover. Look what my freedom fantasy had accomplished in so-called adult life. I pictured myself crawling to Marion, telling her I had returned to my senses. I would plead, sob, resolve to reform myself. I would shake with sincerity. She would cut me down. I would take it. I would honor her fragility. I would speak of Michael and his need for a family. I would throw myself back into analysis. I would reason. I would tremble with sincere, abject apologies. I would beg forgiveness. Was I not the man who had disciplined himself to endure medical school and training analysis? I was skilled at self-abasement. I would consecrate my life to becoming a loving (at least, a more than adequate) husband.

But this was absurd. What I had done to Andrej had reduced me to nothing, but going back to Marion would make me less than that. I was a blight from every angle. The part of me that wished to be married to Marion was nothing but cowardice, a moribund fixation, not genuine feeling. In my self-protectiveness, I was treating her as capital I was struggling to preserve. Yes, admit it! Nothing in my letter, as best I remembered it, was false. If the boy did not recover—a thought I had to force myself to think—if the boy did not recover, why would anything more be left of my marriage than if he did recover? If he did recover, and Milena forgave me, all my reasons for writing the letter would remain valid. If she did not forgive me, my marriage was finished anyway. Or suppose, God help me, the boy did not recover. Was I now to live my life on my knees, groveling for forgiveness, a sacrifice to an unforgiving God in Whom I did not even believe?

If a killer has any right to live, who has the right to tell him how? An unloved wife? An analyst waving categories at me? A marriage counselor?

I got up and went out into the town. The sun was absurdly brilliant. I imagined having looked in the rearview mirror. I imagined telling Milena to watch the boy until I drove away. Behind me, a Deux Chevaux kept smashing into a little boy's head. Dormer roofs stared down at me. From bakeries, delicatessens, and beauty shops, the eyes of women—mothers of children—tracked my movements. Women carrying string bags looked me up and down, then at the last minute averted their eyes and stepped out of my way. I was a zombie. I was a stinking golem. They knew exactly whom they had in their midst. You! The baby killer! The vile, disgusting scum who abandoned his family! Why should you live?

I knew I was projecting, but the projections drew blood and it was my blood. It ought to have been my blood. I avoided as many glances as I could. I passed high-rise apartment buildings where laundry was hanging out to dry. I didn't know where I was, exactly, but headed toward the center of town and found myself approaching a stone bridge, a short one, about forty feet long. Long enough, I thought, stepping onto the walkway at the side of the bridge. This is it. The river beneath was swift, gushing between flat rocks in a seizure. The bridge was not very high. High enough. Flecks of foam spattered upward. This river was invigorated by the seizure it was suffering. The stone wall on the side of the bridge came up to my waist. I leaned over. The stone wall scraped my injured knees. I was glad to feel anything at all. I looked over the edge and heard a shout: Jump! My voice, my shout, my darkness. The water looked cool and bottomless. I closed my eyes.

If I were to be presented with such an account from a patient, I would look for the right moment to suggest in a neutral tone, Such moments are transitory. You are processing very

197

difficult material—very . . . difficult . . . material! You are deny-
ing the horrible truth of what has already happened. The worst
is over.

I listened to the roar as the water rushed over the rocks and
heard the words: I am not done.

Then the word: Love.

Not: Love your wife and cleave unto her. Not: Love, to
the best of your ability, those whom you have ruined, so help
you God. No pointers. No promises of rewards for good works.
Just: Love.

I walked on down the street, past gift shops, banks, tabacs,
and pharmacies with Tudor designs. On a newsstand I saw an
International Herald Tribune headline: "Agnew under investigation." It was startling to be reminded that while I had been
making a shambles of my life, the United States of America in
all its debased splendor had been doing the same. I glanced
at the opening paragraph—something about the vice president accused of a bribe—and felt a little thrill of vindication,
followed by a pang on behalf of Marty DeLong, who would
have rejoiced, had he lived. This was followed, in turn, by an
unwelcome burst of fellow feeling for a bad man whose life
was going to come apart, even if he did deserve it. But I couldn't
concentrate on somebody else's soap opera. I bent down to
glance at a French paper. Something about allegations of torture in Chile. I saw the words "électrode" and "génitales" and
couldn't read any further. I looked up and saw a sign pointing
toward the post office. It was a squat gray concrete slab of a
building in government moderne. I threw open the door. Off
to the right of the entrance were phone booths. A distraught-
looking young woman was shouting into one phone, an elderly
man holding a small jewel box was listening into another. I

could easily have stepped into one of the vacant booths. Marion, I'm coming home. Marion, can you find it in yourself—?

But I had not come all this way to save myself with a lie.

I stepped up to the line that was waiting for stamps, more of a crowd than a line, and, after letting a number of patrons slip in front of me, made my way to the window, held out my envelope—a bit crumpled now—and mumbled, "Par avion, s'il vous plaît," and put down my francs for a stamp. The clerk's smile was piteous, barely different from a glower. He knows! I thought. He knows who is standing in front of him. He refuses to be an accessory after the fact—

"Monsieur?" he said. He hadn't understood me. "Par avion," I repeated, slower and louder. He nodded, said, "D'accord," tore a stamp from a sheet, and pushed it under the grill. I licked the stamp, pressed it on, dropped the letter in a slot marked "Autres Destinations," saw it fall softly onto a pile of the town's mail, the daily business by which G—— maintains itself for another day: gas and electricity payments, wedding invitations, condolences, picture postcards, gossip, misunderstandings, cheerful notes, heartfelt lies. There was a small comfort in feeling myself a member of a vast, disheveled humanity. But the tiny pleasure I felt at having accomplished my mission had sunk to zero by the time I stepped back into the street. Abruptly I stopped forgetting. A mother came along pushing an infant in a stroller. I resisted the impulse to throw myself at her feet, but of course it was absurd to think she could forgive me enough. Cars drifted by. I peered into store windows and pretended to care about jewelry, pâtés, antique lamps. I did not eat or drink. Passersby went on averting their eyes.

Eventually I made my way back to the hospital, to the cracked leather chair in the musty waiting room, and faded into a half sleep. When I more or less awoke, it was dark and as noiseless as a vault. I heard the smash of the car against Andrej's head, and his scream. My jaw was locked in a vise. The hinge in my jaw was taut. It was as if I were biting a gag in my mouth, as if I would grind my teeth to powder. As if I were held hostage. For no ransom at all. No demands. God was not in this room. The thought of God anywhere in a hospital made me want to laugh.

The grave mind is piled high with fresh earth. Rest in upheaval, Chester Garland. What kind of peace have you deserved? Much might be said for and against your recklessness, but the true disgrace is your self-pity.

When the police came to talk to me, I could barely make myself understood. I used the word "accident." One policeman was thin and polite, the other one stocky, with a thick, brutal neck, who looked down at my torn pants with contempt. Derelict, he must have been thinking. "Je suis médecin," I said. The one with the neck laughed. The polite one asked for my passport. I said I had left it at Milena's house because of the—I didn't know how to say "emergency," so I said "disastre." They went off to speak to Milena. A few minutes later, they brought her back to the waiting room. Her eyes were red, but her hair was perfectly in place. She used the word "accident" too. They called me "Monsieur" and "Docteur." Milena translated for them. Madame (pointing at her) said it was not her intention to file charges. If the boy died, I would have to submit to an investigation nevertheless. In any event, I must surrender my passport that day. There were no exceptions in such cases. The policemen seemed reasonable enough. I would do the same as they if I were a policeman. It occurred to me that I should contact a lawyer. It occurred to me that I should call the American embassy in Paris. I decided to do neither. I told the police I would bring my passport to the police station later that day, and I did.

I took a taxi to Milena's house and asked the driver to wait. He wore a white shirt and a tie and exuded efficiency. The fumes of apples hung in the air. The Deux Chevaux was sticking out dangerously far, only an inch or two off the roadway. There was a smear of congealed blood on the bumper, another small patch on the pavement. The keys were still in the ignition. I started the car and pulled as close to the house wall as possible. Inside the house, I took paper towels, dampened them, came back outside, and mopped up Andrej's thickened blood. The taxi driver sat reading a sports newspaper and asked no questions. I told him to drive to the prefecture, where I delivered my passport. The officials were sober and correct and gave me a receipt. Then I went back to Milena's house and stayed there for a few hours of fitful stagnation that could barely be called sleep. I woke up thinking: This is not an interlude in my life. This is my life.

On the morning of the third day, Andrej opened his eyes and blinked.

An ordinary thing, blinking. We do it hundreds of times a day.

Standing at the door of the waiting room, the doctor said, "He blinked, he blinked several times," and a dam burst in me. I was engulfed in tears, and when I was done, I mopped up around my eyes and made a fool of myself thanking the man. He added, with a pleasant smile, "But, you know, it is early to know just what will happen next." His conduct was impeccable. He made no promises. Still, the news was reasonably clear: The boy was coming out of the coma.

I ran, I floated down the corridor to the ward. Murmurs came from within the curtain. His mother's hand rested lightly on his forehead and she was singing softly. Andrej had closed his eyes again, and the bruise area around his eye was a green-black smear. But he had blinked.

Milena looked up and noted my arrival as if I were an orderly, then resumed singing to Andrej in Czech, in English, in French. The English was "Jerusalem": "And we will build Jerusalem in England's green and pleasant land."

Andrej opened his eyes and said, "Mmmah," and drooled out of the corner of his mouth.

I did not know whether to leave or stay. I wanted to share in Milena's relief but I felt like an intruder. She started wiping him off with her handkerchief, and by the time she was done, his eyes had closed again. She stroked his forehead. I was para- lyzed. She mopped her own tears and said to me softly, "You have to go now."

"All right," I said. "I'll come back."

"I mean, you must go and not come back."

There was nothing left of my life to die.

"Milena, you have to listen to me," I blurted out. "I love you. You have to understand. I love you. I won't walk away."

"No, Chester, don't."

"Milena, you are the love of my life!"

She stared at me for a very long time and said, "I am your vacation, Chester, and your vacation is over. Go home. There is nothing more I can do for you."

And, to be truthful, there was nothing else I could think to do for her.

Her face glinted in the dull light and looked strangely lac- quered. "It is finished, Chester."

"Time has to pass, I can see that. Milena, good Christ. I'll go away for a while. But I'll come back. Listen to me—"

"If you will pardon me, Chester, you are speaking nonsense."

"All right, I'm going to go." I dropped her keys into her hand

and started to walk away, then turned back and said, "Promise me that you'll tell me how it goes with him."

"I will—write to you," she said unconvincingly. I left her my address and walked out of her life.

I tried to check into the Hôtel Terminus, by the train station, but the clerk would not let me register without my passport, so I had to go to the police and get a document that would substitute. This took many feeble gestures on my part, and the eventual intervention of the stocky policeman who had quizzed me at the hospital, who chuckled at my embarrassment. The policeman in the back office enjoyed typing the document painstakingly on an ancient manual typewriter, stamping it with equal deliberateness, and bestowing it upon me with a flourish, as if it were a special pass from the local duchy, in return for which I would now owe many favors.

Then, in a room smelling of mildew, I sat in an uncomfortable wooden chair at a plain table overlooking the square in front of the station, and wrote in these pages. I wrote of my life as if it were over. I walked the town in the rain. I lay in bed and watched a crack in the ceiling become Andrej's scar. I raged at Milena. I remembered the circus that had occupied the square, Andrej charging across the sidewalk, about to plunge into the traffic, Milena grabbing him. I raged at Andrej, and raged at myself for raging at him.

Two days later—it might have been three days—the police who had come to the hospital summoned me to a meeting with an examining judge. A young, slender woman in a white blouse sat at the side of his desk and translated. The judge, young, bald, unsmiling, with a thick mustache, told me to describe the incident. I did. He asked whether I had been drinking. I assured him I had not been drinking. The accident had taken place early in the morning, I reminded him. Where was I going? To the post office. Why did I not look behind me? I did look. What was my relation to the young woman and the boy? I was her friend. His eyes gave nothing away.

This was all quite correct.

He asked me if I wished to consult a lawyer. I told him that I did not. Later that night, I wondered if I had done the right thing. But by that time, I had told them the whole story. I had nothing in reserve.

A few days later, there came another summons. The judge told me that there would be no criminal charges and I was free to go. I was not unaware of the joke. I was free to resume a life I had firmly decided to flee. I felt like an escaping prisoner who had lost his sense of direction and tunneled into another wing of the prison. I signed a receipt for my passport and left.

I took a train back to Paris that night and kept writing to save myself.

The next stop down on the train line from G—— is a town with an Hôtel des Voyageurs. I vaguely remembered it from my outbound voyage—how many weeks before?—with Milena and Andrej, when I was a man in a state of grace, a man with a future, not a ghost loaded down with too much past. As the train eased away from that station, a small woman in a long blue dress, her reddish hair gathered in a bun, with a simple silk scarf around her neck and two teenage girls in tow, entered the compartment and sat. The girls were plain, in white blouses. They all whispered in order not to disturb me—the girls didn't even require instruction from their mother on this score—and the rustling of their light French treble was soothing. I was

sacrifice

touched by their consideration. Even a ghost needs silence at times. I closed my eyes for a moment.

The train lurched and the Deux Chevaux smashed into the boy. I heard him scream. The boy was alive and his scream was no less fierce, though not as surprising. The mind gets used to everything, or almost everything. That is its original sin.

The God of the compartment might well have been there—whatever "there" means—in front of Milena's house, that sunlit morning. It was not a God who preserves infants.

As for the wounds I gouged into myself, what were they worth? Nothing. My suffering was an indulgence. No, I thought, wrong; it is necessary. An installment on my debt. I thought, I am becoming a textbook case of trauma. I thought, Steady, Chester, we are early in the recovery process. I struggled to call up a different image. Struggled and failed. The car slammed, the boy screamed, and I broke again.

I may have slept for a few moments. I woke up dulled, sluggish, and the car hit the boy again. I tried something else. When the car smashed and the boy screamed again, I made myself see the boy with his open eyes and his scar, drooling in his hospital bed in G——. I swallowed hard.

Here is a method for keeping one's tears choked off: Apply oneself to theoretical questions. For example, what does it mean to get away from oneself? Who is it who accomplishes such a neat getaway, doctor? These are questions that might well be asked by a man in a prison cell, a man with no hope of parole but possessed of some philosophical patience. These are questions that one would be better off not having to ask in the first place. The sensible-looking composed lady in the compartment with her well-behaved daughters would not ask.

And now, doctor, a question in another key. Suppose that what you wanted in the first place was not to get away from yourself. What if you wanted something a bit more—well,

205

basic? I arrived in France carrying two dead weights: my wife and psychoanalysis. Now I am on my way back to my wife and son with two more. Very bright, Dr. Garland. You changed your life. Now what? You thought you would listen to God whisper in your ear and then relax? You thought you deserved to love?

Everything in the world takes place under the same sky. A man thinks he is free. A child's skull smashes against a pavement.

Do no harm.

God knows nothing, learns nothing, presides over scars and shit. God is. Period. Whatever that means. No absolution. No consequences. The fact, if it is a fact, heals no one.

Gare Montparnasse, late. As the train pulled into the station, a woman in high heels, waving frantically, ran down the platform after another train just pulling out. A small child in short pants ran after her, also waving, more dutifully, and they seemed to run as fast as they could as long as they could, trying to keep up, until the train left them behind.

Taxi to the vicinity of Charles de Gaulle airport. Checked into a featureless slab of a hotel full of businessmen, for a night without hope or sleep. Wrote. Dialed Milena's number for no good reason. Ringing, ringing. Hung up, tried again. Ringing. Dialed the hospital. They did not answer either. Wrote. I am a ghost who writes, a ghost without tears.

Toward dawn, on hotel stationery, I wrote a tortured, abject letter to Milena. I was not so far gone as to overlook the obvious—these laments would prove embarrassing, futile, counterproductive. I tore up the letter. I burned the shreds in the sink, black and abstract as my heart. Before I checked out, I left all my francs under the ashtray for the maid.

I take up space in France. The airport is glossy, extraterrestrial. The escalator is suspended above the ground. The seats and counters, plastic, orange, have the look of coming from nowhere and belonging nowhere. I do not belong here. I am on my way home.

Fathers condemn sons—Abraham and Isaac. They banish sons—Isaac and Esau. They abandon them—Laius and Oedipus. God and Jesus, for that matter. Three forms of sacrifice. Civilization built on the threat to sacrifice the oblivious young. Helplessness of both generations. Devastation of both. Idea for a book.

Here the yellow notebook ended.

Paul closes the cover, and his tears pour through his fortifications. *My thaw at last. So my father came home to the home he burned down. He must have known he would live unhappily ever after. Love, he heard on the bridge. Not love of anyone in particular, just love. Meaning what? Everyone whom he loved, he battered. What it must have cost him to conceal this knowledge for the rest of his life!*

Do no harm.

For some moments he thinks nothing at all. Then he rereads the last paragraph and the verbs slam through his mind: *Condemn. Banish. Abandon. Sacrifice. He left me. To leave my mother, he left me behind too. A devastated man walked away from his whole life. From me.*

And then: *A quarter of a century later, he takes the leap from the subway platform that he refused to take from the bridge.*

I still don't understand.

Absurdly, Paul is tempted to call Howard Spain back—
Dr. Spain, I know what happened in G——, the whole story,
and I'm begging you: Talk to me—but of course this would be
an exercise in futility. Howard Spain isn't going to tell Chester
Garland's son one single thing he doesn't already know. From
the fringes of consciousness comes the thought that the only
other person who might actually be willing and able to offer an
insight is Grace, who has, truth be told, been kind to Paul. And
must have been more than kind to Chester. So kind, so restora-
tive, it was her company Chester chose when he finally abandoned the single life he had settled for after Marion. Paul can
see Grace a bit more clearly now. In his father's eyes, she must
have been the calm after all the storms—not only the anti-
Marion but the anti-Milena. Earnest, devoted, without resent-
ment, without any urge for adventure—or perhaps, for her,
Chester was adventure enough.

But Paul cannot intrude on the widow now. That would be
cruel. And futile. He could never break through her loyalty—
her strong point, after all, as it was everyone's who remained
close to his father to the end, everyone's, that is, except his. All
he can think to do now is pick up *Abraham, Isaac, Esau.*

Father, say more, I can take it.

ISAAC SWALLOWED HIS pride and prayed to the God Who had
once commanded his sacrifice, and his wife conceived. Isaac,
who relished games, and Rebecca, his prize, produced twins,
God's playthings. In Rebecca's womb, the twins, entwined with
each other, wrestled. Rebecca cried out in pain and begged God
for guidance. God spoke to her and told her that she would be
the mother of two nations, and that the elder would serve the
younger. So, when the twins were born and Esau came out first,
reddish and hairy, and the second came out grasping Esau's heel,
Rebecca knew to favor the younger, who was named Jacob.

sacrifice

When Jacob looked down into a pool of water, what did he see? Impenetrable eyes, smooth skin, self-satisfaction. This was a proud youth who needed no one, but who smiled so sweetly that when others beheld him they felt graced by his attention.

Isaac had not heard the Lord's words to his wife. He forgot the fact that he was himself a second son. To him, Esau was the elder, if only by a few seconds, and that was that. Esau, a rough man, grew up to become a hunter of great skill who brought home the raw flesh of the desert, which Isaac loved, while Jacob remained near home, and cooked, and tended the flocks, and calculated, and was lost in thought, like his father, and spoke to anyone who would speak to him. Jacob reminded his father of himself as a young man. Jacob was, moreover, as Genesis says, a blameless youth. There was a warm light in his eyes. It was as if he reflected the glow his mother bestowed upon him. This innocence unnerved Isaac, for he felt judged by it. Isaac knew well the wrong that had been done to his own half brother, Ishmael, and did not want to see the curse against huntsmen passed on to the next generation. For more than one reason, then, Isaac preferred Esau.

Esau came in from the hunt one day, empty-handed, and he was weary and hungry. Jacob was cooking a stew of red lentils, and Esau asked him for a swallow. Jacob demanded his brother's birthright in exchange. Esau said, "I am famished, so this birthright means nothing to me," and agreed, and swore an oath. Whereupon Jacob fed him and gave him water to drink.

When Isaac was full of days, and blind, and knew he might die at any time, he asked his elder son, Esau, to hunt venison for him and prepare it as a festive dish and bring it to him, so he might give him his blessing.

Rebecca, hearing what Isaac had said, told Jacob to go to the flock and bring her two kids, so she could prepare them as Isaac loved, which she did. She took the clothing of her son Esau, and put it on her son Jacob, and put the skins of the kids on his hands and neck. She knew her husband had once benefited from a substitution.

Whereupon, when Jacob went to his father, Isaac said, "The voice is Jacob's voice, but the hands are the hands of Esau," and preferring the evidence of his touch to the evidence of his ears, he blessed him. Yet Isaac remained uncertain. He again asked his son, "Art thou Esau?" And Jacob said he was. And Isaac ate of the kids, finely prepared, which he thought to be venison, and drank of the wine that Jacob had brought him, and repeated his blessing: that he should rule all people and all nations.

No sooner had Jacob departed than Esau came in from the hunt, with the meat he had prepared to his father's liking, and asked his father's blessing. Whereupon Isaac trembled violently, and told Esau that he had already eaten, and accordingly blessed his son Jacob. Esau wept bitterly and cried out for his father to bless him also. But Isaac told him he was too late; his brother, Jacob, had stolen his blessing, and that was that. The thief had taken his words, and words are real and final and cannot be taken back. Isaac knew well the power of words, knew well what it is for a son to be betrayed by his father.

Esau demanded, "Do you have but one blessing?" Isaac, who also knew the power of silence, said nothing. And Esau wept. Esau wept in foreknowledge of the dispossession he would suffer, and his children would suffer, and his children's children, unto the last days.

Then Isaac prophesied that Esau would be banished, that he would have to live by the sword and serve his brother, until such day as he would free himself. Realizing that his father would not be swayed, Esau declared that as soon as Isaac died, he would kill Jacob. Rebecca, hearing this, sent Jacob to live with her brother Laban until such time as Esau's anger should subside. That night, God came to Jacob and renewed the covenant with him and his descendants. He said nothing to Jacob about the manner in which he had received his blessing. In other words, he confirmed that Isaac had done the right thing. Laban cheated Jacob, but that is another story.

The rabbis have strained to justify Jacob's misdeeds. Some have said that, having turned his birthright over to his brother, Esau had no right to expect any mercy from his father. Some have argued that Esau overreached in the first place, that his claim to the exclusive rights of the firstborn was arbitrary and indefensible. In another version, it is Rebecca who is to blame for putting the blameless Jacob up to an evil scheme. According to that interpretation, he becomes the first boy to be the instrument of a manipulative Jewish mother. Others do not think this is fair to the woman.

But here it is time to ask how Isaac's experience on Mount Moriah had molded his idea of what a father was entitled to do for—and to—his sons.

Here is what Isaac thought: From the altar on Mount Moriah I came. I am the son of cruelty. So shall I test my son Esau. He too shall know suffering for no clear reason.

Thus did the God of Abraham beget betrayal upon betrayal, cruelty upon cruelty, punishment upon punishment. His altars do not crumble.

So do fathers bury their sons in history.

You could love the man who wrote those words. Even if he were your father.

Paul hears a high-pitched screech outside, brakes or something sounding like brakes, and rushes to the window, but sees only a delivery truck, taxis, a limousine, no blood, no broken bodies.

Is this what your life felt like when you came back from

TODO GITLIN

*France? Every screech in the street, every slamming car door,
every fire engine and ambulance siren . . . your heart stopping
again and again. And it gave you some relief—was it relief?—to
yank yourself away from your flesh-and-blood son and write a
book about men who abandon, sacrifice, and betray their flesh-
and-blood sons. You would deliver other sons and daughters
from evil. The Hassan Izmets of the world.*

The apartment is filling with moist light. Paul puts on his
sandals, lumbers downstairs to a café as if sleepwalking, orders
his usual large latte to go, and buys the morning *Times*. Back
upstairs, he tosses the paper onto the coffee table with the others that have been piling up, wilting in the humidity, since the
day Chester died. Even at the best of times Paul has next to no
interest in the daily news other than as a heap of ephemera, a
dump of paper shapes and textures, materials for his labors of
assemblage, his caricatures of caricatures. The images of the
week can wait, though. What cannot wait is the tan notebook
resting beside his easy chair. Will this final testament, with the
sweaty stain on its cover and the creases at its corners, crack the
code? He holds this relic of a lost world as if it were a Torah
scroll.

IN THE EARLY New York afternoon, the air was heavy and the
light was congealed. The clouds were long smears, off-white.
The city looked squat and sordid in the late-August heat. Cars,
fumes, congestion—the body of the city poisoning itself. Skirt-
ing the Van Wyck Expressway, the cabdriver took the service
road for miles, past the little yards and clapboards of Queens,
housing uncounted families, each bewildered in its own way, its
pains inflicted helplessly in the name of love or indifference. Silver glints off the distant midtown spires, magnificently false, like
the promise of a new-launched life.

Crossing Manhattan, I was struck by the sheer abundance of

primary colors in New York, the garishness of neon yellows and reds shrieking—look at me! buy here! I exist!—the rusty fire escapes, the bright rolls of razor wire protecting the roofs. New York, city of clamor and high security. Gone from my life were the rosy and tawny pastel stones, the creamy façades, the huge lacquered wooden doors, the fine filigreed iron of balconies, the intricate manhole covers. The black iron on New York streets consists of protective bars. There is too much brick (why does brick look so much more worn than French stone?) and too much noise (why can't New Yorkers suffer their common unhappiness with some restraint?). New York, capital of misfortune and false hope.

False as writing fluidly when your mind is a stop-start stutter.

Misfortune has as many causes as effects, but the effects live longer and shout louder.

Getting on toward four in the afternoon. It's ten at night in France. Lying on an embroidered pillow in Normandy is a woman whom I love and cannot touch.

The apartment. Neat. Nothing has changed.

Slept for three hours, thrashed around in bed, read Kierkegaard and Eliot's "Four Quartets," dozed off, awoke from a nightmare that left no clues, staggered through another hour or two of half sleep, woke again at four, waited till seven, called Marion in Wellfleet, and told her I wanted to see her. She was prepared, formal but not unfriendly, like a diplomat with a bargaining position that (she hinted) might not be final. "Welcome home. I was getting tired of crying my eyes out without anyone to notice except your son."

"You got my letter."

"You always did know how to sum up a situation, Chester." She sounded strangely chirpy. I could imagine starting a life with a woman who sounded like that.

"You know what?" my wife said, surprisingly gently. "I must change my life, too." We made an appointment to meet.

Called Howard. His voice weighed down with concern. He had an hour free in the afternoon, but then, on second thought, insisted on coming over before his appointments—thought I needed a close inspection without any delay. "You don't look bad," he allowed. "Considering," I said. "Considering that I haven't had a decent night's sleep in I don't know how many days." Told him the whole story. Started weeping even before I got to the accident. His reaction indecipherable: sympathy? alarm? analytic objectivity? Imagined that he was jealous— beautiful woman, going for broke, etc. Don't trust my responses. Upright, distinguished Howard asking by-the-book questions. Careful not to disturb me. Trotting out obvious terms: "trauma," "intrusive memories," "hypervigilance." (Don't mean to suggest that these are necessarily the wrong terms.) Mainly he used the word "coping." "How are you coping?" Excellent question, Dr. Spain. When all the theorizing is done, the delicate, elaborate, false reconstruction of a life history out of the rubble of past events, there remains one sublime skill: coping. Mechanisms, strategies, tactics.

"About your—what shall we call it? your recent experiences—a number of us in the psychoanalytic community are concerned," he is saying. Notice that Howard compresses the word "psychoanalytic." Sounds like "psych'alytic." An affectation—the club's secret handshake. Probably I used to pronounce it that way myself. "You've had a traumatic experience," he says. I am supposed to be reassured because the psycho-analytic community can classify my experience.

Psych'analysis will have to get along without me, I tell him. No hard feelings, but I don't know if it works and it doesn't do much for me as a way of life. Feels like so much throat-clearing and ends where it ought to begin. The point is to help those who have suffered the most. I know what you're thinking, I say. You think I'm self-dramatizing.

"The word 'grandiose' comes to mind," Howard offers. "So does 'splitting.' 'Projection.' 'Denial.' "

Asked him what he knows about conducting psychotherapy with victims of torture.

Stony scrutiny. His high forehead higher than usual. Eloquent frowns. Finally: "Don't you think you've made a few too many changes rather too quickly?"

"Too soon to tell," I say.

At Logan Airport, rent a car (thankfully with automatic transmission), make it to Wellfleet before lunch. Splendid, crisp day full of salt air, breezes, twitching leaves—perfect day for a post-mortem. Marion's face lined, lean, curiously relaxed. Trim, pleasant, she reverts to her New England origins. A loose blouse over a one-piece bathing suit. Matron at her ease. A good woman with prospects. Her hair several shades lighter than I remembered it. We kiss cheeks as if we were swatting flies. A relief: We will be civilized.

My son takes his own good time ambling onto the porch, his eyes full of suspicion. He has a crease line in his brow. First he steps up for a perfunctory hug, then veers away. "I hope you had a nice time," he says, obviously a rehearsed line. According to Marion, he has taken to sleeping in the closet.

. . .

The air is drenched with sweet smells. The birds are singing, indifferent to human life.

"Are you all right?" I ask my wife, once Michael has been released to the jungle gym next to the herb garden. We are eating the fresh fruit salad Marion has prepared, sitting on chaise longues, in the shade, four feet apart, keeping an eye on the boy. Her view and my view parallel, not meeting.

"I'm right enough," she says, turning toward me reluctantly. "I was a mess, but I feel better now. I'm clear. That's something."

"That's a great deal."

"You've got a hell of a way of putting an end to half my life."

All I can say is, "I'm sorry for everything."

"I know you mean that," she says dryly. "Me, too. Look, Chester, I want to get on with the anticlimax quickly and painlessly."

I bite into an apple and G—— flies back into my consciousness: the sea, the garden, the wall of the old city, the pavement in front of the farmhouse, the hospital. Andrej's scar. Milena's mouth.

"You look so mournful, Chet, but you know, I think it really is better this way," says my wife. "For you and me anyway. Michael is another matter."

Some things are so true, you don't know what to say.

The sky is huge over the beach, amazingly blue but—if this makes any sense—shallow. The clouds are vague wisps, absences of color. The breezes are feathery.

She says, "I've talked to Howard. Did you know shrinks go crazy more than anyone else?" I see the word "shrink" has entered the household. She knows I loathe it.

I sleep in the guest bedroom. There is no hint of sex, but that's all right; I'm not in the mood. Conveniently for Marion, she ran into a lawyer—someone she went to school with—at the beach. She knows her rights.

She will demand custody of Michael. I will offer no contest. I would not know what to do with the boy. Certainly this arrangement is in his best interest. I say not a word about Andrej or Milena. My best interest. There are no dramatic disputes. I make too much money for that. I will keep the apartment because she wants to start fresh. She will stay on the East Side and Michael will not even have to change schools. Our new lives will fit seamlessly into the old ones. We will make lists of possessions.

We inform Michael together. Oh, we are impeccably civilized! The family meeting is like a government briefing: controlled, full of fraudulent reassurances. Michael stares at me and says nothing. Then he scampers outside. A few minutes later I hear a loud thud, then another. He is throwing rocks at tree trunks.

I write to Milena, special delivery, imploring her to tell me how Andrej is. I urge her to come to the States. I tell her I will put her through her studies. I tell her I will adopt the boy.

I shave the slackening skin of my neck and think about flying to Europe to find her. I will go to London; I will find Andrej's father, Tom. Her skin is still imprinted on mine. When I imagine what I have lost, I can almost wish it had not been offered to me in the first place. Almost.

Even a ghost thinks about his future. I have stopped taking new analytic patients. By attrition I will work my way down from my present load.

．　．　．

I have agreed to spend two days a week consulting with the Society for the Rehabilitation of Victims of Torture. Another two days seeing patients they refer to me. My suffering is nothing.

Every morning, now, I read one chapter of Genesis and another at night. Abraham incomprehensible. Midrash does not help. A lot of straining. Like psychoanalysis.

What does a man want?

All suffering is someone's. Abraham's, Isaac's.

Michael on weekends. He copes. I cannot bear to look him in the eye. He does not know there are sacrifices that are worse than abandonment.

What does God want? The God Who demands loyalty is the same God Who judges that torture is wrong, and puts up with it, and commands us to stop it.

Did Abraham fear to look his son in the eye? Did he always wonder, What does he remember?
     Did he ask himself, Do I deserve to have a son?
     Is a son someone a father must deserve?

sacrifice

Three weeks after I mailed it, my letter to Milena came back stamped "N'habite plus à l'adresse indiquée." No longer at this address.

The journal breaks off here. Paul leafs through the rest of the book, hoping against hope that the words will resume, but the pages are blank.

He's depleted. The city looks airless. The day has come up a pallid blue, and Paul is grateful for the sheltering hum of the air conditioner. Now that he knows what he knows, where is he? His feelings have canceled each other out.

He sips his latte and, for relief, forces himself to concentrate on *Cyberbia* for a moment. Perhaps a weekly anagram feature . . . a visual anagram! Each week they could offer subscribers a trove of images—cropped newspaper photos, snippets from articles, digital photos, found poems—a sort of visual alphabet made up of bits that subscribers could drag around on their screens, juxtapose, and compile into their personal montages. He might as well sort through his unread newspapers and magazines for promising items. He tosses the morning's *Times* to the side and leafs through a few magazines, but feels uninspired by the fashion poses and coy ads. For no particular reason he picks up the metro section of a *Times* from the previous week, this being the least demanding and potentially most surprising part of the paper. On its front, a photo of a bicycle upended, with a van that, according to the caption, has killed the bicyclist, parked behind. No human being in sight. Inside, an attractive woman in a striped dress smiles; he skips the caption. A taxi is half plunged through a store window, a dramatic thought but a visually disappointing display. The drug-dealing son of a movie star hides his face as he leaves a courthouse.

He turns the page and glances at a picture of United Nations delegates stiffly toasting the retiring U.S. ambassador and, though he has zero interest in diplomacy, finds himself reading the caption: "Expressing admiration for Ms. Scott-Croft on her departure were, l. to r., James McCreedy of Ireland, Marthe Hoppmann of Germany, Li Ding of China, and Milena Danova of the Czech Republic." He moves on to the next page but then—for reasons he can't quite explain—turns back to that photograph.

The small dark-haired woman. He knows instantly. The name, of course, and the nationality, but also her large and, even in that dull photo, luminous eyes, and the suggestion— though this might just be a question of camera angle—that they do not point in exactly the same direction. She carries herself like a woman who knows her value. *Handsome* is the word that comes to mind.

United Nations. Forty-second Street. Grand Central.

In later years, he will not be sure why he opened that particular day's *Times*. Was it an accident? Or, to use his father's word, uncanny?

At 9:01, Paul telephones the Czech Mission to the United Nations, but the ambassador is not in. "My name is Paul Gurevitch," he tells the receptionist.

"And who are you with?"

"I'm with Dr. Chester Garland. I'm his son. Tell her I'm his son." He spells the names, and the receptionist, perplexed, writes them down.

An hour later, the phone rings, and Milena Danova's secretary says, "Please hold for the ambassador."

Paul badly wants to sound businesslike but he is unable to

prevent a small transitional cough, *hhmmnnn,* before saying, "I—I am Chester Garland's son."

"Yes. I am told." The vowel has an English intonation: *towld.* "I am very sorry to hear about your father. His tragic passing." Her voice is strong, collected.

"Thank you. The reason—well, the reason I'm calling is that . . . I'd like to see you. I thought—I thought you might be able to help me understand. . . ." He trails off.

"Yes?"

"To understand him, that's all."

"And why would that be, Mr. Gurevitch?" There is the slightest trace of British—or is it routinely diplomatic?— formality.

"Ambassador, Miss Danova—" He stresses the second syllable.

"Mrs. Danova." She corrects him, stressing the first syllable.

"Mrs. Danova, this is awkward. You see, I know about your—relationship. With him." He is thinking, It's crazy to be having this conversation; he is surprised to discover such boldness in his heart, but he is committed to plunge down this path, and without a certain boldness he is lost.

Her voice rises. "I am not sure that I know what you mean. To be honest, Mr. Gurevitch, my duties keep me extremely busy."

"Believe me, Mrs. Danova, I do not mean to intrude. I certainly don't want to cause you distress. It's simply that—I'd better say it directly—I've read my father's journals, the journals he kept, from—from the time when you . . . knew one another. Years ago. I would like to . . . I would very much like to meet you."

A very brief and sharp intake of breath, an interval of silence, and then, flatly: "Yes, I see." Seconds tick off. "I can see you at the end of the day. Six o'clock, in the delegates' lounge. Ask for me at security." Her voice is firm now, commanding.

He thinks the conversation is over, but she adds, "Mr. Gurevitch, let me ask you. Are you certain that you want to do this?"

He hesitates long enough to feel a little embarrassed—not an emotion that comes easily to him—and answers at last. "Absolutely."

The last time Paul visited the United Nations, his father was with him; he had human rights business to do and, while he was busy, left his son on a public tour of the premises. Paul must have been eleven or twelve. He remembers a guide, a dark-skinned woman wearing a sari, explaining that the ceiling was left unfinished deliberately, not to be completed until world peace was in force. Paul was moved by the thought. His father's eyes sparkled when Paul told him what the guide had said. He must have anticipated his son's following him someday into the family mission of good works.

Now Paul is in the delegates' lounge, which is full of men wearing more cologne than women normally wear, and women with shoulder pads as big as men's. There is a friendly murmur of business being done, plans worked up, and if the grand sum of these chats, along with gossip and flirtations, exchanges of advice about restaurants and private schools, is not saving the world, at least it might be keeping matters from getting worse.

She comes striding across the room: a bold woman who knows her attractions, smiling perhaps (it is hard to tell at a distance), and after a single moment of doubt—females who carry themselves like important officials are not as scarce as they used to be—Paul knows this is the woman whom he has come to meet. Short, with a full figure, thickened in the middle. As she approaches, the smile—for it is a smile—flickers. Dark hair, back in a bun. Closer up, the dark eyes, of indeterminate color, slightly misaligned. She wears a simple tailored suit, black, whose label he ought to be able to guess, with a little metallic pin, blue and red, in the lapel. The familiar silver cross hangs from a delicate chain around her neck. Dark hair, round face, long lashes—a tribute to his father's powers of description, although there is a fine web of lines, evidence of wear, fanning out from her eyes, and a fullness of flesh beneath her chin. He would not say she is beautiful, exactly—this is not a large category in Paul's book—but she is more than handsome; she is remarkable. The photograph in the paper did not do her justice.

They exchange expectant looks. She thrusts her hand forward and declares authoritatively, "I am very pleased to meet you." With a wave, she invites him to sit down in a leather chair and follows suit.

"Thank you for agreeing to see me. It is very kind of you."

This is not a woman who hesitates. Her front teeth are slightly stained, but he can picture her young, lush, ripe, more svelte, less bottom-heavy—can picture her walking into his father's train compartment.

"Not at all," she says. "It is the least I can do. Would you like something to drink?"

"No, thank you. I know you're very busy so I'll be direct. I suspect you are the last person to see my father alive."

She stares. Her left eyelid quivers. A smile begins, then dissolves. For the ten-thousandth time in his life he is uncertain of signals. It is as if she's afraid of him. To her, his presence in her life at this moment must be (yes!) uncanny. Surely his father would have thought so. No, perhaps she's only scanning his face for recognizable features. Yes, that's it, she may hear, or think she hears, some speech pattern of Paul's that Paul himself is deaf to.

"I'm sorry?" Milena Danova says.

"I think that you might have been the last person to talk to my father."

"This is—possible," she says. "Highly possible." The quivering in her eyelid is intense. "We met for lunch, you see. The next day, I read in the newspaper— Excuse me. I am . . . distracted. Do you mind if I smoke?"

"Not at all."

She lights a filter cigarette, takes a deep pull, and leaves it to burn in an ashtray.

"What was he like? When you saw him?"

"He was, I have to say, nervous. Grim and nervous. And he was not well. He said that he awoke thinking that every day might be his last. He seemed—well, simplified down to his elements, if that makes sense. To be honest, he was reluctant to see me. I wrote to him, you know. I saw his name in the newspaper. He was receiving a human rights award. We think highly of this activity in my country."

"You sought him out, then," says Paul.

"Of course! I think you are aware that I loved him once, Mr. Gurevitch. He was not a criminal. He was a good man and an old man. I did not want to leave things the way they were. It was no one's fault."

"You are speaking of your son." He leans forward, clasping his hands in front of him, as if in prayer. They are too close to each other, and both uncomfortable, but neither will pull back. His voice is low, confidential. "I am thinking of your son, Andrej—"

"Yes, of course you are."

"I know about—about the accident."

"It *was* an accident."

"This will seem strange to you—it's even strange to me—but

I want to ask you what has become of your son. I do not want to be intrusive, but—"

Looking him in the eye, she is quick to respond, forthright and yet medium-cool, as if she has answered this question for many others, so often that the words have been refined and the manner rehearsed with use. "Andrej is a young man." She pauses. He is tempted to fill the silence with questions but resists the temptation, and after a while she resumes. "He is . . . slow. He moves slowly. He is not normal. He is—well, limited."

Paul listens with a wish that the ceiling would come crashing down and his head would explode and the grief that is in his heart would erupt and pour out of his consciousness to cover the earth, because grief is the lot he has inherited and there is an infinity of it, and always will be, and deserves to be.

"But you know," she says, "Andrej is not unhappy. He has a good life. If I had to choose, in your American way, what to call him, happy or unhappy, I would say he is happy. He is loved. He is well cared for. He has complicated relations with his brothers, but good relations."

"His brothers."

"Yes. My younger children. His younger brothers." Paul's eye is drawn to this woman's small, narrow fingers. On the fourth finger of her right hand she wears a thin plain-gold band.

"And you told my father all of this?"

"Yes, of course. It is curious—or perhaps it is not so curious?—but, you know, he asked me the same questions you do."

"And what else did he ask?"

"What else did he ask? To be honest, he asked if he could see a picture of Andrej. Naturally I showed him."

"And would you show me?"

She wonders—or so it seems to him—at the connection

that binds her to this impetuous, melancholy young man. She must feel so much older than he, older than the entire United Nations, as old as scripture, as old as a continent.

After some moments, she reaches into her purse, pulls out her wallet, opens it, flips back an identification card, pulls out a photo, and passes it over to him. Paul notes the bent smile, the drooping lip, the thick scar slashing down the high forehead. He looks up into the boy's mother's eyes, which are now a strong gray color, and notes parallels: straight hair, a tired expression around the mouth.

"You showed this to my father?"

"Yes, as I said. He asked to see it, like you. I—I thought, well, he should see. He is adult."

"What did he say?"

"He was . . . affected. To tell the truth, he wept. He said he was sorry that I did not contact him during all these years. I said it was too painful. He said he understood. And I could tell that he did understand."

"And what else did he say?" Paul's voice is a hush.

"He said—he said—you know, I am not sure I can tell you exactly what he said, but he said that he thought of him always. *Always.* He repeated this. He said he had wanted to send him money, to care for him. His letters were always returned. Once, years later, he had tried to find me in London, but I had married and changed my name, and I do not know how hard he tried; I did not inquire. He offered money now, actually. I told him it was not necessary. Andrej is not without resources. The boy's father—well, I must tell you, he has been entirely decent. He paid for the operations."

"Operations?"

"There were three. And there was special care. A school for children with deficits—that is the word they use. I stayed in

England with Andrej for that reason. I found work. I made a life. That is what one does."

"If you don't mind my saying so, you don't seem bitter."

"You may think this banal, Mr. Gurevitch, but life is precious. And brief. There are many others who have suffered more. Who still suffer more. I lost my country for many years. I have worked cleaning toilets, and do you know? That too was work that had to be done. To be honest, I have no time for bitterness. Bitterness is a luxury. Forgiveness, if you will forgive me for saying so, is practical." Her voice is firm, and her lips, which are beginning to corrugate with age, close over the last word.

"I know this is painful; I won't keep you much longer. But—if I may, please—one more question. . . . Did you have any idea that he was suicidal? When he left you that day?"

"Suicidal, no, no. Sad. Just sad. And now, Mr. Gurevitch, you will pardon me, but I must attend to an engagement." She stands and holds out her hand, and he passes the photo back to her, and thanks her for seeing him, and she says it was nothing.

And then, as an afterthought, he suddenly says, "You were at the funeral, weren't you?" He thinks he can place her now—the dark eyes at the back of the synagogue, the sense of a woman studying him.

Quietly: "Yes, I was." They exchange flashes of recognition. "Good-bye, Mr. Gurevitch. I wish you well."

"Good-bye."

Paul walks down Forty-second Street in a daze. The heat coats everything, a secretion, like sweat oozing from the pores of the city. The distracted crowds move in suspension: people who meet his look, people with downcast eyes, people in sunglasses; people with grimaces; people who straddle the sidewalk, people who step aside; men in white shirts, their jackets slung over their shoulders; men striding, men taking their time; men going to bars, men coming from bars; men with baseball caps; men with thick hair, and bald men; shoppers lugging plastic bags; women in dark suits and white sneakers; women fanning themselves with newspapers; women of every complexion, short, thin, and plain women, tall women; women attractive to Paul and not; women whom women find attractive, laughing women, defeated women; men who support their children, men who do not; adulterers; those who have left their husbands and wives and lovers, those who will leave next year, those who will never leave. Some have fathers and mothers living, and many have sons and daughters. All will lose those whom they love, or will be lost to them. Few, at this moment, probably none, are thinking that they will die. Few, if any, will die today or tomorrow. A few days ago, his father passed these storefronts and office buildings.

The living Andrej is who he is. Who he would have turned out to be without the accident—this is not to be known. Who Chester Garland would have been is not to be known either.

At Lexington Avenue, Paul goes down into the subway. His father decided not to take a taxi home. He chose the subway on a sweltering day when the platform was an inferno. Today is a few degrees cooler, but the whole subterranean city is still drenched. Dark stains show through blouses and shirts. His father took broken lives, including his own, and did what he could. Somewhere in the city there is a motorman who braked desperately, with all his quickness and strength, the instant he caught sight of a man falling, or stepping, in front of his train. Today, perhaps that motorman berates himself, smacks himself around, demanding whether there was anything he could have done to stop in time. *Don't blame yourself!* Paul demands. "Pardon me?" says an elderly man standing nearby.

Paul is waiting at the express track when the rumble begins,

sacrifice

the onrushing cascade of sound, the hiss as the next train pulls
into the station.

WE LEAVE ESAU here, but we shall not turn our backs on him as
he turns his back on the life he knew and faces the wilderness
where his kindness and vengefulness put him. He plans the
revenge of the weak against the deceiver, and he is alone. He
does not know that he has joined a line of rejected brothers
stretching across time, dispossessed, unsaved, resolute.

He does not know that, many years from now, he will
approach his brother Jacob in fear and trembling, and fall on his
neck and kiss him, and they shall weep, and their tears shall
mingle, and he whom his father would not bless shall receive his
brother's blessing.

Now, as he stands poised at the edge of the wilderness, Esau
thinks of the father who condemned him, who refused to bless
him, who was himself the son of cruelty, who was blinded, who
did shine and laugh because he was faithless. To Mount Moriah
he was led as a boy, and from the bloody altar he descended as a
man, dispossessed of his safety but possessed of his birthright.
He surrendered to his father and to the God of his father, and he
was saved so that I should live, says Esau to the vacant sky. I,
like my father, know the passion and gullibility of a father. And
again Esau weeps burning tears, and curses his mother and his
fate, until he is weary. And he closes his eyes and receives the
heat of the sun that is his to receive, although he is not to be
given of the dew of heaven, of the fat of the earth, of the grain
and wine that have been granted his brother.

The red skin of Esau is hot. He is alert with hope. He sets his
path between two mountains that lean toward each other like a
father and a son, but do not touch.